BACKSTAGE
STUFF

ALSO BY SHARON FIFFER

Scary Stuff

Hollywood Stuff

Buried Stuff

Killer Stuff

Dead Guy's Stuff

The Wrong Stuff

SHARON FIFFER

BACKSTAGE STUFF

MINOTAUR BOOKS NEW YORK

This is a work of fiction. All of the characters, organizations, and events portrayed in this novel are either products of the author's imagination or are use fictitiously.

 For information, address St. Martin's Press, 175 Fifth Avenue, New York, N.Y. 10010.

www.minotaurbooks.com

Library of Congress Cataloging-in-Publication Data

Fiffer, Sharon Sloan, 1951–

Backstage stuff / Sharon Fiffer.—1st ed.

p. cm.

ISBN 978-0-312-60979-5

1. Wheel, Jane (Fictitious character)—Fiction. 2. Antique dealers—Fiction. 3. Women private investigators—Fiction. 4. Murder—Investigation—Fiction. I. Title.

PS3606.I37B33 2011

813'.54—dc22

2010037539

First Edition: January 2011

10 9 8 7 6 5 4 3 2 1

For my friends from the University of Illinois Department of Theater at the Krannert Center, especially the Bored of Directors. Yes, B-O-R-E-D. With love to Thom, Alan, Fred, and all of the people with whom I shared a life in the theater.

Acknowledgments

Writing might be a solitary occupation, but it takes a village to build a book. Many thanks to all those who always answer my questions. Among them: Dr. Dennis and Judy Groothuis; Walter Chruscinski and the entire team at New Trier Sales; Fred Rubin, who refreshed my memory concerning the pit-trap room of the Playhouse Theater in the Krannert Center at the University of Illinois. Thanks, also, to my family and friends who always serve as readers, consultants, and sounding boards: Steve Fiffer, Kate Fiffer, Nora Fiffer, Rob Fiffer, Catherine Rooney, Keiler Roberts, and Susan Phillips. Thanks to Kelley Ragland, Matt Martz, Sarajane Herman, and jacket artists Ervin Serrano and Grace DeVito, and all of the wonderful people at St. Martin's Minotaur. Gail Hochman, you're the greatest!

BACKSTAGE STUFF

1

Jane Wheel couldn't sleep.

Odd expression, she thought . . . *couldn't sleep.*

She *could* sleep. She knew *how* to sleep. She was physically *able* to sleep.

Wasn't everyone?

It was just that this particular night, her eyes opened at three A.M. She closed them, trying to imagine a blank white canvas, a movie theater screen, anything that was empty and neutral and filled with promise. But as soon as she pictured a giant sheet of paper in front of her eyes, she began filling it with words and numbers. As quickly as she tried to erase the words that formed—separation . . . invoice . . . overdue . . . divorce—other words took their place—failure . . . emptiness . . . ending . . . loneliness.

"Forget it," she said out loud, and switched on the lamp next to her bed. This particular lamp wasn't designed to be placed on a nightstand. It was a modern Von Nessen desk lamp, white and graceful. It went with nothing else in her house. She bought it last month at a house sale, in the last hour, on the last day. It had been under piles of clothes in the basement, an odd outcast in a house full of dark Victorian furniture. At least that was all that was left when Jane wandered through the place at the end of the day. She lifted the lamp from its hiding place and held it up, knowing that it was not anything she needed or even wanted. She just knew it was beautiful. It was perfectly balanced, its white metal shade flaring decisively at just the right spot. The fifty-something couple—surely brother and sister, same nose and mouth, matching frowns—stationed with a cash box at the front door, tired out after two days of seeing their childhood home ravaged, savaged, and scavenged, shook their heads when they saw the lamp.

"Have you ever seen that before, Billy?"

He shook his head. "Maybe Mom bought it for you when you went to nursing school?"

"Nope. It wasn't in Dad's office, either. I've never seen it."

"It was in the basement," Jane had offered, trying to help them place it. She knew what that was like, trying to remember the story behind the object. "Under some clothes."

Billy shrugged, barely looking at Jane or the lamp. "How's two dollars?"

"Are you sure?" asked Jane, not wanting to take advantage of these sad people. "It might be a good one."

The woman shrugged and the man repeated, "Two," holding his fingers up like the peace sign.

Jane paid the money and when she carried the lamp out of the dark, sad house, she held it up and studied it. It was dirty but regal. A beautiful modern design that she knew must be the real thing. Quality modern design that her pal Tim would price in the hundreds.

But she didn't give the lamp to Tim to sell. She brought it home, into her bedroom, and cleared off the table next to her side of the bed. With one motion, she cleared the magazines and business cards and junk mail and catalogs and threw them all into a bag for recycling. She cleaned her lamp, looked it up on the Internet, and set it on the table, giving it the position of honor in a house full of objects, all of which had briefly held that place.

She allowed her lamp to be the last thing she saw each night and the first thing she saw every morning. If objects could talk, could feel, could express themselves, Jane knew that all of the Bakelite, and thirties and forties kitchenalia, all of the mission-style oak and McCoy vases would have turned on this modern interloper. Objects, however, don't talk or express feelings or keep their owners from lonely sleepless nights. If one is lucky, they function in the way they are supposed to, and if one is even luckier, they look beautiful as they do it.

What was that sound? Jane heard a thrumming noise from somewhere in the house. Is that what had awakened her? A belt going out in the refrigerator motor?

Jane sat up a little straighter and picked up the notebook she had left lying next to her in the bed. On page one, she had begun to craft a budget, or what she called a budget. It was really just a list, random and arbitrary.

Nick's clothes. Nick's books. Nick's binoculars. Nick's backpack. Dog food. Heisey punch bowl. Did she count the punch bowl if she was going to send it to Muriel or her cousin, Miriam, to sell at their shop in Ohio? Of course not, that should be in a different list altogether. It didn't belong with haircuts, car insurance, shampoo, gasoline, toothpaste.

This was ridiculous. How could Jane have reached this stage in her adult life without understanding basic household finances? She wasn't an idiot. She had worked her way up the corporate ladder before the ladder had been moved, stranding her and the other members of her creative team. When Jane's biggest client switched his account to a new agency, Jane had been asked, politely, to pack up her things and go. It had been a blow, and at the time, Jane felt terrible—marooned on the island of the unemployed. She had been rejected, abandoned by the company she had been with for sixteen years. Even now, several years later, recalling the day she walked through the corridor of Rooney and Rooney for the last time, she felt the same embarrassment, anger, denial,

"Aren't those the stages of grief?" Jane asked Rita. Rita, a giant mass of a dog, was doing her best rug imitation next to Jane's bed, but perked up one ear when Jane addressed her.

How marooned had she been? Lost? Adrift? Not hardly. Her husband, Charley, was a tenured professor and she herself had been given a handsome severance package. After a decent mourning period consisting of sleeping late and eating a lot of bacon dipped in brown sugar, she began hitting the sales, early and regularly. She hadn't planned to find her second career as a picker. She didn't earn much at first, but over the past few years, she had turned over a few excellent pieces of furniture, one good painting, several pieces of jewelry, the odd bits of flotsam and jetsam from weekly sales and rummaging. And the pottery? It turned out that Jane had an eye for art pottery and could spot a good piece from across a basketball court–sized church basement hall. If she made a beeline and grabbed the possible Weller vase without losing her way or getting distracted at the linens table to peek into a promising box of buttons and rickrack, sniffing out Bakelite and decorative needle packages, she could grab a really good piece of American pottery for a few dollars.

"What *is* that?" Jane asked out loud. The buzzing had started again. Was the dehumidifier shorting out? Was the house about to burst into flames?

Jane swung her leg over the bed, digging her toes into Rita's back and allowing herself the moment of sheer pleasure that it gave her. Rita also allowed Jane her moment before creeping into the corner of the bedroom and turning to watch her mistress. Was she getting up for good or roaming the house? Wherever she landed, Rita would go and quietly keep watch.

Jane stood up, gathering her list-filled notebook, pens, and last Sunday's crossword. There was no reason to remain wide-eyed in bed. Better to be sleepy-eyed roaming the house. A loose sheet fell from her notebook. It was one of her rummage sale lists from last week.

Restaurant creamers, Depression glass shakers, wooden frames—primitive, handmade crocheted pot holders, mechanical pencils, pocket shrines, sterling religious medals, Chase, Homer Laughlin, Russel Wright, Raymor, old office supplies, yardsticks, folding rulers, sewing . . .

Next to sewing Jane had sketched a pincushion that Muriel described—a wooden drawer topped with wire posts for thread spools and perched on top, like a second story, a pincushion covered in nappy velvet. Muriel . . . or was it Miriam . . . had a customer who collected pincushions. She had just missed one like this at an auction and now, like an itch she couldn't scratch, she wanted that particular example of cushion. Jane smiled. She had not found it yet, but she would. At the rummage sale last week, when she tried to follow this list, she hadn't found any of the cousins' items, but she had found two fabulous vases. And indeed, she had spotted them from the doorway when she entered the hall.

Tim Lowry, her friend, mentor, bossy know-it-all, threatened to put blinders on her.

"You have a gift, Jane. You can see the finish line, but you're that skittish horse, letting every other little thing distract you from the race. You need to go into a sale and zero in. Those silly little collections of Easter eggs or somebody's crystal bells that you feel compelled to pick up and daydream about add seconds to your race." Tim always shook his head, as if he were one of the owners of this sad little racehorse. "You could win, you know. You have the eye, the speed . . . I've trained you to go in there and finish in the money."

Jane dropped her papers and pens next to her favorite chair in the kitchen. She pressed her ear to the refrigerator. Nothing.

Jane wandered through the house. She paused to look at the small restaurant creamers tucked into a bookshelf in the living room. There were six . . . enough to box up and send off to the ladies to sell. She had enjoyed them long enough. She turned around and scanned the room, trying to be a good, responsible picker. What else was ripe and ready to be sent off to market?

Being laid off had led to full-time picking and then, of course, there were the murders. She was good at solving them, too. Had she not been forced to leave her corporate job, would she have discovered her inner Nancy Drew? Would she have been racing around to garage sales, scrambling to find the best stuff until she stumbled over her neighbor's body? Would she have met Detective Oh?

Bottom line? When she was *downsized,* back before everyone was just fired, before whole departments were demolished, before firms dissolved and disappeared and the people she had known in the corporate world were wandering through interviews and a bizarro world of networking and refitting themselves for a marketplace they no longer recognized, Jane had support. She had Charley and Nick and Tim and even her parents, Don and Nellie in Kankakee, offering her a safe enough haven. And now she had Detective Bruce Oh, who believed in her and believed she had the talent to . . . what was that talent he saw in her?

"You see the objects around people, Mrs. Wheel. You see the space they occupy and the negative space they leave. And where the two spaces intersect, you see the true nature of people and things." *Yeah,* Jane thought, *he sees my talent for whatever that is.*

Jane selected a volume from a Harper and Company Shakespeare collection. These books were in outstanding condition. Well over a hundred years old, but so well cared for. *The Comedy of Errors.* Seemed appropriate. The books had lived on her shelf for six months. If she sold these, the money would pay for the new sleeping bag she had bought Nick yesterday.

The soft *burr, burr* again. An aggravated purr? Had Nick brought home some animal and forgotten to tell her?

Jane had risen from the ashes of her advertising career to become Jane Wheel PPI, picker and private investigator. So a setback like getting downsized, the hurdle of finding new work, the bump in the road . . . Jane was the proof that normally those flies in the ointment set you skittering off, albeit kicking and screaming, on a better path.

And now Charley had set up this new hurdle—had asked her for a divorce—should that be classified as a setback or would it be better described as a bump in the road? If this divorce were a fly in the ointment, it surely couldn't be a small buzzing insect struggling in a teaspoon; it would, at least, be movie actor Jeff Goldblum morphing into a hairy monster, struggling through a roomful of Jell-O. Jane made herself smile at that picture.

"Some detective I am," Jane said. "Can't even find a noise. Maybe it's in my head, maybe something has finally come loose for real. I *am* talking to myself, replaying old horror movies. Maybe it's a lightbulb, ready to blow . . . damn it," she said, looking at the big schoolroom clock hanging in the kitchen: three forty-five. It wouldn't be light for another few hours, but Jane knew any chance for sleep was gone. Time to stop prowling through the house like a cat burglar, deciding what she could sell the fastest to pay this month's bills. Jane went back to the bedroom, grabbed her quilt, dragged it into the kitchen, and threw it into the big stuffed chair. The chair had been a great bargain but hadn't fit anywhere else in the house when Jane dragged it in, thinking its spot in the kitchen would be temporary. The first time she visited Jane's house, Nellie offered her daughter an unvarnished opinion.

"What the hell you want to put a living room chair in the

kitchen for?" she had asked, sitting down in it. "It's going to get all dirty." From its spot in the corner, Nellie could watch Jane's every move in the kitchen. "Dry your glasses better than that, you're going to have spots," she said, putting her feet up on the small hassock. It was the only time Jane ever saw her mother sit down in a kitchen. The chair stayed.

Maybe Jane could nod off there. She curled up in her chair, placed her notebook on top of her laptop, which lay next to her newest device, a smartphone that Tim had bought for her. He had called it her *aspirational* device—Jane should *aspire* to learn to use it, to be as smart as it was. "It will keep you in constant touch," Tim had said, "with Nick and me and everyone." He had given Nick an identical phone and made sure that they both had international calling packages—a hefty chunk of time already prepaid. Jane smiled every time she looked at the pretty thing—not her style—but she could appreciate great design, and it made her sadly happy that Tim was concerned enough to place this object in her hands. To anyone peering in on Jane Wheel, this phone, in addition to the laptop, in her cozy kitchen corner created a misleading tableau. A peeping Tom would have seen a small disheveled woman, still youthful enough, wistfully pretty, wrapped in a blanket, holding a cup of something steamy, surrounded by her modern devices, quite likely ready to type out the great American novel.

Rather than writing fiction, which Jane would have made far less trite, far less cliché than the current nonfiction of her life, she was simply a woman who had been asked to make a proper budget. *A list of household expenses* was the actual phrase. She had to make this budget to give to her lawyer who would, in turn, present it to another lawyer. Jane Wheel was a woman with insomnia whose husband had asked her for a divorce and she was delaying the paperwork. It didn't get any more cliché than that, did it? No . . . a legal separation. She had been told to differentiate. Jane and Charley were not getting a divorce. Yet . . . not yet.

Remarkably, this turn of events, this legal separation, made Jane feel almost exactly as if she had been let go by Rooney and Rooney all over again. The major difference, Jane knew, was that when she had come home with personal things from her office in a paper sack, Charley had been there to dry her tears. This time, Charley phoned her from Central America, explaining that it was he who wouldn't be coming home. He had decided to pursue his passion, but he needed to do it alone, unfettered. *It wasn't anything she had done, he hadn't seen it coming, he was sure it would work out. . . .* And, just like that, Jane was fired all over again.

So Jane, who had neglected all household chores to pursue stuff at auctions and flea markets, garage sales and rummage sales and who, more recently, had been on twenty-four-hour call for Detective Oh as an ersatz partner in his investigation business; Jane, who had happily packed Charley off to this dig and that site for months at a time, missing him, yes, but also cherishing her time alone, was the one who was left. Anyone who had paid attention, who had been keeping score in this marriage would have bet even money that Jane was the one who would snap the line, who would demand freedom to find the treasure and catch the bad guy. Who would have thought that Charley would do the unfettering?

Jane added a few more items to her household expenses list—*cleaning supplies, groceries . . .* Jane didn't really clean all that well or cook regularly, but she often found herself buying supplies.

Five A.M. Jane heard Nick's alarm. He never had to be reminded to wake up on a travel day. She fixed Nick's favorite breakfast. Jane could poach eggs and Nick loved them on top of buttered toast. While the water was heating to a simmer, she grabbed extra T-shirts from the laundry basket and stuffed them into Nick's pack. Scanning the kitchen, she randomly added items, wanting somehow to provide the very thing her son would most need.

"Mom, you're not packing me more stuff, are you?" Nick said, wide awake, dressed for his trip in khaki shorts and a striped knit polo shirt.

"Passport?" Jane asked. Nick slapped his right cargo pocket and dug into his eggs.

She and Charley had made Nick their priority, making sure they never let any stray bits of anger, any clouded moments of grief or regret or recrimination put him into shadow. Nick knew, of course, that this separation of his mother and father was different, weightier than the usual comings and goings, but his parents had lived separate lives and professed happiness at doing so for so long, this legal pronouncement of separation did not carry the jolt it might for a child of a two-parents-in-constant-residence-all-meeting-for-meals-at-the-table kind of family. Did Nick notice his mother's sleeplessness? Did he hear her drift off in the middle of a sentence? Sometimes. But Nick was a teenager, a self-professed geek who could lose himself sifting through soil at a digging site as quickly and deeply as could his dad. And Nick had grown up watching Jane get glassy-eyed, sifting through a tin of buttons, rubbing her thumb over a red plastic disk until she produced the formaldehyde perfume of her beloved Bakelite. Each member of this odd triangle of a family had a method and a madness for getting lost in work, in play, in passion. And Jane and Charley, for all the things they had done wrong in their lives together had done one thing right. They had loved their son, put him first, and made sure he was on solid ground with each of them.

"No-blame divorce," Jane had told Tim, "that's what it will be."

"No-fault," said Tim, correcting her.

"Oh, there's plenty of fault," said Jane, "but we're trying for no blame."

"Too many T-shirts, Mom, I'm dumping these," said Nick, inspecting the main compartment of his pack as Jane pulled the car onto the expressway. "We've got laundry in town and we go once a week."

"I have this new phone, you know, like the one Tim bought you, so we can tech to tech to each other . . ."

" 'Tech to tech to each other'?" Nick said, finally interested in what his mother was saying. He stopped tossing clothes overboard, lightening the load of his backpack, which he had filled with essentials and which his mother, he now saw, had stuffed with extras.

"That's what Tim called it. There's a keyboard and I can type messages," said Jane, shocked and appalled at how quickly they were nearing the airport.

"*Text,* Mom. We can *text* easier," said Nick. "You know that word, you texted on your old phone. You tried, anyway."

Jane realized just how vacant she had been as Tim had handed her the phone. It was such a new, shiny thing, she figured there must be a new terminology for it. Of course, she and Nick could *text* more easily. Tim was trying to think of everything.

"Just kidding," said Jane. "Yeah, I can text or tech—whatever you prefer."

"Sign up for Facebook and Twitter. Tim'll show you how. Dad set up a site for the dig so you can follow what we're doing with pictures of everything. It's going to be cool and it'll be like you're there," said Nick, tossing an extra tube of toothpaste on the floor of the car.

"I'm not always at the computer, honey. I . . ."

"It's on the phone, Mom. That's what makes it so smart. You are always online with it. If you go to Twitter, you can follow what we're doing—and Dad's posting videos all the time, so you can click on the links and see us."

"I promise," said Jane. "I'll sign up for everything you say. Maybe I'll twitter back at you."

"Tweet," said Nick, pawing through the Ziploc bag of snacks and throwing the banana yogurt–flavored bars on the floor.

"Sweet," said Jane.

Jane heard the dull buzz again and wondered if she was getting a migraine. She had never had a migraine before, but if she was ever going to get one, she thought it might be now. She had hugged Nick good-bye at the airport after filling out the necessary paperwork for him to travel alone, returned home, and almost immediately nodded off on the couch. The house was quiet and dark and cool, and now, what the hell was that noise? No wonder Jane couldn't sleep at night or during the day. There was something quietly coming unstrung in her house or in her brain, and now she was alone and there would be no one to find her when her head exploded.

"Jane, are you in there? Open up!"

The dull buzz had morphed into a loud banging.

Tim was standing on the porch, his phone glued to his ear, knocking and yelling.

"Where have you been all night?" asked Tim, still holding his phone, waiting for whomever to answer on the other end.

"Here," said Jane, "and there," waving her hand around the house, "and everywhere. Couldn't sleep so I roamed and fixed Nicky breakfast and took him to the airport . . . damn it . . . can you hear it? Can you hear that noise or am I going all Kafka, turning into some kind of buzzing insect? I'm ready to tear my hair out."

Jane followed Tim, who didn't answer but walked straight back to the kitchen. He scanned the kitchen counter, the small round table. He moved the morning newspapers aside from where Jane had scattered them.

"Help me find this noise. It's not the refrigerator and I don't think it's from the basement although I haven't . . . Are you listening?"

Tim had fixed his stare on the small metal typewriter table next to the comfy chair. He whirled on Jane, almost ready to speak, then flopped into the chair.

"I thought you might be dead, for God's sake."

"What are you talking about?" said Jane. "And who the hell are you calling?"

Tim looked down at the table at Jane's phone, a twin to the one he held in his hand.

"You," he said, pointing to the vibrating, humming, thrumming, buzzing phone. "I've been calling you all night."

Tim picked up Jane's phone, slid his finger across the touch screen, and showed her where to find her missed calls. There were twelve—all from Tim Lowry.

Tim ran his fingers through his hair. He looked as exhausted as Jane felt.

"I couldn't sleep and you said you were up every night, so I thought I'd just call and we could talk the night away—you know, put each other to sleep with old boring stories of our lives. You didn't answer and I thought maybe you'd taken a pill like I told you to and then I . . ." Tim let his sentence drift, then started anew. "It was a terrible idea to drop your land line. You're not ready to depend on a cell phone, I am going to pay for—"

"Timmy, you know I never take pills for anything," said

Jane. "Nellie taught me two things: You're supposed to be in pain most of the time, and if you did manage to stop the ache, how do you know when you're better?"

"Yeah, Doctor Nellie," said Tim. "Anyway, you know how it is when you can't sleep, imagination running wild, and I thought what if you did take a pill or two and couldn't wake up and I knew Nick was leaving and then I got scared all around . . . you've been so . . . sedentary . . . all winter and when you mope around, you get—"

"No fair. It's not moping if you're getting a divorce. Moping is what teenagers do when they can't have the car."

"Anyway, I decided to drive up . . ."

"Moping is what a toddler does when he loses a toy—"

"And what you need is some—"

"Moping is what Rita does when I don't throw the ball for her," said Jane. She stood up as tall as she could. "Moping is what—"

"All right!" Tim stood up and looked directly at Jane. "You're not moping!"

"Damn right, I'm not moping," said Jane. "I am at a normal stage in the grieving process."

"Yeah? Well, I gave you the whole winter to move through these stages and you've had long enough. Time's up. I've got something that will bump you out of that stage, right into the acceptance-and-let's-move-the-hell-on-with-life stage."

"It better be a hell of a house sale," said Jane. "It's going to take three floors of untouched treasures and a basement full of packed boxes from four generations. And an attic full of vintage purses and jewelry and gorgeous old hard-sided suitcases filled with buttons.

"It's going to take scrapbooks and photo albums and autograph books. It's going to take rugs, Timmy, and pottery and so many junk drawers full of string too short to keep, it's going—"

"I got you something better than that, sweetheart," said Tim with a smile.

"Better than a suitcase full of buttons?" Jane asked, aware of a strange sensation. She felt like something had cracked inside, but instead of something breaking, she felt something warm seeping in. Her whole body felt as if it might be thawing. She began to smile.

"Better than Bakelite buttons?"

"Yup," said Tim, patting her cheek. "I got you a murder."

2

HERMIONE: Yes, Detective, maybe you have found the murderer . . . Maybe you're looking into the eyes of the murderer right now. You tell me, are my eyes those of a murderer?
CRAVEN: I think I know something about people, Miss Finn, and your eyes are . . . are . . .

Jane dropped the script and burst out laughing. Real laughter—sunshine after a storm, dessert after dinner, bells ringing, chords striking . . . loud, genuine, joyous laughter.

"Oh, Timmy, this is priceless," said Jane, when she could speak. "I wouldn't have guessed you could find a cornball play that would do this. I haven't laughed like this in— You really do know me. Bring me drivel and you drive away the demons!"

Tim held on to his script, still speaking in the stagy voice he had been using to read the part of Detective Craven. "I wanted you to like it," he said, rising from the couch and crossing to the window, "but you know, it's not exactly a comedy."

"Detective Craven is movie-star handsome, a figure clearly more cosmopolitan than his small town, a sophisticated fish in a backwater pond?" Jane read, stopping again to laugh and wipe her eyes.

"Even the character descriptions are too much. Where did

you find this relic? Library sale? Wait, is it from some old house in Kankakee? Have you really got a good sale?"

Jane poured both of them more coffee from the thermal pot, added a quarter inch of half-and-half into Tim's mug, and grabbed another cookie for herself. Her fourth. Tim never showed up empty-handed. In one hand he had been holding his phone, ready to teach Jane the difference between a ring tone and the vibrate mode, but in the other, he had two bags of Jane's favorite chocolate cookies from Myers Bakery, a Kankakee institution just blocks from Jane's childhood home, and a pound of Peet's coffee, Major Dickason's blend, which Jane did not think he could have found in Kankakee.

"Honestly, this might be the worst play I've ever—"

"Stop," said Tim, "before you say something you can't take back."

Jane froze. The script she held was a bound published script—it wasn't a clutch of random pages in a binder. It had to be real, authentic, and vintage, just from the feel of the paper, the wear on the cover. Even the title, *Murder in the Eekaknak Valley,* sounded like some escapist melodrama from the thirties. But Jane heard defensiveness in Tim's voice. She couldn't be making fun of something he wrote, could she? He couldn't have somehow written this terrible play and had it bound to look like . . . Jane looked at the cover. The author was listed as Frederick A. Kendell.

"Tim, it's not yours, is it? You didn't write this, did you?"

"Oh, now she asks, the insensitive brute," said Tim, striking a dramatic pose at the window. "Am I Freddy Kendell, playwright, playboy, and playground equipment heir? Am I Kankakee's answer to Noël Coward?"

"Just . . ." Jane stood up to brush the cookie crumbs off her lap. "Just tell me where this fine dramatic work came from."

Tim, still in character, whirled on her in his most debonair

Detective Craven manner. "Darling, you've been entombed in this house with your son the entire winter, acting the part of earth mother, as far as I can tell. You've packed school lunches, you checked homework, you've even learned how to dust." Tim stopped to run his finger across the top of a carved Ivorex plaque dated 1908. "And rightly so. I, too, want my godson to emerge from this situation as well-adjusted as possible. But now it's time to emerge from your cocoon and welcome springtime in Kankakee."

"Ah, yes," said Jane, "springtime in Kankakee, when the river rises, the flowers bloom, and Nellie stops making chili at the EZ Way Inn."

"Flowers, shmowers—I got those year-round in my store. It's the estate sales that blossom, honey." Tim returned to his regular Tim voice—earnest, persuasive, and poetic. "I have two houses pending and one enormous fabulous place that I've been trying to sort through and stage off and on for two months. Heirs now want it ready by the end of the month. I knew I couldn't get you to leave Nick this winter . . . I know you and Charley had work to do, but your last message said you couldn't come down this week, even after Nick left, because you were working out a budget. What the hell is that?"

"It's a list of expenses—"

"You know what I mean. . . . You and Charley aren't having a moneybags, high-profile split. Figure out what you want and if it's fair, and it will be, Charley will say yes. You made more money than he did for years when you were at Rooney, so it's all evened out. Just tell him what you want."

After hearing Tim's sensible advice and reading his partial listing of what was in the house he was in the midst of prepping for a gigantic sale . . . *extensive collection of 19th-century children's literature, antique needlework, two Martha Washington tables, each filled with engraved sewing notions—thimbles, sterling silver thimble holders, scissors, etc.—8 bedrooms filled to the brim with toys, dolls, vintage clothing, stage costumes, trunks filled with scripts and props, bric-a-brac from three generations, puppet theater, basement and attic untouched for decades . . .* Jane allowed Tim to pack a bag for her. Tim loved to select her clothes and necessary items, and she loved the surprise of unzipping her old leather duffel and finding a cardigan she had forgotten she owned. Besides, Tim had a much better sense of what looked good on her, what she would need, and what would be appropriate for every occasion. Besides (part two), Jane had a phone call to make.

"Here's what I want. I need to stay on Charley's health insurance policy as does Nick, of course, and I want Charley to continue to pay our life insurance. For now, I want him to continue to pay half the mortgage, but I'll put the house up for sale as soon as there is the slightest break in the market. We'll split any profit on the house fifty-fifty. I want Charley to pay for Nick's travel back and forth to Honduras and anything else Nick needs if I can't afford it," said Jane. She nodded at Tim as he came down the steps with her bag and a small vintage vanity case in which, Jane knew from past experience, he had carefully arranged hairbrush and comb, shampoo, and Jane's pitifully small collection of makeup brushes and products, all of which were samples and giveaways. Jane's only indulgence was lipstick. She regularly splurged on full-sized tubes of an earthy red.

"No. No list, no budget. I'll pay for whatever I need and want. If I don't earn it, I don't spend it, and I certainly don't want Charley paying for household stuff when it's just me here in the household. Absolutely not. You have what I'm asking for. That's it. No. My car is my car . . . bought and paid for and in my name. Okay, put in something about that, that Charley and I will divide education costs for Nick. Oh . . . and send me an itemized bill of the hour you'll spend on faxing this over. No more than an hour, okay, or I'll do it myself. Obviously. Yes, that's right, I won't."

"That sounded more like my in-charge girl," said Tim. "Your lawyer quit, didn't he?"

"She," said Jane. "Yes, she quit. She said I obviously don't know how to take advice. I'll save a bundle in legal fees."

"You really have enough to cover mortgage and utilities and . . ."

"I have enough for this summer, depending on how much you're paying me to help with the house."

"Plenty, plus I have one other teeny, tiny job that I need you for that also pays," said Tim, filling a large canvas bag with Rita's dry dog food and tennis balls.

"I have to call Oh, but I can do it from the car," said Jane, distracted. She couldn't believe how much light Tim had brought into the house. She hadn't admitted how much she had dreaded Nick leaving for the summer, her tenuous and unfamiliar supermom role eliminated for three months. She hadn't even admitted to herself, let alone Tim, how tough it had been to drag herself to sales, fighting bigger and bigger crowds, longer and longer lines. Either everyone had decided to take on picking as their next career or everyone was just scraping for a bargain, but the previous years' fun-loving attitude at St. Nick's Rummage had turned dog-eat-dog, where last week two people stood on either side of a five-by-seven Afghan rug priced ridiculously low, each tugging on a side, claiming first dibs. Jane smiled down at the Bokhara now in her hallway. Okay, so she had won that battle, but did she really want to keep fighting tooth and nail over every textile, dish, and spoon? A month or so of working with Tim would plump up the bank account without involving her in any more near fistfights.

"Tim, the murder you mentioned," Jane said, setting the light timers, "that's just that silly murder mystery play, right?"

"Maybe," said Tim. "Maybe it's just a silly play. But there's this," he said, taking a piece of yellowed paper out of his pocket. "I did find this in my copy of the script."

> People foolish enough to put on this play will die—
> And they will die fools.
> Listen to Old Bumby on this!

"Who's Bumby?" asked Jane, hoping Tim didn't notice her slight shiver. She knew the note was probably a joke, a child's prank, yet the spidery handwriting, the fading ink, the blots at the bottom of the page . . . something about it gave her the creeps.

"Maybe Freddy Kendell's father? I don't think the old man approved of his son the actor/writer/bon vivant," said Tim. "Maybe he thought he'd scare him straight . . ." Tim shook his head at Jane's raised eyebrow. "*Straight* into the family business. Freddy was married, widowed early, had one son who did go straight into the family business, then sold it off, leaving his kids, who are now my clients, richer than God."

Jane handed the note back to Tim, who shook his head.

"You keep it. It's a gift. A silly old play, as you called it, complete with a silly old mystery attached."

"So Lowry got you down here to work on that silly play?" said Nellie, not looking up from the rinse tank she was scrubbing out.

"I'm here to work on the Kendell estate sale," said Jane, parking herself on a bar stool, a front-row seat to the long-running Don and Nellie show that played daily at the EZ Way Inn.

"*The* Kendell? Frederick Kendell?" asked Don, trying to move Nellie aside so he could tend to the rinse tanks himself. Jane's parents had argued for thirty years over whose method was the best, Nellie insisting that Don didn't use enough soap and Don complaining that the rinse water needed to be pristine, no bubbles leftover from Nellie's detergent-heavy zeal.

"Kendell had a kid who wasn't all there, didn't he?" asked Nellie.

Jane's mother, Nellie, was the keeper of many theories, many of them involving wealthy families. She believed first that those with money did not eat. When Jane and Michael were children helping unpack groceries, complaining that they couldn't fit another plum into the fruit drawer, Nellie would suddenly begin to expound upon the grocery-buying habits of the rich.

"You know why they're rich?" she would ask, leaning forward, shaking a stalk of celery or a handy head of romaine. "They don't eat. They don't buy any food. They starve themselves up there in their houses. That's right," Nellie would insist over imaginary protests, since Jane and Michael never questioned their mother's wisdom in these matters, "we might not be rich, but we eat, goddamn it, we at least eat."

Number two in Nellie's list of the secrets of the rich and famous was that all wealthy families had a child who, in her words, "wasn't all there." Occasionally she would refer to the child of a prominent family as having a screw loose or she would simply point to her head and make a clockwise motion with her forefinger.

Once Jane, in a burst of insight, had asked her mother if the damaged child to whom she referred might have problems because of malnourishment.

"What the hell are you talking about?" Nellie had asked. "They're crazy because they all marry their cousins."

"That's why they keep it quiet and don't serve any food or cake at the wedding," said Don from behind his newspaper.

"Really, Dad?" Jane had asked, ten or eleven at the time.

"Hell, no," said Don, lowering the paper. "Sometimes your mom is just a little . . ." He twirled his finger in circles at his temple.

"I heard that," Nellie yelled in from the kitchen.

Nellie now backed away from the rinse tanks, wiping her hands on her apron. "Lowry's got you working on the Kendell house while he's doing that silly play then? That's okay—you probably got the better job. That theater thing . . ."

Nellie pronounced theater *the-a-tor*—long *e*, long *a*, long *o*, and with as much disgust as she could muster.

Jane did not like to admit she wasn't in the loop, but clearly

Nellie knew something about Tim's springtime exploits that Jane did not. What theater thing? *Doing* the silly play? How could she find out exactly what was happening without giving her mother the opportunity to dangle what Jane didn't know in front of her face, baiting her to the point of exhaustion?

"What makes you think the play is so silly, Mom?" Jane asked.

"Well, it was written by Freddy Kendell, and I told you he might have been a few sandwiches short of a picnic," said Nellie.

So Tim had shown her that script . . . not just to cheer her up . . . but because . . .

"Is that it? That's no—"

"And," Nellie said, drawing out the one-syllable word, "Venita, down at Pink's, says everybody knows Tim's no actor."

"Yeah?" said Jane, clearly treading water.

"Yeah, the Cartwright boy wanted to play it and he's been in two plays and does the commercials on Kankakee cable for his granddad's lumberyard, and he should have gotten it. That's what everyone's saying."

"How about you, Dad?" asked Jane, trying to hack through the brush and find the path into what the hell Nellie was talking about. "Do you agree with Mom?"

"I don't go in for gossip, Janie," said Don. "But," he said, chuckling, "Phil, at the barber's, said he heard Lowry rewrote it ten years older so he could do it, you know, so there weren't references to him looking like a college boy and all. I don't even think Timmy could pull off being in his twenties," said Don.

Jane was ready to turn over all the cards and give up when the screen door swung open and Francis walked in. Francis had delivered bread and buns and snack cakes, supplying the EZ Way Inn kitchen and bread rack, for as long as Jane could remember. Even though he was now retired and Don and Nellie didn't serve any kind of regular lunch, Francis still showed up late morning and Don and Nellie still referred to him as Francis the bread man.

Jane nodded to Francis and he nodded back.

Nellie poured him a cup of the thick viscous liquid that the EZ Way Inn promoted as coffee. Jane had ordered coffee in every diner, every chic coffee shop, every franchised fast-food dive, always curious if anyone made coffee that tasted like her mother's. Nellie used two glass bubble pots, boiling the water that shot up through the metal funnel-like device filled with grounds, then dripped slowly back into the carafe. The resulting semiliquid poured like molasses, and Jane had often thought that she should melt a little chocolate in it and bottle it as an ice cream sauce. There could be a fortune in it.

Don thought there might be more money in using it as a home remedy.

"We put it in cough syrup bottles, Janie, and peddle it from the trunk of our car with your mother as the pitchman. That's where the money is."

Tim had suggested an infomercial to promote it as a fixative in a jar. "Holds false teeth in place, hangs posters without unsightly nail holes in your walls, and . . . patches shingles better than tar! No mixing required. Call now and we'll throw in a jar of de-caf-goo-to-you, too!"

Francis, on the other hand, just showed up every morning and drank a cup. He made the same acid grimace that everyone made at the first sip, then settled into drinking Nellie's bottomless brew, seemingly intent on removing the lining of his ample stomach.

"Hullo, Janie," said Francis.

"Hi, Francis," said Jane. "How are you?"

He shrugged. It was the all-purpose Kankakee answer.

"Visiting?" he asked.

Jane shrugged back. When in Kankakee, she believed in speaking the language.

"She's here to work with that Lowry, selling off the Kendell place," said Nellie, topping off Francis's cup.

"Gonna be in the play, too?" asked Francis.

Of course, that was it. Tim must be putting on that terrible play. That's why he had the scripts. And he was going to get Jane to act in it! Jane hadn't stepped onstage since college. She had started school as a theater major, had several roles in university productions, been a member of a comedy troupe. She had loved it. But after school, there was Charley and that wonderful job opportunity at Rooney and Rooney, where they welcomed theater majors, art school dropouts, poetry students with music minors . . . "creative types . . . we love you creative types," they had said. And Jane had never looked back. Correction—Jane rarely looked back. Every once in a while, when she happened to catch the Tony Awards or Oscar night on television, she recalled her acceptance speeches. She and her friends "in theater" had all written them and every year, at Oscar parties, they would dress up and deliver their heartfelt thank-yous to one another for "being there during the lean years," and "supporting their art."

And now that sweetheart, Tim Lowry, was going to take her mind off her mundane real-life troubles by asking her to resume her too-short career, cut off in her prime, and Jane Wheel was once again going to trod the boards!

Could she do it? Could she memorize lines, walk confidently across a stage, not laugh at the silly dramatic dialogue in Kendell's play?

"There she is," said Tim, entering the EZ Way Inn through the seldom-used front door. "Kankakee's answer to Helen Hayes, Sarah Bernhardt, and Thelma Ritter . . . my leading lady!"

Jane laughed, feeling her cheeks grow warm. Had she missed being the centerpiece of someone's life so much that being asked to star in a Kankakee Community Theater play was enough to lift her out of the swamp? How pathetic was that?

"Lowry, is that all you can talk about now? That damn play of yours?" said Nellie.

"You've heard, Janie, right? You know why I showed you the script, you know I'm directing Kendell's play for the Community Theater?" asked Tim. "I know it's creaky, but I thought it would be fun to 'discover' a seventy-year-old play written by a Kankakee resident from a famous Kankakee family."

"Was Kendell famous?" asked Don. "I thought he was just rich."

Nellie approached Francis with the coffeepot but he shook his head and covered his cup with both hands. "He invented the monkey bars," said the bread man.

All conversation stopped and all eyes landed on Francis.

"That's what my wife said," he explained, shrugging his shoulders.

"He manufactured and sold playground equipment," said Tim. "I'm not sure what he actually invented or if—"

"He didn't invent the monkey bars, Francis," said Don, laughing.

Nellie nodded vigorously. "How can you be so gullible? Monkeys invented the goddamn monkey bars."

All eyes turned to Nellie.

"What? You don't think a monkey swinging through the trees invented the monkey bars? Jeez, where's Rita?" asked Nellie.

"I left her at the house," said Jane. "She told me you two had been up all night trading animal secrets."

"Very funny," said Nellie, turning to head back to the kitchen. "Who wants pie? I got cherry and lemon cream."

"Okay, as I was saying," said Tim, "I'm directing the play. It has a perfect part for me, so I'm acting in it, too. I'm tweaking and rewriting a bit . . . it's public domain so nobody's going to complain. Nothing beats working with a dead writer. And all that's left is to cast my leading lady."

"Tim, I think it's flattering, but . . ." Jane began.

"You're going to have to do some wooing," said Don.

"That's why I brought these," said Tim, producing from behind his back an enormous gift box of Godiva chocolates.

"That cost a fortune," said Jane. "No one buys a five-pound box of Godiva." Jane felt her hands begin to tremble. For someone like herself who never bought retail, who thrifted, scavenged, and scrounged, buying an overpriced luxury item like this produced shivering and a cold sweat. "In this economy, Tim? Godiva chocolates? It's obscene."

Nellie returned with a piece of cherry pie in one hand and a slice of lemon cream in the other. She set the plates on the bar and glanced at the gold, beribboned package. Then, just as Jane, shaking a little, reached out for the chocolates to take a closer look, Nellie rocked back on her heels, then forward onto her toes, and snatched the gold box away from her daughter's hands.

"For me, Lowry?" said Nellie, smiling slyly.

"If you say yes to being my leading lady, Nellie," said Tim.

Jane felt faint, like little lights were being turned off all around her head.

"All right, I'll star in your goddamned play."

“Nellie is not the leading lady,” said Tim. “She’s playing the dying dowager head of the family. She lays in a hospital bed onstage during the whole third act, comatose. I just needed someone like Nellie, you know, to get on board.”

Jane whipped out her notebook and rummaged through her tote for a pencil.

“Let’s get this show on the road, Tim. Where do you want me to start at the Kendell house?” she asked. “You’re obviously going to be busy down at the auditorium, rehearsals and all, so . . .”

“I didn’t think you wanted to act anymore. You’ve said a million times you were through with all that. I might know you better than you know yourself, but even I cannot read your mind!”

Jane put down her pencil and began applauding, one slow clap at a time.

“So Timothy Lowry finally admits that there is something he can’t do? Let’s hear it for the boy!”

“Sarcasm is so ugly on you,” Tim said. He picked up the fork she had next to her plate and broke off a bite of the cherry pie Jane had claimed for herself. Seated in a corner of the EZ Way Inn dining room, Jane and Tim were speaking in low voices, neither wanting Nellie to overhear them, albeit for different reasons. "And I planned on asking you to help with the play, but you were so snarky about it when we read the scene together, I just figured you wouldn't want anything to do with it."

"Let's get over to the Kendell place so you can show me around," Jane said, giving up on finding the pencil. "I don't want to have this conversation in front of Nellie."

"Fine."

"Fine."

The drive to the home of Frederick Kendell took ten minutes. In ten minutes' time, one can accomplish many things: read ten or more pages of a book, prepare a microwave rice pilaf, boil an egg, run a mile. In these particular ten minutes, Jane Wheel and Tim Lowry accomplished the following: Jane Wheel set a record for the most minutes she had ever remained silent in the company of Tim Lowry; Tim Lowry set a record for the most words spoken in the face of uninterrupted silence from Jane Wheel.

"Now just hear me out, okay? I started the clean-out, right? The first walk-through was amazing. You'll see when we get there. No one has lived in the house for fifteen years and it's been untouched since the day the parents left. Before that, the mother's parents and the father's parents and two great aunts lived there with them—with all their stuff. These two kids—a little older than we are—are the heirs and they want nothing out of this house. They're done. They want a sale, hoping that some of the big items make money, the paintings, the piano, the harp . . . that's right, there's a harp. The grandfather made a fortune and married a fortune and the son—the grandfather of these heirs, Frederick Junior—sat around on pillows made of money and wrote plays and this one actually got published. I think it was the equivalent of self-publishing because I've never heard of this place—Knarp Press? Have you?"

Jane shrugged.

"So anyway, I find twelve of these scripts and I just took them home, looked them up, and saw no one had ever bothered with a copyright and decided to make a case for putting this play on as the spring community theater production. Naturally, I'd direct, and who else could play the lead? So . . . long story short . . . I'm getting a little flack about directing and starring, so I needed to get some new blood involved—you know, people who don't usually participate in stuff like this. So I suggested to the board that I could get a whole element of the community to attend if I got Nellie to be in the show and so they kind of agreed that it would widen the circle—they're tired of being accused of being cliquey. And if Nellie's in it and the whole EZ Way Inn crowd comes, well, that's a wider circle for sure.

"And I thought you might want to get involved, too," said Tim, finally stopping for a breath.

Jane looked at him with one eyebrow raised. She had been practicing Detective Oh's no-eyebrow-raise-eyebrow-raise and she could feel it working its magic.

"I know you need money, and acting in the show doesn't pay—it's community theater—but there's a stipend for tech stuff, so I thought maybe you'd . . ." Tim stopped and looked over quickly as he turned into the long drive leading up to the Kendell mansion. Jane still hadn't spoken. Tim took a deep breath and finished his question. "I thought maybe you'd agree to do props?"

Jane was looking out her window. The house was enormous—even by the standards of old-money houses on the river, this one was special—gigantic. Without turning back to Tim, she asked, "How much?"

"All of them," Tim said, sounding a little confused. "It's a three-act play."

"How much is the stipend?"

"Five hundred dollars. I know it's not much, but it's four weeks' work and I figured we'd find most of the stuff right here at the house, borrow it for the production, then bring it back in time for the sale. Freddy earmarked the props he wanted used. Family won't care. I've got a great carpenter building the set and if you were to dress it and—"

"Design and props? And I have to run the show?"

"I figured you'd want to and that way maybe you could help with the vintage clothes and—"

"So aside from hammering in the nails myself, I'd be in charge of everything? Props, basic set dressing and design, costumes? How about makeup and hair?"

"Diane down at Waves said she'd handle all that," said Tim. "Janie, don't you think it would be fun? We haven't done a play together since *Antigone* senior year of high school."

"This is the other teeny little job you had for me, right?"

"Yeah," said Tim. "I thought you didn't hear me when I said that."

"I hear everything," said Jane. "I'll think it over."

"Think fast, because I already told the theater board you'd do it."

"Tim!"

"Look, it will be fun, you'll get paid, oh . . . yeah, there's one more thing," said Tim.

"You want me to hang the lights or sew a new stage curtain?"

"No, no, I almost forgot the most important part. I just heard this morning that the year after he finished the play, Freddy Kendell collapsed just like the character in the play. They found him out like a light in the garden. Just like the end of the first act? The cousin is found poisoned, collapsed in the flower beds. That's where they found old Freddy," said Tim, looking through an enormous ring of keys to find the one that would unlock the massive oak front door. "They said it was a heart attack, but it's possible he was poisoned."

"You're making this part up, aren't you?" said Jane.

"You could solve the Freddy Kendell murder!"

"Murder in the Eekaknak Valley?

"That's right. You design it, prop it, and solve it—a perfect summer project!" Tim turned the key and swung open the heavy door.

"You know, we detectives have to be hired by someone, paid by someone to solve a case. It's not a hobby like . . ." Jane's words stuck in her throat. The light was dim, filtered through sheer curtains made less sheer by several decades of dust. While Tim was wrestling with the heavy door, trying to get the lock to release his key, Jane stepped over the threshold. The entryway was a round foyer larger than most dining rooms. Although this space was cluttered with stacks of sealed boxes, and several folding tables marked T & T SALES leaned against the walls, it was still imposing, grand, and spacious. The floor was patterned in an elaborate mosaic design of tiny shards of blues and yellows and gold. The walls were painted with angelic murals, clouds. It was churchlike except for the one unholy sight that made Jane's skin crawl, a picture so horrific that she couldn't make the smallest sound let alone the scream that ached to come forward. Jane clutched at Tim's arm with her left hand and pointed to the chandelier—an enormous crystal-laden behemoth, the kind you might see in an opera house or the lobby of a grand hotel.

"Tim," Jane finally got out, squeezing his arm so violently, that without thinking he shook free before looking to where she pointed.

"What, what the . . ." Tim began, then followed the arrow her body made as she reached out both hands and leaned forward.

"Chandelier," Jane said, knowing that this word was not the one she intended to say. "Chandelier," she repeated.

From one of the chandelier's gigantic prism-laden arms swung a small body. A child hung from his neck by what appeared to be several colorful scarves knotted together. The door opening had caused the prisms to shimmer and shake and the body now continued to sway, seemingly keeping time with Jane's lurching heartbeat.

"Get a ladder," said Jane, after what felt like years of being frozen in place. "Tim, get a ladder and call the police."

Tim, still paralyzed, didn't answer.

Jane suddenly let out a breath. "Dummy."

Tim looked at her, apparently not comprehending.

"Dummy. It's a dummy."

Jane walked over to the light switch and pushed the heavy round button in. The chandelier lit up, illuminating the foyer, causing the gold-flecked floor to shine and the mirrors hanging on the walls to ricochet light around the circle of the room.

The brightness helped Tim see what Jane had just figured out.

The body swinging from the chandelier was not that of a child, but instead a ventriloquist's dummy—a boy with red hair and freckles and what would have been a giant grin on his face, had the mouth mechanism not dropped open, changing the mindless jolly expression of the doll's face to one of slack horror. Now that the room was lit, they could see that the clothes, the blue-and-white-checked shirt, the baggy dungarees, and the shiny black round-toed shoes were plainly those of a doll, a vintage doll at that. Now that the chandelier illuminated the space, the dummy looked so unlike a human child, instead of relief, they were overcome with the kind of anger that only strikes when one feels he or she had been made a fool.

"Get the ladder anyway, Tim. We can't leave it there to give the next person a heart attack."

"I want to know who in the hell thought this was funny," said Tim.

Jane set up the small stepladder that Tim had stashed with his folding tables. Rummaging in one of his supply boxes, she found a pair of heavy scissors and climbed up to the light fixture, ready to cut through a fuchsia-flowered scarf.

"Don't cut. Untie if you can," said Tim. "Most of the clothes here are really good. I'll bet those scarves are silk and—"

"Damn," said Jane, her fingers tangled in a knot. "This one isn't just silk, honey, it's Hermès."

Jane handed the designer scarves to Tim, who smoothed them out, clucking over the wrinkles. Jane held up the dummy by its shoulders in front of her.

"What was so bad about your life, buddy? Why'd you try to end it all?"

"Oh, sweetie, please don't open the door to jokes about all those strange hands up his—"

"Right. Being a ventriloquist's dummy would be a hell of a life . . ."

Jane brushed off the doll's clothes. A tag on the inside of his collar read: MR. BUMBLES. Underneath it, in italics, was written *Bumby*. "So you're Bumby," said Jane. She held him up and gave him a shake. A halo of dust radiated out from the doll.

"Well, Bumby, unless I find a suicide note, I am unable to rule out foul play. This could be attempted murder."

"Out of curiosity, Madame Detective, how do you tell when a ventriloquist's dummy is a victim of murder or just attempted murder?" asked Tim.

Forgetting her anger, Jane laughed, closing the dummy's mouth and laying it out on a mahogany console table. It was true that the difference between a dead dummy and a live dummy was, on the surface, negligible.

"He just doesn't look depressed enough to end it all, does he?" asked Jane.

The dummy was one of those clones of the early television brash boys of ventriloquism. Not quite Howdy Doody, not quite Jerry Mahoney, but close enough to present to your child as a recognizable TV toy and creative prop for playtime.

Peering over Jane's shoulder at the laid-out Bumby, Tim shuddered. "They are so creepy. Honestly, dummies give clowns a run for their money when it comes to a what-were-my-parents-thinking-when-they-handed-me-that-nightmare-provoking toy?"

Jane nodded, also wondering what parents actually wanted their child to show a knack for ventriloquism. Wouldn't the ability to throw one's voice just push a child into the class clown role at best, the class pariah at worst? If your son was *bad* at ventriloquism, you would be doomed to watching his little play-lets, sitting on the couch pretending not to see his lips move. And if he was *good* at it? Even worse. He might grow up to be a ventriloquist!

"Hello, Bumby, what's this?" Jane said, straightening the kerchief in Bumby's pocket. She pulled out a folded piece of paper.

"If you tell me that it is a suicide note, I'm giving up this sale," said Tim, backing away.

ASK ME ABOUT THE MURDERS

The words were block-printed on a lined piece of paper, a page, Jane noted, that was ripped from a small six-ring binder, a calendar book, a Day Runner–type organizer.

"Okay, I'm officially creeped out," said Tim. "Anyone who plays this kind of game is a little too sick to mess with. Maybe I should give up the sale and the play."

Tim had stepped away from the dummy and Jane until his back was against the wall on the other side of the foyer. Directly above him hung an austere portrait painted in a stiff, unappealing style. This was not a painting old or ornate enough to be one of those collectible instant ancestors one finds at a flea market, nor was it folksy enough to be painted by a wandering itinerant artist or a family member hobbyist with a palette and a smock. This gentleman was professionally painted, but the work was completely devoid of emotion or affection. The painting looked as if it might belong in a row of past company presidents whose portraits might line the hallways of corporate headquarters.

Jane did not think it was the right time to point out to Tim that he was standing beneath a painting that, in an old horror film, would have eyes that followed you wherever you moved. She also had had enough time to cast her eye into the parlor off the foyer that was filled from parquet floor to cove-molded ceiling with antique tables, needlepointed stools, dusty books, and a plethora of fascinating small collectible items crying out for a dust rag and a price tag.

"I'll need a copy of the play, an expense account, and a boatload of cleaning supplies."

"You're taking the job," said Tim, exhaling in relief.

"Ssss," said Jane. "Jobs, plural. I'll start by reading the whole play tonight and making the props list, then working here tomorrow to see what we might use. We can clean and price as we go."

Tim nodded, rummaging through his leather bag to find her a copy of *Murder in the Eekaknak Valley*.

"I'll need a list of everyone who has a key to the house, too, so we can put a stop to any more practical jokes," said Jane, laying a protective hand on Bumby's shoulder. "I want the cast of the play and the cast of the house."

"Yeah, hey," said Tim, handing her the script. "I can't

believe I just got this. The title? *Murder in the Eekaknak Valley?* Eekaknak? It's Kankakee backward."

Jane looked at the script, then at Tim. She had just agreed to become props mistress for an amateur melodrama starring Nellie, cut down a suicidal ventriloquist's dummy named Mr. Bumbles, and decided to solve a possible seventy-year-old murder.

Jane was definitely in Kankakee, and as usual, life was definitely running ass backward.

Jane clicked through the new photos posted on Nick's Facebook page. She enlarged the picture of Nick standing next to Charley, both of them holding special narrow-bladed shovels. Jane leaned in toward the screen and moved the cursor to the thumbs-up symbol. Is this what exchanging letters had become? A picture had always been worth a thousand words, but her return of "Like"? Wasn't that just worth one word? Jane tapped out a Facebook message to Nick, telling him briefly about the play and the Kendell house, leaving out any mention of Mr. Bumbles. If there was a mystery to solve, it was a little too tangled to explain just yet. Nick would just be happy to know she was working with Tim, staying with Don and Nellie in Kankakee, and not rattling around in the house alone. Jane logged out and settled back into rereading the script.

It had been a while since Jane had done props on a theatrical production, but, she reasoned with herself, how hard could this show be? Even though MITEV, which was her shortened version of the bulky *Murder in the Eekaknak Valley*, was a three-act play, heavy on the deco set dressing, it was an almost-closed-room kind of murder mystery. No real scene changes.

Myra, a famous actress, retires and moves back to the Eekaknak Valley of her childhood, buys the biggest house in town, and invites all of her relatives and ne'er-do-well friends to live there with her. A cousin who resembles Myra is found murdered in the herb garden, laid out with flowers and leaves decorating the body, and a detective sets up shop in the gazebo, ready to solve the mystery and woo Hermione, Myra's daughter.

"Who's playing Hermione?" said Jane out loud. "Why in the world wouldn't Tim offer that role to me?"

Rita, resting under Jane's bare feet, sighed and groaned. It wasn't the first time that the dog had heard the question.

"Okay, maybe I'm too old for Hermione, which means that Tim is too damn old for Craven, but if not Hermione, I could have played Myra—aged it up a bit."

Rita had been listening to Jane mutter and mumble and watched her scribble notes to herself for three hours—twenty-one hours in dog time—and enough seemed to be enough. The dog rose, stretched, and trotted off toward the kitchen in search of Nellie and leftovers and a tall, cool drink, not necessarily in that order.

"Yeah, go ahead. Just like in college—everybody wants to hang out with the actor. Who wants to be with the techie?"

Jane had read the play twice, making a list of all objects required to be on the set, which thankfully did not change through the acts. Freddy Kendell had spent more time specifying props and set dressing than he had on believability of characters. Jane was delighted to see that her work, in the form of a meticulously detailed props list, was practically done for her.

A formal and ornately decorated living room with three entrances: One, in the rear opens onto the garden. Stage left is the entrance from the dining room; stage right leads to the front entrance of the stately home. There is a staircase in the rear leading to the upstairs bedrooms and living quarters of Myra, Hermione, and all of their relatives, friends, and hangers-on.

The fact that the set remained the same except for the hospital bed set up on one side during the second act when the room is converted into Myra's mother, Marguerite's sick room simplified the set dressing somewhat. Curtains, rugs, furniture would all remain the same. A bar set up downstage left would be fun. Jane already had the glasses, cocktail shaker, and decanters sketched out—all from Tim Lowry's private collection. Jane knew he'd balk at letting his Chase cocktail set out of his house, but those were the sacrifices an actor-director would have to make for his art.

"I told you I'm not interested. Do you see the sign there? I printed it myself, and . . ." Nellie's voice was rising steadily. Jane hadn't heard the doorbell but had heard her mother open the front door and start talking before any sounds came from the other side. Jane pitied the poor child who might be selling candy for his Little League team or, worse yet, the earnest college student collecting signatures for a worthwhile cause.

Jane had set up shop in the small room one step down from the living room, which her mother referred to as the breezeway and her father referred to as the den. It was neither breezy nor denlike; it was just a convenient and tidy little room that led from the attached garage into the small dining area and living room of her parents' early-fifties, almost-ranch-style house. The house was a one-story with a deep basement, laid out like a ranch, but with touches that were definitely pre-fifties ranch explosion—a fireplace alcove, a built-in china cupboard. Cape Cod meets California? Jane's parents had moved to this house during Jane's senior year in high school, so it was and wasn't her childhood home. Jane had lived there, occupied a bedroom across from her parents' room, and tried to entertain friends in the finished basement, but only for a year. This house had never stuck as her real home. She always felt like a tourist when she stayed with Don and Nellie, except when she worked on a project in the breezeway. Jane had claimed this room, the one that was neither fish nor fowl, as her own space. The knotty pine wainscoting was right out of the forties, and although the windows on both sides had been updated, the wooden venetian blinds were old-school—fat, real wooden slats—installed long before mini blinds were a gleam in some metal fabricator's eye. Jane had found a comfy old stuffed chair with hassock and dragged in a small wooden side table to use as a makeshift desk. An open corner cupboard held plants—ropy philodendrons and ivies cascaded down the front of the shelves. Nellie claimed that she had never killed a houseplant. *Even when she tries,* Don would always add. Nellie always claimed that houseplants just grew for her, and although Jane had pointed out the excellent light sources, windows on both sides—southern and northern exposure—her mother had shrugged it off.

"It isn't the light that makes my plants grow," she said, nodding. "I've got secrets."

Now Jane could hear her mother growing more agitated at the front door. When she heard Rita give her low, almost inaudible growl of warning, Jane shoved aside her notebooks and hopped up.

Although Nellie seemed to be treating the four people standing on the porch as a cross between door-to-door missionaries—"I got my own church"—and vacuum cleaner salesmen—"I don't need anything you're selling"—Jane could see right away that they were neither.

The only male in the quartet looked the least disturbed; he seemed to be amused by Nellie's bum's rush. Although it had been more than twenty years since Jane had seen the man, she recognized him right away. Still tall, of course, but also still handsome—all the girls had thought him pretty dreamy when he started teaching freshman English at Bishop McNamara during Jane's senior year.

"Hi, Mr. Havens," Jane said, trying to edge around Nellie, who, tiny as she was, seemed to grow in every way when she was bent on blocking the doorway. Before he could answer, the woman who Jane now realized had been doing all the talking, who had taken Nellie on, eyeball-to-eyeball, turned to Jane and began laughing.

"I think you can probably drop the 'mister' stuff now, Jane. Still afraid of getting a demerit?" Although Jane might not have recognized her face, she would have known the voice anywhere. Low, throaty, always sounding as if she knew a delicious secret. Twentysome years might have changed the face and altered the body, but that voice was unmistakable. Mary Wainwright.

Why is it a universal truth that no matter how far one travels in life, no matter how much material and professional success one achieves, when one is confronted with one's high school nemesis who could always reduce one to a stuttering clown, one . . .

Jane's highest thought process could not finish on a high note—damn it. Now that Jane was face-to-face with Mary Wainwright, no matter how hard she tried to think herself onto the high road, to reflect on youth with lofty language, it clearly wouldn't work. When Jane thought about her four years of high school, sitting next to Mary Wainwright in class after class, competing for grades, boys, class offices, and the leads in every school play, Mary Wainwright was, and Jane now realized, disappointed in her own pettiness, would probably always be "the bitch who tried to ruin my life."

"Do you know Patty Horton?" Mary asked, introducing the dark-haired woman, perhaps five or six years older than Jane and Mary. And with a gesture to her left, she indicated the fourth member of the group, a gray-haired woman who looked embarrassed to be standing there. "And this is Rica Evans."

Nellie had remained quiet during the introductions, partially, Jane was sure, out of curiosity. Her finely tuned antennae would have picked up Jane's agitation and Nellie, always delighted to observe discomfiture, especially, Jane thought, in her daughter, was willing to wait a few minutes longer before slamming the door in the faces of her visitors.

Just then, Tim drove up in front of the house and slammed his Mustang against the curb, his signature parking style, and jumped out waving both arms.

"Nellie! Sorry I'm late. I've been trying to call you to tell you the cast was coming over to meet you. Your phone must be out of order."

Tim was lying. Jane knew he hadn't tried to call Nellie because Nellie would have told him she didn't want to meet the goddamn cast and hung up on him. Much better to tell everyone to show up—in a group—and then dash in, breathless, as the hero, to smooth things over. This would allow Tim to explain away Nellie's crusty exterior as part of a mix-up rather than what the other actors would discover soon enough—that her crusty exterior was the outer manifestation of her crusty interior. Jane tried to catch Tim's eye so she could convey to him that she knew what he was up to even if Nellie was fooled.

"Well, you're here anyway, so come in." Nellie stepped away from the door, wiping her hands on her apron.

Don slammed his recliner forward, changing from man-dozing-under-the-newspapers to awake-affable-host as his chair shifted him into second.

Don and Nellie stood awkwardly as the cast filed in. No bar, no rinse tanks, no rags in hand, no tap, no cooler, no jukebox in the corner—Jane realized that without the fittings and fixtures of the EZ Way Inn, Don and Nellie had no idea what they were supposed to do in the company of other human beings. Used to serving drinks and offering plates of food, at ease with the patter of conversation as customers filed in and out, Jane saw her parents now totally bewildered. People were in their house. What next?

Jane suggested everyone sit and make themselves comfortable, while frantically trying to make eye contact with Don, who seemed frozen in his spot.

"Dad, don't we have some iced tea or something? Mom, some cookies? Some . . ."

That did it. Orders. As soon as he realized he could serve them up glasses of something, anything, Don thawed and beamed before heading to the kitchen. Nellie, still wiping her hands and looking at these people as if they were museum specimens, did not move.

"So who's who?" said Nellie. "Don't tell me your real names again," she added, holding up her hand like a traffic cop as both Tim and Mary started again with introductions. "Tell me who you are in the play and I'll just call you that. It'll make it easier for me to remember."

"In that case, from now on, I am Detective Craven. Phillip Craven," said Tim. "Rica is playing Myra, the actress who returns to the valley after a successful career and buys a huge mansion and moves her mother in, that's you, Nellie, playing Marguerite. Myra wants to reconnect with both her mother and her newly divorced daughter, Hermione, played by Mary. Chuck plays Hermione's jealous estranged husband, Malachi. Patty is the cousin who invites herself to stay in the house, but is—"

"Jeez, Lowry, I told you to make it simple. I've read the play," said Nellie.

It was Tim's turn to be shocked. He cast Nellie as a bit of whimsy and as an inclusive bit of politicking between the town and the amateur theater group, and he expected he would be able to plant her onstage for the weekend of three performances with little or no interaction on her part. He had hardly expected her to read the play.

Jane was delighted to see Tim squirm a bit. She had carried her legal pad in with her to investigate the front-door debacle and now held it in front of her mother. After finishing her preliminary list of set props and design notes, she had listed the cast members in preparation for determining their personal props, scene by scene. Now, next to the character names printed in large block letters, she added the names of the people sitting in front of Nellie.

MYRA: *Rica Evans*
HERMIONE: *Mary Wainwright*
DETECTIVE PHILLIP CRAVEN: *Tim Lowry*
MALACHI: *Mr. Havens—Jane scratched out "Mr." and wrote "Chuck."*
COUSIN FLIP: *Patty . . . Jane hadn't caught her last name*
MOTHER/GRANDMOTHER MARGUERITE: *Nellie*
COOK: *tba*
PERKINS THE GARDENER: *tba*
DINNER GUESTS/NEIGHBORS: *tba*

"What did you think of it, Nellie?" asked Tim.

Nellie studied the legal pad Jane put in front of her, looking at the names, then up at the faces of her guests.

"The play, Nellie, what did you think of the script?"

"Not much, to tell you the truth. Seemed like Myra was kind of a sap, letting all those people live off of her. She must have felt guilty about something to let the town run over her like that," said Nellie.

Before Tim could defend MITEV in front of his cast, Rica, who had kept her head down, even as they all sat down, looked up at Nellie.

"I feel the same way, Nellie. I've thought about it a lot and I think Myra must have felt that she deserted her mother or that she left something undone or unsaid when she went to New York to pursue her dreams. I think she is consumed by guilt. Much more interesting than thinking about her as someone ditsy and naïve who doesn't see others taking advantage of her," said Rica, looking down as soon as she finished.

Don entered with iced tea for everyone, balanced on a large modern wooden tray that Jane had never seen before. She realized she had never seen her parents entertain anyone in their home, so it would make sense that anything passing for "partyware" would be hidden away.

Everyone stood to reach for their glasses so Don wouldn't have to step through to their chairs, and as Patty reached for hers, she looked down at the legal pad Nellie was studying and in a squeaky voice asked, "What's that?" pointing to Jane's doodle in the corner of the page.

Tim, perched over Jane's chair, looked down and studied Jane's sketch of Mr. Bumbles hanging from the chandelier. "Oh God, the strangest thing happened—" he began.

Jane, shifting the tablet, managed to spill iced tea on Tim's perfectly pressed khakis. She quickly handed him a napkin so he could dab at the spot while she folded the tablet over on the coffee table and stood up.

"Just the remnants of a hangman game I was playing earlier."

"So are you still acting, Jane? I lost track of your career after college," said Mary.

"Advertising," said Jane. "I went into advertising."

Tim remembered that he had not only arrived in time to save the day, to protect his cast from getting the heave-ho from Nellie, but he also had a tray of sandwiches and cookies and cupcakes in the car. He ran out to fetch as Nellie gathered plates and napkins.

"Help me get this stuff, Jane," said Nellie in a voice Jane had never heard her use. Part sweetness, part helplessness, adding up to one hundred percent phoniness.

"Wasn't that Wainwright girl the one who took your boyfriend in high school?" asked Nellie, pushing Jane away as she tried to help get small plates from a high cupboard shelf.

"Yup," said Jane, standing back as her mother grabbed napkins and sugar, and found a lemon in the refrigerator and began slicing it for the iced tea that Don had already served.

"And she ran against you for vice president of the school, right?"

"Student council," Jane said, nodding.

"She made your life miserable, right?"

"She tried," Jane said.

"She sure has gained a lot of weight, hasn't she?" said Nellie, grinning maliciously.

"Mom!" said Jane, happy beyond measure that Nellie in her meanness was giving her best motherly attempt at protecting and defending Jane. "I hadn't noticed."

"Tim should have put you in that part."

Nellie had finished gathering everything and insisted on carrying it all out on the second tray Jane had never seen. Jane gave her a minute to make her entrance before following her into the living room. Things always work out, she thought. If Tim hadn't asked her to do props, if he had cast her in his play, Jane would have never gotten to hear Nellie champion her. This was beginning to feel like it was all worth it.

"Oh yeah, she's solved lots of crimes. Murders even," said Don.

Don, on the other hand, never tired of championing Jane, and although she was appreciative, she had hoped to keep the fact that she was doing detective work a secret for the time being. Jane hadn't really thought much of Tim's ruse to get her interested in helping him—the mysterious death of playwright Freddy Kendell would not amount to much, she was sure. But the fact that Mr. Bumbles had been swinging from the end of a Hermès noose this afternoon signaled that someone concerned with the Kendell estate was up to some mischief. Much easier to find out who the someone was if no one knew she was looking.

Don, however, was beaming at Jane as she stood in the doorway. When Jane was a little girl, all dressed up for church or a party, Don always called her "Miss America." Now he smiled at her as if she were wearing a sash proclaiming ACE DETECTIVE."

"Dad, I just help out a bit on some investigations. I'm not—"

"They were going to do a movie about her," said Don,

Jane caught Tim's eye as he set down the tray full of goodies he had put together from a trip to Myers Bakery and the deli counter at the supermarket and gave him the pleading head-to-one-side this-is-your-bright-idea-of-a-get-together-so-get-going kind of look.

"We have a few more cast members on the way," said Tim, "but we can get started, you know, getting to know each other."

"Why?" said Nellie. "What's the point of that, Lowry?"

"Actors have to trust each other, Nellie. It's important that we know a little bit about who we're going to be performing with and—"

"Seems to me Marguerite has to know Myra and vice versa. They have to know what makes each other tick. Doesn't matter a damn if Rica knows me as Nellie or Santa Claus. She's got to know me as her mother, Marguerite," said Nellie. "We should be talking about the play. We only got a few weeks to get this show on the road."

Nellie's understanding of theater, the press of time, and the importance of the characters connecting to each other onstage impressed Jane. As far as she knew, Nellie had attended six plays in her whole life—two when Jane had appeared in them in high school and four of the productions Jane had been in at college.

Chuck Havens cleared his throat. He looked amused, but Jane wasn't sure if he really was or if his slight smile was the residual coolest-guy-in-the-room expression that he had always used in the halls of Bishop McNamara. Jane realized that he must have been only four or five years older than she was, but the distance between high school senior and recent college graduate was enormous. Jane looked at his left hand—no wedding ring—and told herself it was just a reflex. An observant, trained detective always checked for the obvious.

"Marguerite?" he said, looking at Nellie. "I think you're quite right. And although Myra and Hermione would address you as Mother and Grandmother, I think I wouldn't have been the kind of grandson-in-law who would have adopted the Grandmamma address. You would be Marguerite to me, and even if I were scheming about how to stay in the will after Hermione divorced me, I think you and I were friends and I would be truly sorry to see you ill and unable to communicate your wishes."

"Yeah, even though you try to put words in my mouth that will help you get your hands on the family money," said Nellie.

"Touché," said Chuck, laughing.

Jane was impressed with how well Nellie had studied the script. She could see Tim was appalled. Interpretations seemed to be flying fast and furiously past him. Had he ever directed a play before? Jane was pretty sure he had not. And if he couldn't take control soon, establish his vision of *Murder in the Eekaknak Valley,* Tim wouldn't exactly be directing this one.

The rest of the cast arrived. A husband and wife whose claim to fame was that they had appeared in every Kankakee Community Theater production for the past five years—always as "dinner guests" or "chauffeur and maid" or "neighbors 1 and 2," but nonetheless took their roles seriously and loved their lives in the theater. Another married couple was introduced as Kendell cousins who were going to cover a few small parts. And Henry Gand, whom Tim introduced as Perkins the gardener, arrived just as Don came in with a full pitcher of iced tea to offer refills.

"Henry." Don nodded.

"Don." He nodded back.

"What the hell are you doing here, Hank?" asked Nellie.

"I am Perkins," he said with a slight bow and smile at Nellie.

Jane might have squirmed a bit when she saw Mary Wainwright at the door, but it was nothing compared to the stiffness Jane saw in her always hospitable father. And Nellie? Either her mother had just been stung simultaneously by several insects or placed her feet on a bed of hot coals or . . . was it possible? Nellie was blushing?

There were enough people talking past each other and over each other that the community theater gossip and chatter covered any personal relationship confusion that might have emerged due to Tim's surprise prerehearsal, but Jane filed away this little play-within-a-play for later discussion.

Jane managed to take down everyone's name and even talked costuming, writing down some sizes and measurements to share with the costumer Tim claimed to have in the wings and made some notes about who might own what as far as personal props for their respective characters.

Except for the frost that formed between Don and Henry, everyone seemed to get along, and as far as accidental rehearsals go, Jane thought Tim might be able to deem this one a success. Actors picked up their plates and glasses and brought them into the kitchen, then picked up scripts and notebooks as they said their good-byes, promising to take up where everyone left off the next evening when rehearsals began in earnest at the cultural center.

Although she had enjoyed the novelty of an impromptu party at Don and Nellie's secret lair, Jane was getting anxious to grill her parents about Henry and some of the other townspeople who had attended. The last person out the door, Rica Evans, pulled Jane to one side, lightly tugging on her sleeve.

"Your hangman doodle?" she began. "I saw that you had written 'Mr. Bumbles' on it."

"Oh, that?" Jane stalled, trying to decide quickly whether she needed an elaborate lie or just something simple and elegant, a little black dress of a lie.

"I found this in my script," she said, withdrawing a scrap of dingy lined paper from between the pages of her copy of MITEV. "I just thought it was a joke, a child's prank, but maybe it's something else? Your father said you were a detective?" Rica sounded apologetic. "I was using it as a bookmark."

Written on the paper in large block letters:

DO NOT PUT ON THIS PLAY.
IT IS A "CURSED PLAY."
YOU WILL BE SORRY ALL YOUR DAYS.
LISTEN TO ME.
YOUR FRIEND,
MR. BUMBLES

Tim offered to wash the dishes. It was the least he could do, he told Nellie, and Nellie, who never let anyone near her sink, nodded and agreed with him. Nellie handed Jane a dish towel and motioned for her to stay in the kitchen with Tim. Nellie walked into the living room and gave Don a stern stare while he pretended as long as he could not to see it. However, since she stood directly in front of him, arms folded, as he sat in his chair concealed behind the front page of the *Kankakee Daily Journal,* he finally had to give in.

"What?"

"You know what, Don. Henry Gand, that's what," said Nellie.

"I don't know what you're—"

"Can it," said Nellie. "Let's not have any nonsense about this. It was all over between him and me when I met you and I didn't know he was going to be in Lowry's idiotic play."

Don set the paper aside.

"I know, Nellie, it's just that Henry's an educated man, a successful man, and I'm afraid I never—"

"Can it," Nellie said again. "Never would have worked. His family didn't approve of me. I was a factory girl and he was going to college. He just wanted me to be in those plays of his because I could remember lines, not like some of the twits in his usual crowd. Besides . . ." Nellie stopped.

"Besides what?" Don asked, starting to sound more like himself.

"You know damn well. I didn't love him."

Jane hoped the gasp she felt escape from her wasn't as loud as it sounded in her own head. She and Tim were crowded into the doorway, watching Don and Nellie play roles for which they never would have been cast—at least not by Jane and Tim.

"And you loved me at first sight?" Don said, his big grin returning.

"I didn't say that," said Nellie. "But you've been all right."

Nellie turned around and trained her laser-beam eyes on Jane and Tim. "I told you both to do the dishes and stop staring." Don, behind his wife's back, winked at them.

Jane now remembered that she and her brother, Michael, had come across a rare souvenir of Nellie's youth once when leafing through the giant *North American Atlas,* one of the few books in their home. Jane was helping Michael—or maybe Michael was helping Jane—with a geography project, and pressed between Illinois and Indiana they found an old folded paper with hand-drawn illustrations, carefully lettered and with their mother's name in it. They figured it was a joke of some kind—some bit of ephemera from the EZ Way Inn, a piece of nonsense or doggerel courtesy of Slats, the poet of the bowling league, or a prank from Sy, a printer who often made up joke posters to hang on the tavern wall. Nellie had snatched it away from them and said it was nothing, just some silly old play she and her friends were going to put on. Now, with all of tonight's theatrical planning going on in the house, the memory came back to Jane. Those names on that dusty piece of paper were a cast list. It was a theater program. Of course. Apparently

Murder in the Eekaknak Valley would not be Nellie's theater debut.

"Your mother is a woman of many secrets," said Tim, finishing up the last of the glasses.

"As if I didn't know," said Jane. "Charley calls her the 'dig' because there is always something to uncover. A shard here, a shard there."

Jane knew Nellie didn't believe in reminiscing or telling childhood stories. Nellie moved forward—no pause, no rewind, no slow-mo. She didn't believe in looking backward. Any time Jane or Michael questioned their mother her answer was always "Who cares about that old stuff?" or, if the question was personal, "That's none of your business." Even if Jane had recognized the old program for what it was, Nellie would never have taken its discovery as a cue to sit down and regale them with stories of her youth.

Jane had filled Tim in on where she stood with props, managing to avoid commenting on his choice of her old rival Mary Wainwright for the role Jane should have been playing. It was odd, though. Tim had been Jane's best friend, staunchest ally, and unrelenting supporter through high school, even if he had also been her sternest critic and tyrannical stylist as well. Jane relaxed her shoulders, which she realized had been bunched up around her ears all evening, and took Tim's arm to lead him into the breezeway.

"Okay, we've got some weird love triangle going on with my parents and Perkins the gardener, and you've managed to get Mr. Havens, everyone's high school crush, to join your cast, and you somehow forgot to mention that you cast Mary Wainwright in the part I should be playing, but I'm willing to forget all about this since we've got something much more important to worry about," said Jane.

"Mary Wainwright needs this play," said Tim. "She's had nothing but trouble—"

"Not now. You make your excuses and apologies later," said Jane, handing Tim the note given to her by Rica Evans.

"A cursed play?" said Tim. "Come on. Somebody's just—" Tim stopped. "Isn't that what they call *Macbeth*? The cursed play?"

This was just like Tim Lowry. Pay attention to something negative just long enough to find something that could be twisted into a positive, a compliment. Jane could see his wheels turning. Somehow this threat was morphing into a comparison of the play he was directing for Kankakee Community Theater and the work of Shakespeare. Only Tim Lowry would be able to see the hand of the bard in *Murder in the Eekaknak Valley.*

Jane had asked Rica not to mention the note to anyone else in the cast. Neither confirming nor denying that her "hangman doodle" was anything more or less than she said it was, Jane took the scrap of paper from Rica and promised to make sure that it was nothing more than a joke and a coincidence.

Actors are superstitious. Even actors in community theater productions will not say the name of Shakespeare's "Scottish play" backstage, and if someone does make the mistake of uttering "Macbeth," determined to show how silly all the hoopla is? Someone else will be just as determined to make the offender turn around three times, go outside, and perform a variety of tasks to lift the bad luck he or she has invoked. The last thing Tim Lowry needed for his production of *Murder in the Eekaknak Valley* was any link to the cursed "Scottish play."

Jane went over her notes on the necessary props for the play. She almost felt guilty about accepting the tech stipend, since there wasn't going to be a lot of work to dressing the stage. Freddy had been specific about the props, including notes about where they could be found, boxed up in the attic of the family home. He wrote his own possessions into the play, both in a note at the end of the script and throughout, within scene descriptions and stage directions—paintings, silver sets, furniture—everything was annotated. Jane knew from reading the stage directions and descriptions that the painting of Myra's father that was supposed to hang over the sofa was the portrait that hung in the entry hall of the house. If everything at the house had remained as untouched as Tim said—and that is how it looked—the gathering of props for *Murder in the Eekaknak Valley* part of Jane's job was going to be easy . . . practically paint by number.

Since she could pick up most of the stuff for the play at the house, Jane told Tim her work hours for the Kendell house could be pretty much nine to five. She handed him an estimate of the time she would need for props, trying to formalize her role, but Tim waved it away. Instead, he offered his own notes in trade: a list of all the Kendell relatives and those who had keys to the house.

"Who's Penny Kendell? Why does that name sound so familiar?" asked Jane.

"You just met her," said Tim. "Penny and Bryan carpooled here with Henry Gand. They're playing dinner party guests, then Bryan will be one of the cops in Act Two and Penny will be the visiting nurse. Bryan's a second cousin or something to the Kendells and Penny has a key to the house. She was helping them sort through things before they called me in. Likes antiques and thought she could help, but was overwhelmed by sheer volume."

Jane drew a lopsided star next to her name. Might as well prioritize. Here was a Kendell who had a key to the house and was involved with the play. She had been in the house, could have slipped a note into a script.

"The thing is," said Jane aloud, "that note looked really old.

It was either put there years ago, in Frederick's time, or someone went to a lot of trouble to make it look old," Jane stopped when Tim's cell phone rang and he fished it out of his pocket. He held up one finger as he answered, but Jane finished her thought. "The good news is that Mr. Bumbles pulls pranks but hasn't really caused any harm. Nothing bad—"

"Oh my God," said Tim. "Where did they take her?"

"Vanilla okay?" said Nellie over her shoulder to Don as she walked through the kitchen door, hand already holding an imaginary ice cream scoop. "I think it's all we got."

"What?" said Jane, looking at Tim.

"What?" said Nellie, looking at Jane.

"What?" said Tim, looking into his phone. He turned it to the side, stared at the screen, then held it back up to his ear. "It looks like them. Sure. Before noon tomorrow. Please give her our best. I'll be up to see her."

"That was Bryan Kendell. He and Penny are at the hospital. She walked into their bedroom and as she was turning on the light she slipped on some marbles and hit her head; they think she might have fractured her leg."

Jane studied her list of names.

"Marbles?" said Nellie. "Who the hell has marbles . . ."

"Penny Kendell. She collects marbles. Has jars of them all over the place. But these, the ones on the floor, were antique clay marbles. When Penny was at the Kendell place and the cousins asked if she wanted anything, she said she wanted the jar of clay marbles that she saw in the playroom and they said as soon as everything was inventoried she could have them. She said she'd buy them from the estate sale, just save them for her. Bryan said the marbles on the floor looked just like the clay ones from the house."

Jane held her cast list in one hand and the list of people with keys to the Kendell house in the other. "Any chance one of your Kendell clients, Bryan's cousins, dropped them off? Do they have a cat who could have knocked over the jar?"

Tim shrugged. "Don't know about the cat, but Bryan found a note next to the jar."

"Yeah?" said Nellie. "Stop being so dramatic. What the hell did it say?"

"Here are your marbles. Don't lose them."

Nellie finished scooping Don's ice cream and licked the bowl of the old serving spoon before dropping it into the sink.

"So somebody from the family dropped them off and made a little joke. Then the cat knocked them over and the joke isn't so funny," said Nellie.

"We don't even know if . . ." Jane stopped when she saw Tim staring at the picture on his phone. He passed it over to Jane.

On the screen was a surprisingly clear photo of two clay marbles on top of a block-printed note that said just what Tim had reported. The note was signed *Your friend, Bumby.*

The two Kendell heirs no longer lived in Kankakee. According to Tim, they never really did. Both had attended boarding schools and had never really deeply dug in and lived in the family mansion. Margaret, who, as a child, went by Margie, and Frederick, who thankfully did not add to any Fred/Freddy confusion and went by Rick, were the great-grandchildren of Frederick Kendell, the lumber baron, construction magnate, and outdoor equipment fabricator; the grandchildren of Frederick "Freddy" Kendell Junior, the playwright, author of *Murder in the Eekaknak Valley;* and the children of Frederick "Fred" Kendell III, who died after selling off his namesakes' companies and redirecting the family business into stocks, bonds, property—ostensibly retaining the fortune while ridding the family of the messiness of day-to-day work. Both lived at least part-time in Chicago. Frederick Kendell IV, Rick, a lifelong bachelor, divided his time between a high-rise in the city and an oceanfront mansion in Florida, and Margie, now divorced for the second time, spent half the year in London. It had taken the brother and sister well over a year to agree to sell the mansion and allow Tim to begin prepping.

Those were the facts Jane culled from the messy explanation of the children Tim had given her. Apparently Margie and Rick didn't like each other much. Since they had boarded and summer camped separately for all of their younger lives, Jane wondered how they even knew each other well enough to know they didn't get along. The brother and sister finally agreed that the house and its contents must be sold and finally concluded that some of the fine art and a few of the museum-quality furniture pieces could be shipped off to auctions in New York and London, but they continued to argue about who would supervise the Kankakee sale. Neither wanted to let it go and neither wanted to be totally responsible.

"It's like this in almost every sale I've ever done," said Tim. "The sibs tell me to sell it all, they're done with it, then one of them shows up and sees an old Martha Washington sewing stand with $195 price tag on it and decides maybe he should take it home to the wife. Then the sister shows up and hears that the brother took the sewing table that she never wanted in the first place but she has to have something comparable so she finds the father's antique pipe rack and decides it would be just the thing for her husband's office. Brother pops in while I'm prepping and asks about the pipe rack since he's decided he might like to smoke a pipe, finds out that Sis nabbed it and all hell breaks loose. I've had to cancel sales because the brothers and sisters start snatching back objects one by one to keep up with each other. And don't get me started on the wives and husbands of the siblings . . . they can get just as competitive and twice as grabby."

Jane had been up early, working on a list of the Kendell family members as well as finishing up her costume and props lists, so she could get to the bottom of the Bumby mischief. Actually, now that Penny Kendell was undergoing surgery for a badly broken leg, Jane upgraded mischief to malicious mischief. Tim had his fingers crossed that the cat-knocking-over-the-marble-jar explanation would pan out, but Jane was sure that unless the cat was named Mr. Bumbles and wrote a passable cursive, they would not be able to blame the family pet for Penny's fall.

The Kendell family tree was an easy sketch. A straight up-and-down birch rather than a spreading oak. Frederick and wife begat Freddy; Freddy and wife begat Fred; Fred and wife begat Margaret/Margie and Frederick IV, who shuns the first half of the family moniker altogether and calls himself Rick. Jane had asked Tim if Margie had children who were involved in the estate sale. She didn't. Rick was unmarried and Jane knew that didn't preclude having children but felt she could safely assume none of his offspring would be carved by name onto the family tree. Jane looked at her drawing. Margie and Rick were the end of the line

"Wait a second," said Jane, talking to Rita, who had been wandering around the house all morning, searching and sniffing, before settling at Jane's feet in the breezeway. Rita seemed disappointed that Nellie and Don had already left for the EZ Way Inn by the time Jane got up and showered. When Jane and Rita had visited before on the weekends, Nellie had been first up, cooking bacon and eggs and pancakes, all of which made an appearance in Rita's bowl. But this was midweek, an EZ Way Inn morning for Don and Nellie. Jane had slept in, made coffee, skipped breakfast altogether and filled Rita's bowl with an uninspired cup of dry dog food. Rita now looked at Jane as if to say, "Now you expect me to listen to your nonsense? On a kibble breakfast?"

"How can Bryan and Penny Kendell be Kendell cousins?" asked Jane. "Only child, only child, only child?"

"Easy," said Tim, when he arrived to pick Jane up. "I told you, they're like third or fourth or something. Frederick the first had a younger brother who had kids and that line continued, not as rich, not connected with the business. Bryan's great-great-uncle was Margie and Rick's great-great-grandfather," said Tim. Then he added, "I think that's how it goes."

"And they're close?" asked Jane.

"I don't know about that," said Tim, picking up her bag and gathering her notes. "But Margie gave them the go-ahead to walk through the house and they seemed to be somewhat familiar with the place when I showed them around. Now let's get moving, sweetheart. I want to start getting that house inventoried and I was wondering . . ."

"Let me guess. The carpenter you hired moved to South America and now you want me to actually build the set," said Jane. She knelt in front of Rita, reassuring her that Nellie would be back early afternoon to overfeed her. "Play your cards right, and she'll be bringing you cream pies."

Jane pointed at her giant tote, which Tim handed over. Opening it up, Jane ticked off aloud, "Notebook, measuring tape, flashlight, string tags, loupe, large magnifier, antiseptic, Band-Aids, pens, pencils, gloves . . . do I need anything else?"

"Nope. I've got all this stuff, too, honey, you know that. And the stage carpenter's fine and staying put. You'll like him, great guy. Marvin's an old professional who's moved back here and does this all out of love. But I do need a little assistance with something else."

Jane stayed mum, waiting. She didn't want to help him out with another sarcastic remark or by asking another question. If she made another wiseass comment, it would only make it easier for him to answer back in kind. She was trying to put into practice what Detective Oh tried to teach her. "Your silence, Mrs. Wheel, makes everyone else around you so much noisier."

"I need a little help with blocking," said Tim.

"How far have you gotten?" asked Jane. She was thinking that Tim might have a handle on this directing business after all. Tonight was an early read-through and he was already planning ahead, preparing to move his actors around on the stage.

"What?"

"What scene are you on? How many scenes have you done?"

"Let me rephrase the question," said Tim. "What *is* blocking?"

Jane caught herself before laughing—his timing was so perfect she was sure it was a joke until she looked at him, clutching his script in one hand and a worn library paperback called *Directing the Director.*

"Everyone in this book talks about blocking—how it is important, how it isn't the most important or how actors should have input or actors shouldn't have input, but"—he took a deep breath—"no one really says what it means."

"How about we *exit by way of the garage* and I'll explain on the way over to the Kendells'."

Jane described blocking as choreography onstage—getting the actors on and off the stage and around the furniture—adding movement to enhance the storytelling and keeping the stage picture balanced.

"We won't be putting all the furniture on one side of the stage; we'll make areas of interest and you'll have to move the actors around accordingly. No one moves on anyone else's line or steals focus. You have to make sure the nonspeaking actors are actually listening when others are talking and let the script tell you what to do. Follow the exits and entrances that old Freddy Kendell put in already for you," said Jane. "I can talk you through it. And Freddy was generous with this directions and notes. He told you how to stage it. And another thing," Jane added, "let's consolidate Acts One and Two. Easier to make one intermission. And in the long run? Less blocking."

Jane tossed her bag into the backseat, allowing her old more-than-distressed leather tool satchel to mingle with Tim's tonier, albeit vintage, work bags. Between them and their carryalls, they carried all that any picker needed to measure, authenticate, clean, test, or dismantle. When Jane climbed into the front seat, she was caught off guard by the look Tim gave her. He held up one hand as if in surrender and with the other, took hers and squeezed.

"Janie, I'm sorry I didn't ask you to be in the play," said Tim. "I really didn't think you wanted to be onstage. I just figured you wanted to be busy and have some fun, you know, no-pressure fun."

Jane knew he meant it and welcomed him back into her heart with a nod. She hadn't really locked him out, just wanted to keep on the porch for a while until he acknowledged his missteps.

"I get it and I think I get it about casting Nellie, although I think you're in deep trouble there, but what I don't get is—"

"Yeah, Nellie seems to be a little more hands-on than I expected. I mean, I knew she'd talk trash and all, but she actually seems to know a little about the play and about being in a play," said Tim.

"Yup, she's trod the boards, and God help the director responsible for her comeback. I'll dig around later and find the program Michael and I saw with her name in it. It's one of those little Nellie things I totally forgot about after I saw it, because she never gave us any details, no explanation at all. Michael and I saw her name and she snatched away the program and stuck it back into the bookshelf and we just knew that it was never going to be spoken of again. But she's not the actor I question," said Jane. "What's the deal casting Mary Wainwright?"

"Oh, honey," said Tim, turning onto the block of the Kendell mansion. It was the only house on the block and across the street there was a private park with stone benches and manicured gardens that edged the Kankakee River. Although the house was located in the heart of the historic district of the town, it might as well have been a country estate, since no other house was visible from the property.

"Mary's had nothing but trouble since college, and when I

heard about it and then she showed up for the auditions, I just couldn't hold on to the teenage bitchiness part of the memories anymore." Tim parked and began unloading his bags as Jane came around to help. "Lost both her parents in the same year. Cancer. And she took care of them both. Her husband took off when it became clear that her parents' illness was going to take what was left of the family money. Remember how we thought she was rich?" asked Tim.

Not waiting for any confirmation from Jane, he went on. "She always acted like she knew it all and had it all, but it turns out that her dad lost a lot of people's money—lots of bad investments—and before he could actually be blamed or maybe even prosecuted, he got sick. The wife had been ill for years. There wasn't a lot of sympathy for the family but Mary held her head up through it all. I just sort of felt sorry for her."

"What does she do?" asked Jane.

"Sells real estate, but nothing's happening on that front around here these days. Lives in a tiny apartment over Roy's Hardware. Now she's working as a substitute teacher," said Tim.

"She works as a sub? Okay, now I'm sympathetic," said Jane.

Jane told Tim she wanted a rundown on everyone in the play, but it could wait until later. One job at a time, and this morning, she wanted to pay attention to the Kendells and the Kendell mansion.

"The sooner we get everything laid out the better," said Tim. "Margie called and she wants to come down in a day or two to see what we've got done. I warned her that she wouldn't like what she saw once we really got going."

Jane understood. When they prepared a house for a sale, it wasn't pretty. Similar to turning a garment inside out so that all the seams and stitching and mistakes showed, a house being prepared for a complete "everything goes"–type sale was turned inside out. Closet doors were opened and if there were too many clothing items, Tim would set up freestanding clothing racks and they would hang the clothes so that crowds could paw through and go over every inch of Grandma's sheared beaver coat with a fine-tooth comb. Drawers were emptied or at the least, opened, and everything from slips to sweaters was available for rifling. Linen closets were emptied out onto the beds and the family monograms were scattered throughout so that customers could hold them up, count out the napkins, search for holes in the tablecloths, and ask for a better price if they found a tiny stain or two.

Every shelf and chest and drawer would be ransacked. Jane and Tim would cull the best books from the library shelves and lightly pencil in prices based on Internet booksellers' listings. The range was often so wide—an early edition of a Steinbeck novel might range from $2.99 to $299—that Tim usually priced the book somewhere in the middle with a little room to come down on the second day of the sale. If he penciled in $125 and the book guys started yelling, Tim would calmly unfold a printout from the Internet site that listed the price range.

"But those aren't the right prices," the book guys would yell. "No one *gets* those prices, they just *ask* those prices!"

Tim would then draw out a second sheet with book auctions that had already closed and he would point out the "sold for" prices, also noting that the shipping and tax might even add another $10 to that price. Tim would then smile and ask what the book guy wanted to pay, if not a fair price, then how much?

The book guys would sputter and mutter and usually walk away. For every seller who did his homework, there were so many others who would simply mark all hardcovers for a dollar or two and even give better deals if someone bought a box. The longtime book guys, those in it forever, the ones who had been picking through shelves for decades, selling books out of the trunks of their cars and still hoping one day to find that elusive Jack London or Steinbeck with the printing mistake on page 68, those guys would walk away and head out to the next sale, the library cart with the donated books or the garage sales with the boxes of books laid out on the driveway. The book guys knew it was a tough market and if they didn't buy their stuff for next to nothing, they were going to be stuck with a heavy and not so portable inventory. Jane didn't blame them for the way they felt, she just hated dealing with them. Unlike any other picker or dealer, a book guy got mad when he saw a decent price on a book. Even if he knew somewhere in the back of his head it was a fair price, he knew it wasn't a good price for him. A book guy took it personally, especially the book guys who were female. Jane had seen more than one woman with a canvas bag full of modern firsts slam down what she considered an overpriced vintage cookbook on a counter and storm out the door.

And the book guys, as hard as they were to deal with, were nothing compared to the owners, the sellers, the heirs. When Margie walked through the house after Jane and Tim effectively turned it inside out and began hanging string tags on the valuables, taping signs to the walls for group pricing of linens or men's ties, Jane and Tim both knew she would go through the owner's four stages of dealing with their own estate sale—denial, embarrassment, anger, and greed. In other words:

"No one is going to want to buy that."

"I wouldn't want anyone to see that."

"Why wouldn't someone want that?"

"We should have charged more!"

When Jane and Tim had entered the house, both had stepped over the threshold carefully, Tim finding the light switch immediately, no fumbling. Both looked first at the chandelier, then to the console table under the hall mirror where Mr. Bumbles thankfully remained.

"Even when he's not hanging around, he creeps me out," said Tim. "Do you want to take him up and start in the toy room?"

"No way. I'm almost a PI, but I don't carry anything that protects me from ventriloquists' dummies," said Jane. "Or clowns," she added.

"Okay, how about we stay together, emptying the bedroom closets. I've already got a good start in the master—we'll finish and move on to the other four on the second floor. If we can get those laid out today, it'll be a good day's work. The downstairs will be more fun and the attic and basement of course, but those bedrooms will be fast and we can finish them. I could use a little closure."

Jane agreed. Bedrooms were usually easy enough that they could talk, and she could explain blocking and go over his rehearsal plan for the evening. They were almost through with what was probably Margie's room when she lived at home—a mishmash of a teenager's clothes from thirty years ago and a closet filled with vintage thirties and forties winter coats, a few furs, probably saved from various family members. The dressers were filled with more clothes; however, Jane was more interested in a few high school yearbooks she uncovered and a jewelry box that held several charm bracelets.

"Probably not Margie's. These charms are from an earlier generation. So sweet," said Jane, unscrewing what appeared to be a tiny ivory egg and finding an even tinier carved ivory chick inside. "I'll buy this," said Jane.

"No shopping yet," said Tim. "It's too early."

They had been working side by side in Margie's enormous bedroom, leafing through books, shaking out clothes for more than two hours when Tim's phone buzzed. He read the incoming text to Jane. "From Bryan. Penny's leg in a cast below knee. Okay after plenty of phys therapy. Sorry you'll have to recast me, too. Will have my hands full."

"You want to play the cousin? Penny's part?" asked Tim.

"Nope. I'm perfectly content in my offstage role, Timmy boy. How about asking Margie if she wants to go onstage in her grandpa's play? It appears she's had experience."

Jane was leafing through a school yearbook and had found a bookmark placed on the drama page. Margaret "Margie" Kendell had played major roles in two of the year's offerings. Because it was an all-girls school, Margie had the distinction of playing the male lead, Beany, in *Leave It to Beany*, the fall play, and the slightly off-kilter dancer in *You Can't Take It with You*. The bookmark was a theatrical program for *Leave It to Beany*. The school had sprung for pricey color printing and the programs included the student actors' bios.

> Margie Kendell (Beany) comes from a theatrical family. "My grandpa is a playwright and he writes a show for us each Christmas. My brother and I played everything from Santa's elves to Tiny Tim by the time we were twelve!"

"The Margie Kendell I met is not going to want to hang around town to appear in Grandpa's play," said Tim.

"You never can tell," said Jane. "I'd like you to ask her."

"Janie, you know what a hassle that would be—her poking around here every day and then every night . . ."

Tim was sitting on the bed folding table linens and pinning blank hang tags on them with the tiniest of gold safety pins. Jane placed the yearbook on his lap.

"Just ask her and see what she says," said Jane.

Tim looked down at the yearbook. On one page there were snapshots of various acts in the school variety show. On the opposite page there was one large photo of a pretty blond girl sitting on a stool smiling at her partner. Under the photo, the caption read: *Margie Kendell and her friend regaled the audience with songs, stories, and jokes!*

Jane leaned over Tim's shoulder.

"If you don't want to cast Margie, maybe you can find a part for her friend," said Jane, pointing to the familiar-looking wooden doll who sat on Margie's knee. "I wouldn't mind knowing where Mr. Bumbles is every night."

Nellie wasn't one to spend a long time in front of the mirror. As she had told Jane many times, she didn't believe in makeup, special facial scrubs, creams, moisturizers, cleansing grains, Retin-A, wrinkle removers, line fillers, mud packs, clay masques, facials, steams, or herbal peels.

"Soap and hot water's all you need," said Nellie. "And lipstick."

Lipstick. Nellie barely ran a comb though her gray-streaked waves and never bothered with anything that came with a wand or a brush, but, daily, before leaving the house for the EZ Way Inn, she did apply a soft red lipstick. Whenever she saw Jane, bare-faced and ready to leave for work with Tim, a house sale or basement clean-out, dressed in her grungiest work clothes, Nellie would shake her head and growl at her to "at least put on a little lipstick for God's sake."

Nellie's advice took, for the most part. Nellie noted that Jane did carry a tube of color with her and often remembered to apply it. If Nellie saw Jane wearing a little Angel Red or Earthy, she nodded. Jane might not even see the slight head movement, but Nellie never failed to give her signal of approval. If her son earned a living and her daughter wore a little lipstick, she had done her job.

Because of Nellie's spartan approach to primping, Don

wasn't used to seeing his wife stare at herself in the mirror. He knew she was studying her face this morning, because at the EZ Way Inn, the tiny bathrooms marked "Men" and "Women" were carved out of the barroom using the smallest space possible, allowing them to be used solely for what was to be their only use. A small hand-washing sink, paper towel dispenser, and wastebasket were positioned just outside the restrooms, in full view of patrons and proprietors. A mirror was mounted over the sink. Pity the kitchen help who tried to avoid washing hands before returning to work. On the other hand, if Nellie had ever consented to hiring anyone to assist her in her kitchen, pity the employee. Period.

Because Nellie stared at herself and Don stared at Nellie staring, Francis the bread man stared at Don, wondering why he was chewing the inside of his cheek and not offering him more coffee or any news of the day. Baseball season was in full swing and surely Don had an opinion on this year's White Sox and surely he would be interested in Francis's opinion of the Cubs.

The back door, the one that led directly into the kitchen and the one that all the regulars used, swung open, the screen banging against the frame, and Boxcar Neilson powered through the kitchen into the barroom. The jury was out on why Boxcar was called Boxcar. There were those who surmised it had something to do with the railroad, and there were those who figured that it had something to do with shape and heft. Jane had asked both her parents about why he was called Boxcar and Don had raised one eyebrow and shrugged. "Just his name," he said, winking and tossing a smile to Nellie.

Those were the kinds of secrets they shared, thought Don. How people got their nicknames, who they slipped a buck or two to make it until their next payday, who brought them the bags of prelottery gambling tickets they occasionally tucked under the bar for the regulars to unfold and dream over. So why now was Nellie staring into the mirror, looking very much like someone keeping a secret to herself?

"Don!" shouted Boxcar. "Wake up. I need a shot."

"Yes sir, Box," said Don, pouring out a measure of Walker's DeLuxe and setting it down with a flourish.

"Too early for that," said Nellie, giving herself a final nod in the mirror, then stopping at the coffee counter outside the kitchen and pouring out a cup of sludge. She set it down in front of Boxcar. "Have this with it for God's sake."

"Not going to believe who I saw late last night at the Moonlight Inn," said Box, downing the shot and nodding at the coffee.

Don raised his chin in the silent version of "no, who?" but Nellie just folded her arms and waited. In her experience, no one who wanted to gossip ever needed encouragement.

"Henry Gand! I thought he'd moved to California, but he said he's been coming back summers for a few years. Thinking about staying year-round. Said he needed winter back, made him feel too old to be out there in the sunshine all the time. Retired, and he's fixing up his parents' cabin out by the state park. Was a nice place—we used to raise some hell out there, remember Nell?"

Boxcar was one of the few old friends who got away with calling Nellie Nell, since he never paid any attention to her paralyzing stare whenever he said it.

"Don, you know Henry, don't you? He and Nellie went around together for a while, didn't you, Nell?"

Francis leaned forward. This was much more interesting than going over the sixth inning of last night's game.

Nellie grunted and went into the kitchen. The three men heard her drag down her biggest kettle, banging it loudly against the other pans on the open shelf.

"Nellie's going to make soup," said Francis. "Oh boy."

Since the Roper Stove Factory had closed, Nellie made a

pot of soup only when the spirit moved her, and something, they all noticed, was moving her now.

"Henry said you and him was going to do another play," said Boxcar, directing his comment into the doorless opening to the kitchen. No one could see Nellie but they could hear her, opening and closing the large two-door institutional-sized refrigerator that used to be full of supplies when the lunch business was in full swing. Now it held only what Nellie considered essential—milk, cream, eggs, cottage cheese, and lots of vegetables kept in fresh rotation that could be cut up on a moment's notice.

"Is that so, Nellie? You going to be in that play?"

They heard the swinging metal doors on the bin that held potatoes on top and onions on the bottom squeak open and slam shut.

"Yup," said Francis. "That florist shop guy, Tim, the one Janie runs around with, he brought Nellie chocolates and she said she'd be in his play."

Bang. Nellie's large cutting board crashed down from its hook onto the counter, and in a moment of quiet, Don knew from the faint scratchy paper-folding sound that Nellie was peeling onions, easing off their brown parchment coverings before she began to chop.

"That's something, ain't it, Don?" asked Boxcar, holding up his shot glass for another pour. "Nellie's going to be up onstage again. And with old Henry, too. It'll be like old times when they used to put on those stage shows at the park building over there on—"

A heavy rasping sound came from the kitchen. Don knew Nellie was drawing her knife blade back and forth, angled against the sharpening stone.

"I didn't know Nellie acted before," said Francis.

"There's a hell of a lot you don't know, Francis," shouted

Nellie. They could hear her chopping the onions, and then there was a tearing sound that Don thought might be the separating of stalks of celery. Had vegetables ever sounded so violent?

"Here's something else you don't know," said Nellie. "This play I'm going to be in? It's about a murder. And the best part," she continued, still out of sight, all the while *chop-chop-chopping* on the wooden board, "is that just when you think you know who did the murder . . ."

Nellie stepped into the doorway, wiping her left hand on her apron. "Just when you get comfortable in your little velvet seats, someone else comes along and commits another murder!" As Nellie said the word *murder,* she threw her head back and cackled, whipping out her right hand from behind her back, brandishing her vegetable-chopping butcher knife.

"Jeez, Nellie," said Francis, spilling half of the coffee out of the cup that he had lifted halfway to his mouth. "You scared me."

Boxcar nodded at Don. "She's still got it, ain't she, Don?

"Yup," said Don. "She's got something all right."

Jane, still paging through yearbooks and scrapbooks chronicling Margie Kendell's early years, heard music. Was it a harp? Tim had told her there was a harp in the Kendell house, but this strumming was coming from the outside pocket of her tote bag. She found her phone and tapped on the screen. Finding the right spot, more by accident than design, the music abruptly stopped, and she raised the phone to her ear, letting a startled "oh" escape as she composed herself to answer the call.

"Yes?" said the caller.

"Oh?" repeated Jane.

"You knew it was me, Mrs. Wheel? The telephone Mr. Lowry bought for you is easier to understand?"

"Detective Oh," Jane said. As comfortable as their relationship had grown, Jane couldn't bring herself to say "Hi," which, when directed toward Oh sounded even more frivolous and inconsequential than it normally would.

Once, when she expressed a desire to curb her tendency to fill in empty space with chatter when questioning suspects, Oh had suggested she imagine that every word she spoke cost a dollar. Jane, frugal to her core since she had become a picker, found that the "dollar a word" game worked very well when she found herself surrounded by persons of interest. When she began a conversation with Oh, however, remembering the value of words often rendered her tongue-tied. Jane wondered if she needed to invent an entirely new language to use exclusively in conversation with Oh.

"Mrs. Wheel, you left for your parents' home in a hurry? I hope nothing is amiss."

Amiss was the perfect word. No murder, no mayhem, no provable crime and yet things were definitely amiss. A creepy ventriloquist's dummy hanging from a chandelier, ominous notes, and a possibly arranged accident that sent Penny Kendell to the hospital were not exactly the great mystery of Jane Wheel's career, and yet she felt that things were definitely off-kilter. The fact that Tim was directing a terrible play with Nellie in the cast, not to mention Nellie's old boyfriend showing up, contributed to the "kilter" being off. Jane took a deep breath.

"Tim has dragged me down here for two projects. I'm helping him prep for a huge sale and also helping him work on a play he's directing for the community theater."

"Back to your theatrical roots, Mrs. Wheel?"

When had she ever told Oh about majoring in theater? She must have been babbling about it when they were on a stakeout or driving to meet a client or . . .

"You mentioned your dreams of a career on the stage when we were in California and you were being courted for the movies."

Oh was helping her save money for future words by reading her mind.

"I'm a designer and tech person for Tim, which was not my strength or forte, but he needs me and there's something interesting . . . amiss . . . going on here that I think I need to figure out before something even more serious happens, before someone—"

Jane stopped because she could hear Oh's wife talking loudly in the background and sensed a distraction on the other end.

"I apologize, Mrs. Wheel, but Claire must leave the house and is asking to speak with you."

"Jane, is Tim doing the sale at Margie Kendell's parents' house? I won't tell anyone how I found out, but I have to know. Please."

Had haughty Claire ever said "please" before? Tim hadn't told her the Kendell sale was a secret and since the contract had already been signed, Jane saw no harm in filling her in.

"I'm sitting in Margie Kendell's bedroom right now," said Jane.

"I knew it! Just because he lives in that pathetic little town doesn't mean he should have exclusive rights to those kinds of antiques, those furnishings. The art alone . . . why in the world didn't she hire someone from the city, someone whom she had known for years, for heaven's sake, I went to school with her. I found her mother all of the lighting for the parlor twenty-five years ago when I was starting out. I have receipts, provenance . . . I have paperwork!"

"Claire, I don't know how—"

"Is she there? I haven't been able to reach her for weeks! Did Lowry get her to change her number? Does he have her locked in a closet?"

Jane could hear Bruce Oh murmuring in the background.

"I will not be calm, not this time. She promised me this property years ago when her mother and father were gone, she'd have me in there to do a complete . . . wait a minute. It was Rick! Her lazy brother hired Lowry, didn't he?"

"Why don't you call Tim, Claire. I'm sure he knows more than—"

"Oh yes, I'll talk to Lowry all right."

There was a pause, then Oh was back on the phone.

"I am so sorry, Mrs. Wheel."

"I understand the frustration. This is quite a houseful of

stuff—and if you knew about it and thought you were going to get it and didn't, it would definitely be a blow."

"It's more than that, Mrs. Wheel. Claire and Margaret Kendell were close friends in boarding school. I met Ms. Kendell when Claire was leading a group of collectors to London for a shopping trip. Margaret spent the night at our home before their flight the next morning. She was a lovely woman, very quiet, and she seemed to be a good and loyal friend of Claire's. I believe that although my wife becomes passionate about the objects in question, this time she is more concerned about her friend's broken promise," Oh said. He paused before continuing. "I think Claire believes that with this sale, something is amiss."

Oh promised to call back after speaking with Claire. He said his wife was in need of some calming and a cup of tea, which he felt called upon to provide. Jane sat where she was, staring at the phone still in her hand. If Tim had made the ring tone for Bruce Oh a harp, what might she expect when other calls came in?

How did Tim get this sale if Claire was such a buddy of Margie Kendell? Not that Claire did house sales; she was too much of a high-end dealer to actually prep a house, dig through boxes in a watery basement, or shake out moths from clothes stored in the dust and must of an attic. No, Claire would have come in and assessed the good stuff, shipped it off to auction as Tim had already done, then she would have probably hired someone like Tim to prep the house. But the key is she would have been in the house first, she would have pulled the strings.

"Some lunch, dearie?" said a squeaky voice. Jane looked up and with some real effort, squelched a scream. Tim was dangling Mr. Bumbles in through the open door.

Tim always packed great lunches on house prep days. He went to Pink's and coaxed the cook there to make homemade potato chips that were to die for, although no one ever would have ordered them had Pink consented to put them on the menu. A small bag of commercially produced chips was good enough for the average Joe Kankakee, who wouldn't have wanted the more expensive crispy and irregular homemades. Tim claimed that most of Pink's customers were too timid to try anything the excellent cook could and did prepare for private customers like him.

In the Kendell kitchen, Tim now warmed up two ham and cheese sandwiches on brioche rolls, dumped a large bag of the homemade chips into a bright green Pyrex bowl, the second largest size from the nesting primary color bowl set on which Tim would soon stick a price tag, and poured out tall glasses of peach iced tea. Jane felt cared for as soon as Tim put the plate of food in front of her. Afraid he might snatch it back if she began to question him too much about his dealings with Margie Kendell, she decided to eat her fill of chips before launching in. Instead, she suggested he make plans for tonight's rehearsal.

"After you all read through the play tonight, you should be prepared to give everyone a schedule for the week, you know . . . what scenes you'll rehearse and when, so that not everyone is tied up for the entire night, every night. Have you broken down the play like that yet?"

Tim shook his head.

"Look at my script, Tim," said Jane, fishing in the bag at her feet. "I've broken it down for props. You'll see where I suggest the act break. You need to make notes—figure out how to maximize your time with everyone. Give them dates for memorization—you know, tell them they have to be off book in ten days or whatever. You don't have all that much time."

Jane helped herself to more of the chips. "I'll help you with the play, Tim. I promise. But you have to be straight with me. How did you get this sale? Claire Oh is fit to be tied, she's an old friend of Margie Kendell's—they went to school together and . . . Yikes!" said Jane, putting down her sandwich.

Jane held up one finger and told Tim she'd be right back. When she came racing down the back stairs from the second floor, she was carrying Margie Kendell's yearbook. She began paging though while telling Tim about Oh's call and her conversation with Claire.

Either Tim was a better actor than Jane had suspected or the news about Claire and Margie was a complete surprise.

"I have to tell you, she didn't even say she was talking to anyone else. The only back-and-forth about this job was between her and her brother, Rick. Of course, it was Rick, pretty much, who hired me. She told me she never wants to be at the house at the same time he is. Each of them had to sign the contract . . . they faxed them to me. Neither of them tried to drive a hard bargain, they just sniped at each other whenever I talked to them on the phone."

"Here, this must be her."

Jane placed her finger under the picture of Claire Landow, who didn't look that much different from the current Claire Oh. She wore her hair down to her shoulders, with a clip at the side, rather than pulled back in a tight bun. Other than that? Same tight smile, same unflinching stare. Under her senior picture, her quote was "Act like you've already won."

"Whoa," said Tim. "No self-esteem issues there."

"Look at Margie," said Jane. In the photos from the plays, Margie looked animated in that hokey high school drama way, larger than life in costumes slightly too big. And sitting with Mr. Bumbles on her knee, she looked happy and in control. In this, her individual picture, her eyes were vacant and she was unsmiling.

"'Make 'em laugh?' That's her quote?" said Tim. "She looks like the grim face of death. Who lets that be published as her class picture? They offer retakes for these things. I mean she's no barrel of fun now, but she's not tragic-looking."

"Yeah," said Jane. "Maybe she was trying to be funny—you know, ironic. Making that face with the quote."

"Oh, honey, irony's for college. High school is pure. This was one sad girl. Look up teenage angst in the dictionary and this is the picture."

"When was the last time you talked to her?"

"A week or so ago," said Tim, eating the last of the chips. "We e-mail back and forth, though. She's only been here to meet with me twice. Took forever for her to make up her mind on the sale, and now she wants it done in two weeks. I got the impression she was under some pressure from her brother to get it all done."

"How many times has Rick been here?"

"I never met him. Faxed me the prelim stuff, then left a final signed contract for me here. I couldn't get here the day he came to the house and he couldn't stay over. About two weeks ago, I think. He called and said he was taking some of the books and a painting from the library—nothing special—and said he'd try to get back here before the sale date. Told me Margie could deal with the details."

"What do you figure this sale will bring?"

"Gross? Conservatively . . . upper five figures or . . ." Tim focused on something Jane could not see, seemed to be adding in his head. "You know, we could easily go six figures, give or take, even without the antiques and paintings I sent to auction—that's where the big money is. There's a motorcycle out in the garage—have to see if it's worth anything—and I still have to check the garden sculpture. I'm trying to calculate numbers based on everything being just okay, nothing being stand-out. If everything turns out to be ordinary and we're dealing with sheer quantity—for example, if all the hardcover books in this house are all two-dollar hardcovers—we're talking fifty thousand and up with all the furniture and china and the quantity of . . ." Tim broke off again. His eyes almost rolled back in his head as he tried to concentrate on the items he would be pricing for sale. Jane thought she could almost see him teleporting himself to the various rooms and closets. He began again. "Like if you find a Hemingway first edition or if some of this pottery turns out to be special . . . the figures rise accordingly. Or if one of those guitars up in the playroom turns out to be a vintage Martin . . . I haven't gone through all of the silver. . . ."

Tim went on cataloging what would bring money and how much, interspersing every prediction with a mordant comment about the economy. No one knew how things, or what things, would sell at estate sales anymore because no one knew who had money left and who was willing to spend it. High-end antique and art dealers might survive the downturn if their high-end banker clients continued to collect their bonuses. Middle-of-the-road dealers like Tim and junkers like Jane, however, were fighting for every disposable dime and unnecessary nickel.

"Margie and Rick are millionaires, right?" asked Jane.

"Well," said Tim, looking down at his phone, buzzing to tell him that he had a text. "Hmmm," he said while pushing keys.

"So they didn't need to bicker over selling all of this stuff—they could have just donated everything to charity. Why go through the bother?" asked Jane.

"You've been Dumpster diving too long, honey." Tim said, clearing their lunch plates and rinsing their glasses. "Have you really looked around this house?"

Tim threw open the kitchen cupboards and crossed over to a large pantry and opened it. Stacks of plates, glassware, serving pieces, measuring spoons stuck into colorful ceramic flowerpot holders, measuring cups, mixing bowls, vintage copper pans, kitchenalia of every kind was jammed into every possible corner of storage.

"Every room is like this. They have so much stuff stuffed into this place. Don't you see? If they decided to donate it, someone would still have to sift through, separate the wheat from the chaff, bag it, box it. They would have to trust someone to be on the premises and to take care of all the packing and getting it to a charity. The truth is, it's an overwhelming amount of stuff—one local thrift store couldn't handle it—they'd want someone to run a sale on premises, reduce the volume of stuff, and then benefit from the proceeds. Rick and Margie want to sell the house, so they need it cleaned out and spruced up—at least cleaned out—and who better to do that than someone who has a vested interest in getting all of the stuff sold for a profit. Then I'll let them pay me to do a complete clean-out—or rather pay me to hire and supervise someone who can haul away everything that's left."

Jane picked up the yearbook with the teenage Margie Kendell and Claire Oh so Tim could wipe the table. As Tim explained why he was hired and what he was doing, Jane's mind raced ahead. If Tim was right and he was hired to sort through and find the good stuff, maybe there was some stuff that someone didn't want him to find. Why try to creep someone out with Mr. Bumbles unless whoever the prankster was thought Tim would walk? And what about the warning notes in the scripts of *Murder in the Eekaknak Valley*?

"Do Margie and Rick know you're directing their grandfather's play?"

"Sure. I mean I told them I found the scripts and all," said Tim.

"But did you ask them if they minded if you put it on. I mean they own the scripts and it's their family and—"

"I told them I thought I might propose it to the community theater board and Rick didn't say I shouldn't."

"Do they know you're putting on the play or not?"

"I didn't really talk it over with Margie, but I know she knows. I told Rick I was going to do it and he didn't think it was a great idea," said Tim.

"So he doesn't approve," said Jane.

"He said it was a bad idea because he thought something bad happened the last time the play was put on. What did he tell me? Let's see . . ." Tim stopped rummaging through the cupboards and turned toward Jane. The usual confident Tim face had been replaced with a less familiar expression.

"I didn't even think about this before. I think he said the play was unlucky."

"And you're just remembering this now?" said Jane. "Did you ask him why?"

"It wasn't a serious conversation."

Tim sat down to check the e-mail that had just buzzed in. He muttered something and looked up at Jane. "Trouble. Margie says the paintings and furniture that went to the auction house can't be the right pieces. Estimates are too low. She says that . . . whoops, here's an e-mail from Rick," Tim paused. "Same thing. Rick said they expected bigger money from the auction items."

Tim left the kitchen. Jane heard him on the stairs and assumed he was headed back to the bedrooms. Apparently, their conversation, which Jane did consider serious, was over.

"Why's Tim being such a pill?" she asked aloud, directing the question toward Mr. Bumbles, whom Tim had propped up into a sitting position, his legs dangling over the counter.

Jane brushed some sandwich crumbs off of Bumbles's brown suit pants. She straightened his tie and adjusted the lapels on his jacket, smiling to herself.

"Look at me sprucing up a creepy ventriloquist's dummy. What's next, Bumbles? I actually learn to throw my voice and sit you on my—" Jane broke off as she pulled the dummy's pocket square into a sharp point.

"Are you talking to me?" yelled Tim from the top of the stairs.

"What was Bumbles wearing yesterday, Tim?"

"What? Who?"

"I'll tell you what," Jane said, looking directly into the carved glass eyes of Mr. Bumbles. "You were wearing a plaid shirt and dungarees. And today, you're wearing a suit. How in the hell did you manage to change your clothes?"

There is an old theater adage that proclaims a bad dress rehearsal signals a good opening night. There are those who actually believe that the superstition works in a reverse proportional way—the worse a dress rehearsal, the better the show. If one wanted to take this old theater wives' tale and push it to its extremes, one might say that the play's entire success depended on the failure of the rehearsal process.

And if this extrapolation had even a shred of truth in it, thought Jane Wheel, *the Kankakee Community Theater production of* Murder in the Eekaknak Valley *was, after only a few weeks, destined for Broadway.*

The problems began the first night of rehearsal. Tim directed the cast to read through the play, but since he was busy getting into character himself as Detective Craven, he found it difficult to drop the quasi-British accent he had adopted as part of this character.

"We need to hear the truth behind what you're saying, Myra," Tim would say in a voice that seemed to originate from somewhere around his knees and emerge as a cross between a Noël Coward leading man and the character of Lady Bracknell from *The Importance of Being Earnest.* Instead of taking it as direction from Tim, all of the actors scanned their scripts to see where this line came from and tried to figure out how they had lost their places.

By the end of the first week of rehearsal, Chuck Havens, in his role as Malachi, the would-be-ne'er-do-well-bon-vivant-possible-murderer, had adopted a strange tic of stroking his beard every time he spoke. Problem? Neither Chuck Havens nor Malachi had a beard. Problem number two? The gesture effectively covered his mouth in such a way that each of his lines came out a cross between a mutter and a mumble at the beginning and end of his beard stroking. When Malachi spoke, one didn't wonder so much whether or not he might have committed the murder, one wondered if he was speaking from a cell phone with bad coverage.

Henry Gand as Perkins the gardener was a passable actor, actually quite believable. In the second act, however, he delivered a monologue to the comatose mother, Marguerite, played by Nellie, in which he confessed his unrequited love and during which Don, who had taken to staying and watching rehearsals when he drove Nellie over, coughed and hacked, making it impossible for anyone to hear Henry's speech straight through.

At the end of the second week of rehearsal, it was clear that Mary Wainwright could not memorize the part of Hermione. In fact, she seemed totally distracted, and most nights read her lines from the script, which she refused to relinquish, with a kind of hysterical edge. She ended each sentence with a questioning up-speak quality, as if her character were always on the verge of laughter or tears and wanted someone to tell her which would be more appropriate. Even when announcing a meal—*Mother, oh Mother, breakfast is ready*—Mary turned *Breakfast is ready* into a maniacal existential query.

Rica Evans, a good actress—and in her one scene with Henry Gand a more than good actress—owned the stage. Jane hadn't really immersed herself in a theatrical production since college, but she remembered the thrill of seeing people who became real onstage, merging a kind of empathy for character as well as a kind of energy that told a story above and beyond their written and memorized lines. Jane could see that in a good play with an adequate cast, Rica would be a star. In *Murder in the Eekaknak Valley,* she did the best she could to underdramatize the overwritten lines and to make the unrealistic plot ring true.

Jane found Rica's scenes with her comatose mother, played by the one and only Nellie, especially poignant. Since Nellie had no lines to speak and was ordered by the script and faux-British Tim to lie as still as possible in her hospital bed, Jane could imagine her mother listening to a daughter's confession of love and misplaced affection throughout her life and, finally, asking for forgiveness and understanding. Rica's plea to her mother, just before the murderer was revealed, never failed to move Jane, even if she was busy polishing silver or replacing handkerchiefs in pockets or repositioning plants backstage, which were seen through the open French doors, representing the garden to which characters retired in almost every scene.

Actually, Jane was moved only on the nights when Nellie didn't attend rehearsal and her part was played by two pillows covered by a Victorian crazy quilt, since on those nights, Rica was able to finish sentences and build the emotion properly so that her final confession, a combination of human suffering, wry acceptance, and daughterly love, could be delivered. Corny and sentimental as the speech was, it got to Jane every time.

On the nights Nellie was called to rehearsal and Don coughed through the second act, Nellie herself was impossible in the last scene. Unable to lie still, she tossed and turned, making her coma look more like an epileptic seizure. Every time Rica confessed her indiscretion with the son of the town's prominent banker, the result of which was pregnancy and her flight from the small town, Nellie would grunt and snort until Tim called cut and begged her to lie still.

"Stop worrying, Tim. You can just give her a Tylenol PM during the show," said Mary Wainwright.

Jane looked at Don, sitting in the third row, who had also heard the remark. They smiled, both of them knowing it would take an elephant tranquilizer to quiet Nellie down.

After two weeks of rehearsals, just over a week before opening night, Tim once again began his nightly pleading with Nellie.

"I can't stay still, Lowry. The scene doesn't feel right."

"Nellie, please," Tim said, holding up his hand.

"The words seem all wrong," said Nellie.

"What are you talking about?" Jane asked. Tim had already stalked off to the back of the stage where he usually retreated when things began to go south, busying himself rearranging plants and complaining that they needed watering.

"All this pap Myra's saying? It isn't right. Myra's supposed to ask about Hermione and what she was like as a little girl since she had left her. Marguerite, me, I raised that girl for her. And all the money Myra sent home? I used it to protect them from all these vultures. Myra's supposed to come home dead broke and Marguerite's supposed to save the day."

Jane looked at Nellie, who seemed dead serious. Jane had never known her mother to claim to have one creative bone in her body. Why now was she trying to rewrite Freddy Kendell's play?

Tim came back to the front of the stage to address the cast.

"We don't have that much time left, people. We have a beautiful set, thanks to our carpenter, Marv, and Henry, of course, who's really pitched in and helped to build everything. And thanks to Jane, who's made sure everything looks good and works right. But, actors! Please. Mary, you have to learn your lines. Patty, you have to make your lines real. And Nellie, you have to lie still. Rica has this beautiful speech and you are stealing the entire focus from the play's big moment."

"I'm trying to tell you it shouldn't be the big moment, Lowry, it's—"

"Mr. Lowry."

Everyone turned to the back row of seats. With a few lights on the stage and the rest of the houselights dimmed, it was difficult to make out any more than what might have been a human shape standing in the aisle near the main entrance to the theater.

"Mr. Lowry, a moment?"

Tim excused himself and whispered to Jane as he headed back to the shadows. "Maybe that's the custodian, finally, to finish up the lighting stuff. Take over for me. Pep talk them or something."

Jane was more interested in the person whose imperious voice could get Tim to respond so obediently, but she nodded and cleared her throat.

"We're going to take it from the second-to-last scene. Where's Henry?"

"He's working out in the parking lot with Marv on the latticework for the garden," said Chuck. "I'll get him for you." Havens headed backstage where there was a door leading directly to the large parking lot that adjoined the cultural center.

"Places for scene four," said Jane. "Marguerite, you can take a break—we'll probably use your stand-in pillows in this scene anyway, since the bed is pushed to the back." Jane asked a few of the dinner guests to make the slight adjustments to the furniture.

Jane hopped onstage and recentered the black urn supposedly containing the ashes of Marguerite's late husband. Freddy had specified this particular prop and Jane smiled at how perfect it was for the job—both macabre and trophylike at the same time.

Nellie, still shaking her head in imaginary conversation with Tim, walked over to Don, whispered something, and together they stepped out one of the side doors. It was after eight, according to the clock at the back of the house, not totally dark outside yet. Mid-June, it was already warm enough for midsummer. Jane and Tim had propped a few of the side doors to the auditorium open to get a breeze and now Jane noticed a moth at play in front of one of the stage lights.

Jane had one of those giddy romantic moments where all things real fell away. She had no past life, no almost ex-husband, no son with whom she could communicate only via computer messages, no obligations, but was just a college girl again, directing a play in a summer theater. The hammering from the parking lot had stopped but there were voices still drifting in. The clicking of Rica/Myra's heels on the stage as she paced back and forth, going over her lines, provided a beat, and Jane remembered what it was like to be eighteen years old, dreaming about a life in the theater. As unreal as she knew her fantasies about it had been, every once in a while life gave you a moment like this when it felt like the romance was the one true thing.

This particular romantic moment was interrupted, as moments always are, by something real; often something small, like a hammer to the thumb, a broken stiletto heel, a lightbulb popping as it burns out in its socket. In this case, though, on a warm June night in Kankakee, the something real was a scream of bloody murder, a shout for help, and Jane's mother, Nellie, yelling that someone had murdered Henry Gand.

11

By the time Jane got out the rear door to the parking lot, everyone in the cast was standing in a semicircle. Jane pushed her way past the cast members and saw her mother kneeling next to the body of a small older man wearing a plaid shirt and jeans, pressing her apron against the bloody wound on his head. Don also knelt next to the body, feeling for a pulse, asking calmly if anyone knew CPR.

Tim shouted that the ambulance was on the way. Rica Evans seemed to remain in character as Myra, regally commanding everyone to step back and go back inside to the theater so the ambulance could get through. Mary Wainwright and Chuck Havens, both pale, were clutching each other. And Henry Gand, who wandered out from the theater tucking in his plaid shirt, asked what the fuss was about.

"Marvin?" Henry asked, seeing his friend lying on the ground. "What happened to Marv?"

"I thought it was you, Henry," said Nellie. "When did you two start dressing like twins?"

There was a park behind the cultural center with a walking path and a sculpture garden. In the clearing between where the parking lot ended and the green space began, Marv, the carpenter, had set up his power tools with thick extension cords running along the ground into the backstage area. He had stacked lumber, plywood sheets, under two tarps. Several large wooden beams, eight to ten feet in length, were propped against a giant oak. Jane saw that one beam—the one that must have struck Marv on the head—lay on the ground next to him, apparently pushed aside by either Don or Nellie, whoever had reached Marvin first.

Jane walked over to the oak, stood next to the beams, and looked up. The tops of the boards were firmly stuck into the fork of two branches. There was nothing precarious about their placement. Either Marvin had not planted this beam as firmly as the others to prevent it from being blown down or dislodged by passersby, or someone had come along and pushed the board over on top of the man.

If Nellie were ever made into an action figure, thought Jane, she would be the opposite of a nodder. Nellie was a shaker, a perpetual-motion doll whose primary movement was the negative head shake. She moved through her life disagreeing with people out loud and silently to the voices with whom she argued inside of her own head. But now, Jane noticed, her mother was shaking all over. Don had lifted her to a standing position and kept his arm firmly around her shoulders. Nellie looked up and around the group for Jane and when Jane caught her mother's gaze, she expected her to look upset, shocked. She did not expect the eye-narrowing, flare-throwing anger that crossed her mother's face.

"Who in the hell killed Marvin?" said Nellie. "You couldn't find a sweeter man than that one right there."

"A beam fell, Nellie," said Henry. Jane noted he was shaking, too. "See how he had them stacked there? He must have just put that one up and not secured it. I was helping, then I went to go use the bathroom. Maybe if I'd . . ." Henry's voice broke.

Jane saw her mother start to answer, but whatever she was going to say was drowned out by the ambulance siren.

The cast and crew of the play stood aside in small groups next to the theater, waiting and watching. The police arrived and began taking statements, beginning with Henry Gand, who was, by this time, openly weeping, apologizing and blaming himself for not securing the beam that had fallen and killed his friend Marvin. Jane saw the policeman who seemed to be in charge signal to one of the paramedics to come over and assist Henry.

Jane studied the gravel on the parking lot side of the tree where the beam had fallen. She had a million questions to ask Nellie, who was talking a mile a minute to Don, but there was a sea—okay, pond—of people between them, and Jane wanted to memorize the angle of these boards before it got too dark to see anything. She remembered that her fancy phone had a decent camera and she wedged it out of her jeans pocket and snapped a shot of the boards just as she heard a familiar voice.

"It seems unlikely that if a beam fell, it would come down cleanly without dislodging any of those branches or stirring up this gravel. Also, how could it have been angled so it would fall that way?" asked Detective Oh. "The rest of these boards are placed just so . . . that weeping gentleman couldn't have placed it at an opposing angle so it would fall . . . there would be no room for him to do so. Is that what you were thinking, Mrs. Wheel?"

"Yes. That's what I was thinking," said Jane. She smiled at Oh, wanting, of course, to ask how he managed to arrive at this moment, but waiting to see if the scene told her what she wanted to know. That is what Oh always advised her. Look to see what the scene tells you before you ask a question.

Beyond the groups clustered around the police and the ambulance, Tim Lowry was being questioned by two tall female inquisitors who, it appeared, could teach the Kankakee police a thing or two about good cop/bad cop. Apparently they believed in bad cop/bad cop, as they took turns asking questions, one woman beginning to talk before the other finished. Tim was looking back and forth rapidly, unable to get a word in edgewise.

"Over there, with Claire?" Jane nodded her head in the direction of the trio, after allowing the scene to tell her what she needed to know. "Margaret Kendell, I presume?"

As anxious as Jane was to meet Margaret Kendell, she needed first to talk to Nellie, who was now telling a young police officer that someone had clobbered Marvin Gladish and they better check the walking path because whoever it was might have cut out fast through the wooded path.

Although it was now dark, Jane could sense the officer's eyes rolling from where she stood. To him, Nellie was an excitable old lady upset about the accident that had befallen her old friend. Since no one had been working with Marv except for Henry, who had gone in to use the backstage bathroom, the logical supposition was that the beam fell on Marv as he bent over his makeshift worktable. An accident, without a doubt.

"Claire finally reached Margaret, who had been at her London flat until yesterday. She offered to accompany her here, to see how you and Tim were doing with the sale. There is a problem, it seems with the auction items," said Oh. He also watched Nellie talking with the police officer. "That problem, however, pales when compared with tonight's accident."

Jane turned back to Oh, but before she could correct him, he nodded.

"Yes Mrs. Wheel, you're right. *Alleged* accident."

After the police and ambulance left, Jane was reminded that unlike what happened in fiction, in real life, after death, accident or not, someone was always left to clean up. In the movies, after the ambulance disappeared down the street, the next scene involved principal characters talking, snooping, questioning, debating, driving, kissing . . . in some way *investigating* something. Rarely was any name-above-the-title character left to sweep up debris, scrub up a stain, or put away props and lock up backstage cabinets.

Jane mulled this over as she packed up the borrowed bar set and cocktail shaker used in the second act, the crystal champagne bucket, and the costume jewelry they had tried out tonight for the third act reveal of the thief's bag. Jane wanted a real treasure trove of jewels to spill out onto the carpet and she had gathered the shiniest baubles she could find to see what carried visually to the back of the house. None of the stuff was real, although some of the signed costume pieces were highly collectible. Jane counted the brooches, bracelets, and rings, borrowed from Tim's inventory along with two long rock crystal necklaces from the Kendell house. Freddy had specified so many of the props he wanted to use for his play and Jane had actually found two huge boxes in the third-floor ballroom marked *Eekaknak stage props*. Even the paintings and statues were stored as

Eekaknak props. Jane discovered that the first trunk had almost everything she needed, which made her hunting and gathering even easier. She added the jewelry to the other borrowed props and locked them into the backstage cabinet. She would have to take another look at them before deciding what they would use—that is, *if* the production of *Murder in the Eekaknak Valley* was going to go on as planned.

"Almost finished, Mrs. Wheel?" Detective Oh had walked from the stage out to the rear parking lot and back several times, counting steps. He had also paced the walk to the dressing rooms, lobby restrooms, and the front parking lot.

Jane knew he was gathering information, but she was also sure that after she had waved everyone on ahead to meet, comfort each other, and debrief at the EZ Way Inn, Detective Oh had decided to stay behind so she would not be alone in the theater. Even after she assured him that the custodian stayed on the premises until midnight and there was a police officer assigned to the parking lot—a bone thrown to Nellie, who insisted someone must have come out of the woods to dislodge the beam—"dislodge the beam" being the language that the police substituted for Nellie's more descriptive "clobber Marvin," although no one in uniform believed anyone had come from or fled to the wooded area. Since no one had seen any strangers around Marvin's workspace and everyone in the cast and crew was accounted for when the beam had to have fallen, the police had, so far, unofficially declared Marvin's death an accident.

Jane nodded, again reflecting on the aftermath of Marvin's death in the parking lot. She knew only the most basic facts about the man. He was born and raised in Kankakee, a widower nearing seventy, with no children, who lived alone in a small cottage on the west side of town. Tim had described him as a wonderful carpenter and she had seen firsthand that he was. He was modest, Jane could tell, by the way he turned away from compliments offered every time a new piece was added to the stage. He was cautious, always wore his safety glasses, and only allowed Henry, who was an experienced woodworker himself and an old friend, to help him. Otherwise, he made sure actors were out of harm's way. Jane had been surprised at how professional he was, and Tim had explained he had actually been a stage carpenter in Chicago before retirement, and since returning to his hometown had worked on many of the community theater productions. Jane had heard him joke with Henry about their early days in Kankakee, wanting to go professional, waiting for their opportunity to flee to the big-time. Both had flown, Jane thought. Henry had gone to California, and although it seemed he had given up his theatrical dreams, he had made his fortune. And Marvin had been successful in Chicago. Over the last several days, Jane had watched him work, admired his skill and steady patience, and now regretted that she'd never said more than ten words to him. Guilt. That was something else you didn't see too often in the fictional aftermath of death. Simple guilt that here, just a matter of hours ago, someone was alive—one who had a history, a life, a family, accomplishments, joys, and sorrows and you hadn't spent even a moment getting to know him and now he was gone and you never would.

"Maybe this play is unlucky, Mrs. Wheel," said Oh, walking up behind her as she slipped the key to the padlock for the cabinet back into her pocket.

"Why unlucky? Why do you use that word?" asked Jane, turning to face him. Hadn't Tim used the word *unlucky*?

"It's the word Margaret used on the drive down. Her grandfather, the playwright, was pleased with his work. He told his grandchildren that his play would be their legacy, that it would make the family fortune. He expected it to be a great success, she said. Then, because of unforeseen circumstances that occurred just before the premiere, the production was canceled."

"Did she say if the play was ever a success?"

"I don't know if it was ever performed. When Freddy—that is what they called their grandfather—became ill, the original production was canceled. More than that, I don't know."

"Didn't they already have a family fortune?" Jane asked, fishing her car keys out of her bag. She turned on the stage light and wheeled it to the center of the stage and motioned for Oh to follow her out through the lobby so she could tell the custodian they were leaving.

"Interesting question, Mrs. Wheel," Oh said, taking her bag from her and putting it into the backseat of her car. He then held the driver's side door for her before letting himself into the passenger seat.

"Do you have an interesting answer?" Jane asked, backing out of the parking lot. She stopped the car abruptly, shifted from reverse to drive and pulled forward, around to the back of the cultural center. She shifted the car into park with her high-beam lights trained on the four-by-fours leaning against the tree.

Jane had parked in the lot on the side of the building. The gravel continued around to the back, where double doors opened onto the backstage area. Delivery trucks could drive around to the back, unload, and have enough space to turn around. Marvin had set up his worktable and power tools on the edge of the wooded park.

"I should cover those tools," Jane said. "Marv was careful with his equipment. He had special tarps for the saw."

Oh got out and together they pulled the heavy fitted covers over the power tools and tied them under the table. The legs of the table were anchored with sandbags and weights. Marv had said that only the most determined thief would be able to get away with his stuff, so he hadn't minded leaving it under the trees, as long as the tools were unplugged from their extension cords running into the building and protected from the elements. "If some jerko makes off with this table saw, why, he really, really needs a table saw," Marv had said.

While they tied the last corner, the motion detector lights on the building flashed on and the entire area was illuminated.

"Too bad it wasn't quite dark enough for those lights to go on when Marv got hit. Nellie would have seen the phantom in this spotlight."

"Yes, it was that twilight time of night where nothing is dark and nothing is light," said Oh.

Jane nodded. "Just what I was thinking. An impossible time to see anything well. So why would a carpenter, a good and careful carpenter, one who wore a sweatshirt that said 'Measure twice, cut once' be out here working with dangerous tools in the almost dark?"

"Maybe he had come out to put things away. From where the beam was rolled away on the ground, from where your mother sat with him," Oh said, bending over the table saw. "He could have been beginning to cover this corner when the beam fell. If he had his head down, he wouldn't have seen it coming."

Jane stepped over to the base of the tree next to the remaining lumber.

"If he were standing the way you are, whoever pushed the beam down wouldn't have had a very good view of him, either. The way those branches hang down, you could barely make him out. He was wearing dark jeans, a dark plaid shirt," said Jane. "Just like what Henry was wearing. Henry's been dressing like Perkins the gardener since the night of the first read-through. A method actor, I guess." Jane paused and squinted, trying for a better view of Detective Oh from where she stood just about ten feet away. "Not a very precise way to kill someone," she muttered.

Jane stepped back from the work area and took stock.

"Okay, tools are covered, power cords are disconnected. I put them backstage earlier. We're done here," said Jane.

Jane drove them to the EZ Way Inn, where the bar was, by weeknight-in-Kankakee standards, hopping. Tim and the rest of the cast filled the table area and Don was moving from table to bar and back with drinks. Carl, the evening bartender who was used to one or two regulars nursing a beer or two, was completely befuddled. Who were all these people and why were they ordering drinks with names? Carl knew the basics. If pressed, and if he could find any olives, he could turn out a martini, but what was a cosmo? And what did they mean by wine by the glass? How else would you drink it? And who did they think they were asking about house brands and bar brands and naming vodkas by the dozen? Did they really expect him to believe that there was a difference between one tasteless glass of alcohol and another fancier-named tasteless glass of alcohol? Again, who were these people? Carl was used to a quiet evening with Francis or Burt, both of them sitting side by side at the bar watching television until eleven or so and Carl could close up and go home. But more than twelve people on a weekday night, all ordering different drinks? This was madness. Carl had not signed on for big-city life in the fast lane. If he had wanted to be in the thick of the action, he could have stayed in Danville, where he grew up.

Don and Nellie began working the bar and Nellie pushed their bartender toward the kitchen.

"You look like a damn deer caught in the headlights. Carl, go home. You're too old for all this excitement."

Without a word, Carl pulled on the navy blue cap he wore winter and summer and left by the back door. He wouldn't bother to remind Nellie that he was one year younger than Don. He would, however, as he did several times a month, call them tomorrow and announce that he was quitting.

Jane knew there was no bottle of Grey Goose behind the bar of the EZ Way Inn. She also knew better than to ask her dad what brands he did have. Instead, she just asked him to pour her some vodka over ice and throw in a few olives if he had any and vowed not to look at the label. What she didn't know wouldn't give her a hangover.

Jane surveyed the dining room of the EZ Way Inn. It wasn't exactly a separate room, just the other half of the space opposite the barroom. Ten round tables with four to six chairs pulled around them were clustered into the space. Jane remembered the old days, when the Roper factory boys and office girls, for they would always be boys and girls to her parents, crowded into the dining room at lunchtime. Now it was an unusual sight to see three of the tables filled in the evening. Jane knew no one would mistake this for a party . . . no cardplaying, no loud interruptions, no laughter.

At the table closest to the bar, Chuck Havens was listening to Mary Wainwright tell the story of Marvin's set for the musical they had done two years ago. "He was so proud of the turntable. It took six of us to tug that rope and revolve the stage, but when we did it, you could hear the gasps from the audience. They applauded the set every night! Marv always said we shouldn't be underestimating how much an audience appreciated hard work," said Mary.

Bryan and Penny had joined the theater group, arriving through the front door only a few minutes after Jane and Oh had entered through the back. Penny looked pale, but maneuvered well on her crutches. When Jane asked how they knew about the gathering, Bryan nodded toward Henry. "He called us. We had all worked on lots of shows together and Pen and I just thought we'd like to be here."

Jane noted that Bryan and Penny seemed surprised to see Margaret but did not make much of a fuss over their distant cousin. They exchanged hugs and pats, but none of the three had much to say to each other. Bryan and Penny seemed anxious to get over to the table where the actors sat exchanging their stories.

As far as Jane knew, no one had ever determined how the jar of marbles had spilled in their home. Or who had left the note from Mr. Bumbles. She had tried to pursue the question, but Bryan had shaken his head and told her to chalk it up to an accident and they were just relieved that Penny was okay. He told her they did have a cat, and although nothing had ever fallen before, maybe it was Pumpkin who knocked down the marbles. There was no need to make a fuss.

Oh had joined Claire and Margaret at a table where Marvin was not the topic of conversation. The two women flanked Tim and continued to question him. Jane decided it was time she met Margaret Kendell.

"Lowry, we know you're honest, there isn't a question about that, but those paintings you sent to auction, the Scottish watercolor, at least . . ." Claire was talking to Tim but looking down, consulting a small black leather-bound notebook.

Tim allowed himself to exhale when Jane arrived, his oppressed expression almost giving way to gratitude.

"Margie, this is Jane Wheel. She's worked at the house with me all this week. Tell her what you told me."

Jane reached across the table and shook Margie Kendell's hand, then sat down in the empty chair between Oh and Claire. She was torn when she saw Nellie sit down with the cast members since she didn't want to miss Nellie's version of what happened, but Margie looked like she had her own compelling tale. Her face, years older, of course, was still that of a sad-eyed girl. Her yearbook quote, "Make 'em laugh," might no longer be her motto, but her yearbook expression hadn't changed a bit.

"I've heard about you from Bruce, too, Jane. I'm glad you're here to help out with this mess."

"It's been a night of messes, Margaret. You're going to have to fill me in from the beginning."

"The valuable paintings from the house and a few of the silver pieces—the pieces I've always been told are the valuable items . . . objects my grandfather said . . . the pieces that we could count on to retain . . ." Margie didn't exactly stammer, but Jane noticed that in trying to choose her words carefully, she had a difficult time getting out even one coherent sentence. Jane was, by nature, a sentence-finisher, one who tried to supply the missing words, to finish the half-formed thoughts, but Oh's presence made her conscious of what he called "listening discipline." He taught her that no matter how close she might come to what another intended to say, when she helped them to say it, she would not learn as much from her own words as she would from theirs, no matter how haltingly the other person's words came out.

Claire Oh, however, either had not had the same lesson from her husband or she chose to ignore it.

"What Margie means is that there were valuable paintings, some silver, some Kalo silver pieces—large ones—and I have them all documented right here. I helped find the silver, as well as some Chinese porcelains, for her mother over twenty years ago. These are the pieces Rick and Margie knew they could count on to bring in some money when the estate settled. It turns out that the auction house has determined that all the pieces we sent in are either not authentic or not that valuable. They are moderately priced antiques or merely decorative reproductions."

"Did you see them before they went to auction?" Jane asked. "Are they the same . . ."

"The two paintings I purchased for Margie's mother were authentic. I delivered them to the house and helped her place them myself. The large silver bowl was Kalo, two water pitchers, a set of plates. I have the receipts from when I purchased them. The total value of that silver should be well over fifty thousand, and that's allowing for this economic climate. Let me make it clear that I am not accusing Lowry, but I need to know the timeline of when these pieces were boxed and sent—"

"But you don't know if what you purchased twenty years ago was what was boxed and sent to the auction house. You weren't here, and if there was a switch—"

"Of course there was a switch, whatever and wherever."

"Now I understand," said Tim, sounding almost relieved. "You've been peppering me with questions for over an hour, but you never exactly explained what had happened. You think I switched the items? Boxed up fakes and sent them to auction? I stole the Kalo and swapped it for cheap plate and thought I'd fool the auction house?" Tim's relief disappeared and was replaced with anger. "I'm not sure whether to be insulted because you think I'm dishonest or because you think I'm that stupid."

"I think you are neither, Lowry," said Claire. "However, someone was duped."

She was interrupted by Margie, who shook her head and said, "Not either one, Tim. I knew right away I could trust you. Claire had advised me on pieces to send for auction, but I didn't think she'd want to do a house sale. I thought it would be beneath—" Margaret caught herself before she branded Claire a snob and Tim a lowly house sale guy and began again.

"Right away when you came to the house, I knew you understood there were lives and histories in that house and that you . . . you had an understanding of how things— I mean, I said yes to this silly play idea of yours and I wouldn't have if— I trusted you. I mean, I *trust* you."

"But," said Claire, "we need to know exactly when you sent those pieces and who packed them, if you had help," Claire turned and looked at Jane pointedly. "You love Kalo silver. Did you help pack it for the auction house?"

Had Claire totally forgotten that Jane had cleared her name and reputation when Claire herself was accused of selling an expensive forgery?

Jane took a deep breath. Looking at Tim and Tim only, putting on imaginary blinders to screen out both of the women who insisted they weren't accusing anyone of anything, she asked, "What's the story?"

"I had met with Margie twice at the house and the paintings and silver weren't there. She was having them independently appraised."

Margie nodded while Claire shrieked. "You didn't tell me they had left the house. Who appraised them?"

Tim continued talking directly to Jane.

"When the house keys were turned over to me, it wasn't by Margie, it was Rick who was in town and who left the keys for me. He was going to meet with the appraiser and have them sent directly to auction. I never saw these items, although Rick left the photographs of the Kalo . . ."

Jane raised an eyebrow.

"Yes, it was fabulous," said Tim. "But I was never in the same room with any of the stuff pulled for auction."

"Nicely done, Mrs. Wheel," said Oh, who had been watching all the parties in action. "Claire, you could have gotten to the bottom of this much faster if you had allowed Mr. Lowry to answer any of the questions you hurled in his way."

"Right as always, Bruce," said Margie. "I see it now, don't you, Claire?"

And at the same time that Margie said, "My brother, Rick," Claire said, "that scumbag, Rick."

Tim had been right when he described the greed that divided siblings. But didn't Rick and Margie each inherit a bundle of money? How much would be enough?

"Here's the other silver bowl," said Margie, holding up a photograph. "This one was in the family forever and Freddy . . . my grandfather, Freddy . . . said it was better than all the rest of the stuff in the house. Is this one that my brother Rick showed you, Tim?"

Tim shook his head. Although this was an old photo and the quality was not great, it did look magnificent—a large double-handled bowl.

"I would have remembered seeing it," said Tim. "It's a grand piece."

Jane nodded as the photo was passed to her. She repeated, "a grand piece," and looked up at Tim. "Why does this look so familiar?"

Claire's facial features grew even more symmetrical as she pulled herself up straighter in her chair. "Perhaps you've visited the Metropolitan Museum of Art?"

"No, I mean, yes, of course I have." Jane was too absorbed in the photo to be insulted. "This does look like a museum piece. *A grand double-handled silver bowl.* It reminds me of one that I've seen." Jane looked up. "There's one in the Metropolitan?" she asked.

Claire nodded.

"Freddy said it was by Cornelius Kierstede. Eighteenth century, American. Would be worth millions now. Maybe it's still at the house. Maybe in one of the large cabinets in the hall between the dining room and the butler's pantry?" said Margie. Those cabinets were fitted with locks so mother could lock up the valuables and maybe Freddy told her to lock it up. . . ."

Jane and Tim both shook their heads.

"There was good stuff in there. Gorgeous silver serving

pieces and candlesticks, but not this. I would have called you if I'd found—"

"I'd like to say something," said Henry, standing and raising his glass, half-filled with what looked to Jane like whiskey and water.

Although he had been sitting with a drink at the table of actors, Jane thought he still looked alone, shaken. She had seen him sitting still, half-listening to others, but had not seen or heard him talking about his friend or the events of the night.

The sight of the small elegant Henry standing erect, head held high, silenced Claire and Margie, and the entire roomful of people waited.

Jane noticed her father stood behind the bar with his arms folded, chewing on the inside of his cheek, looking as if he might be deciding something. Jane hoped he would not decide to begin the coughing and sneezing routine he had perfected at rehearsals.

"Marvin was a good friend and an excellent craftsman. We went to school together and worked on our first play together when we were just about fifteen years old. We really wanted to do a bang-up job on this play . . . for Freddy Kendell, as much as for ourselves. He was a great old man, a real mentor to me and Marvin and all the kids in the theater club. So now, I'd like us all to do a bang-up job for Marvin. It's what he'd want us to do. To our friend, Marvin!" Henry threw back the whiskey in his glass and sat down. There was a moment when all was quiet, then Don, slowly and solemnly, began clapping his hands. Everyone joined in and ordered more drinks, and once again, began trying to outdo one another with stories about Marvin, which gave way, as stories do, especially among theater people, to stories about themselves.

Jane saw Nellie get up from her seat at the actors' table and walk over to Don behind the bar. She whispered something short and most probably not sweet into her husband's ear, then grabbed a towel from the stack next to the rinse tanks and started to wipe down the bar.

Jane excused herself from her group and joined her parents behind the bar. Jane touched her father's arm.

"It was nice of you to be so respectful when Henry made his speech, Dad. I noticed you started the applause."

Don, still looking thoughtful, gazing out at all of the patrons gabbing away in the dining room, smiled down at his daughter. "Oh sure, honey, Henry's a hell of an actor. Always was." Don walked to the opposite side of the bar and began gathering up glasses and bottles.

Her mother, still cleaning the bar, worked her way toward Jane. Nellie looked so small and fierce as she wiped down the worn wood. Jane had an odd feeling that if her mother stopped her motion, she would fade away and disappear. It appeared as if Nellie's frantic movement was what kept her earthbound. If she stopped, she would simply become untethered, invisible. Jane badly wanted to put her arm around her mother but knew from past experience that the gesture would not be accepted in the spirit in which it was given.

"What are you staring at?" said Nellie, not even looking up to see Jane staring at her.

"I'm just sorry about your friend, Mom. You saw a horrible—"

"Don't you say accident, because it sure as hell wasn't an accident," said Nellie.

"Okay," said Jane. Maybe she should apply Oh's listening discipline to Nellie. Maybe Nellie would talk more if Jane questioned and commented less.

"It wasn't an accident, and it's going to be up to you and me to find out who did it, because the police sure as hell didn't listen when I told them somebody clobbered old Marvin. And none of these bozos seem to care very much even though they act like they do. They just want to be in this silly play. If I hear one more idiot say Marvin would have wanted the show to go on . . ."

"Do you think Tim should cancel?"

"Hell, no. But not because Marvin would have wanted it that way. Who the hell knows what anyone would have wanted? Especially when they're dead? People just say that because the dead person can't argue back. I sure as hell hope you don't start saying what I would or wouldn't want once I'm dead. Tim shouldn't cancel the damn play because it's important to keep everyone together."

Jane was touched that her mother was thinking about all of the nerves and anxiety that had erupted with Marvin's death. It probably would be better for everyone if they continued the play. It would be therapeutic to finish what they had all started together.

Nellie folded her arms and looked around the room. "Yup, keep everyone in the same damn place every night until we find out which one of these phony bastards murdered Marvin."

We find new things every day and it never gets old.

Starting to really like plantains.

Margo taught me to make cowboy coffee. Still don't like coffee.

Jane had taught herself to enjoy Nick's tweets. Complain as she might about 140 characters offering anything substantial in the way of information, she realized that Nick's distilled comments did offer pocket descriptions of his life with Charley in Honduras, his day-to-day observations. And after all, a teenaged boy didn't usually speak in whole sentences and tell his parents stories with beginnings, middles, and ends anyway, so having these nuggets from a son on a daily basis would probably make many mothers envious. Plus, she had the Facebook postings. Either Nick or Charley put up new photos every other day. It didn't make up for her son being so far away, but Nick had kept his promise to stay in touch.

Jane kept her promise, too, tweeting back about the play, the treasures she was finding in the Kendell house. Jane wasn't quite sure what her message would be today, though, since she wasn't sure one could communicate anything as serious as

Marvin's death through a post or a tweet. Some pieces of information were just not appropriately passed along through social media. Nick's tweets, however, were perfect. Jane thought of them as her daily haiku from her son, usually repeating them over and over after receiving them, often with a smile on her face. A few days ago she was repeating to anyone who asked her that Nick was starting to really like plantains. Today she found herself asking, Who's Margo?

She also found herself with a list of questions concerning Marvin's death, not the least of which was whether or not it was a deliberate attack as Nellie insisted or an accident. She, too, might be persuaded it was deliberate because of the way the wood had been placed against the tree. But the why and who of the question remained unanswered.

The rest of today's list of questions? So many and pointed in so many directions. What happened to the valuable antiques and paintings that were supposed to be sent to the auction house? Did Margie's brother steal them, sabotage the sale, subvert the share-and-share-alike plan between the siblings?

There was another question that was unanswered. Jane had asked Oh about the Kendell fortune. She had wanted to know if Rick and Margaret were as rich as everyone had assumed, but Oh had not answered her. Jane knew that no matter how large a fortune the brother and sister had inherited, they would still be concerned over forgeries and fakes. They would still want their property to be valued as it should be . . . and yet there was a whiff of the desperate in Margaret's manner when she spoke about the missing items. She had seemed so nervous, so lost . . . not angry or puzzled about the news from the auction house that the silver and paintings weren't valuable. Claire was livid, but Margaret seemed defeated. She didn't have the aura of privilege that one might expect of someone as wealthy as she and her brother had been portrayed.

The Kendell place was close to being finally prepped for the sale, so Bruce and Claire Oh and Margaret were staying at a motel on the outskirts of Kankakee, rather than at Margaret's family home. Jane and Tim had arranged to meet them all at the house around noon. That would give Margaret the morning to try once again to reach Rick and try to get to the bottom of at least a few of the questions that were beginning to hover over this sale.

Jane, after e-mailing Nick, avoiding the subject of Marvin's death altogether and trying to respond to all of his tweeted information with a little of her own, decided to take Rita for a long walk. The dog deserved some attention. Nellie, whom Jane had assumed never liked the messiness of dogs or any other animal who couldn't control its own shedding or sweep up after itself, had turned out to be Rita's best friend, but during this visit, Nellie was distracted. This morning she did manage to prepare bacon and scrambled eggs for Rita before leaving with Don for the tavern but was not her usually Dr. Doolittle self, talking away and communicating with the dog on some Nellified plane of consciousness. Rita knew something was wrong. The giant-eyed dog sat completely still, watching Nellie move from refrigerator to stove to sink. Rita's whole doggy being seemed to quiver with a question. Jane wasn't sure whether the dog wanted to ask *What troubles you, Nellie, my friend,* or *What? No pancakes?* But clearly there was some canine curiosity in the air.

Rita also deserved a decent walk before Jane took off to spend a long day at the Kendell house, then, Jane presumed, another long night at rehearsal. The cast had been so discombobulated after the "accident," there was a lot of catching up to get back to where they were in the rehearsal process. Which wasn't far enough. Jane knew she could use a little purposeful exercise herself to clear her head before her day of writing down prices and folding and refolding linens . . . since she knew that

Claire would unfold each piece and examine and question the prices agreed upon by Jane and Tim. Even without a possible murder to solve, it was going to be a full day.

Snapping on Rita's leash, Jane locked the door of her parents' house behind her. They set off, Jane choosing the destination but allowing Rita to decide the route. Since this neighborhood had not been Jane's territory growing up, she didn't have favorite spots or secret childhood haunts to revisit. Instead, she allowed Rita to follow the scent of the lilacs still in bloom and the flowery trails of yellow forsythia that was beginning to spend itself, leaving the lawns littered with gold. Fall was Jane's season, particularly when she visited her hometown, where the crayon-box colors of maples along the Kankakee River filled her with joy and longing, a heady mix to which she had long been addicted, but today, walking through this Kankakee neighborhood on a spring morning felt equally seductive. The palette held more green and blue, rather than red and orange, and Jane saw its lively beauty. In fact, as she walked briskly, trying to keep pace with Rita, who sorely needed the exercise, Jane felt a curious sprig of a spring blossom take root inside of her.

Maybe all that new-beginning-spring-has-sprung-hope-is-eternal nonsense was beginning to sort itself out in Jane's head. She had spent a long winter reconciling herself to the divorce with Charley. Even though she usually referred to their split as a separation, she knew in her newly minted spring heart that it was a divorce. Her marriage, although not her motherhood, was definitely over. But instead of the lingering good-byes and endings of fall and the weight and shiver of snow and ice, she felt something else now. Blooming, blossoming, growing? Well, that was a bit much. But there was a sprig of something . . . a sprout of something new. Change? Hope? Beginning?

Jane couldn't answer her own musings since she and Rita

had arrived at the spot she had intended they visit when they began their morning walk. Rita's muscle had pulled Jane along for seven blocks in a zigzagging walk past houses, a church, a park with tennis courts, and Jane had pulled back, directing the dog to where Jane herself had wanted to go. They arrived in front of the Kankakee Cultural Center, both breathing a little harder, both feeling like they had won the tug of war. Standing in front of the large building in the daylight managed to drown out Jane's personal reflections and brought back all the chaos of the night.

As much as Jane preferred to stand still and re-create the events leading up to Marvin's death, she couldn't resist the tug of the leash. Rita wanted to explore the wooded walking path behind the center and Jane couldn't blame her. Trees, bushes, blooming shrubs, and, best of all, squirrels, lived back there, and Rita deserved to sniff and lunge and think about everything she could do if dogs ruled the world and she weren't at the end of this ridiculous leash.

Instead of walking through the parking lot, where all of the actors including Nellie had entered and exited the building, Jane allowed Rita to tug her around the other grassy side of the building. This was lawn and trees, a wide swath of green before reaching the rear of the building, where the wooded walking path wound around. Jane noted that Marvin's tools were all still neatly covered and the canvas still snug and tied as she and Oh had left them. Rita sniffed along the path and, just for a moment, Jane let herself fantasize that her dog would look up at her, bark once or twice, and then lead her mistress on a romp through the woods, ending at the very hideout of the bad guy who had killed Marvin, and—why not if it was a fantasy—had also stolen all of Margaret Kendell's valuables and hidden them away in his lair.

However, although Rita was a large empathetic animal, part German shepherd and several parts dog unknown, and a sweet, smart, loyal pet who more than once had earned her place as top dog in Jane's heart, she was, indeed, a dog, not a detective. Instead of sniffing out the bad guys, she buried her nose in the mulch of the path alongside the table saw, then barked once, shaking her muzzle to dislodge pieces of bark and grass. Jane noticed something clinging to her and reached down for it, thinking it was something vinelike and stringy coiled around her ear.

Jane straightened up, holding not a natural piece of debris but instead a piece of fabric with a part of a clip still attached. Blue-and-green polka-dotted grosgrain—a hair bow—that had fallen out of the braid or ponytail of some little girl who had walked this path with her parents or friends . . . probably recently, this spring for sure, since the ribbon was not faded or stained as it would be had it lain under a blanket of snow or been stepped on through several seasons. No, it was a spring hair bow, this spring . . . but more than that, Jane couldn't tell. Rather than toss it back on the ground or into the large garbage barrel that was between the saw and the tree where the pieces of lumber still rested, she slipped it into her pocket, since Jane Wheel, magpie-at-large, had never found a broken bit, a lost thingamajig, a worn scrap, or a discarded odd and/or end that she didn't, at least for a short while, slip into her pocket and keep.

"Ready to head back?" Jane asked Rita aloud. She wanted to jot down a few notes and check her props list before driving over to the Kendell house. If the show truly must go on, there were still a few prop spots to fill.

"Almost."

Rita was an intelligent animal, but even Jane, who was prone to flights of fancy, had never heard her speak before. She turned around at the familiar voice.

"Mr. Havens? God, I mean Chuck," said Jane, feeling her face grow hot.

"Sorry, Jane. Didn't mean to scare you. Just finishing my run, decided to cool down on the walking path here. I live just over on Fraser. You can almost see my house from here."

"You didn't scare me. I just have a hard time with the name change," said Jane. "I'm not sure if I'll ever be able to call you Chuck without feeling I'm about to be smacked upside the head by Sister Kelley."

"First of all, I'll bet Sister Kelley never laid a hand on any of you girls, right?"

Jane nodded.

"Second of all, turnabout's fair play. You think I didn't get red in the face every time I passed a gaggle of you giggling senior girls my first year teaching? I was twenty-two years old, only four years older than all of you. I could hear you whispering . . . oh God, it was awful. So, if you get caught now feeling a little uncomfortable considering us as equals in the world, I'm actually okay with that."

"Fair enough," said Jane, adding, "Mary seems to have overcome any student-teacher awkardness." Jane hoped that didn't sound as snarky as she thought it might.

"We're friends. She sold me my house and there's nothing like contracts and frank discussions about money to banish embarrassment. I mean, once you have to confess your pathetically low teacher's salary, you have to give up any cachet you might have had as the new young English teacher. Besides, I'm one of the oldest teachers there now. And, since the school is coed, the old gaggle of girls has been replaced by coed groups who don't pay attention to teachers now that they get to pay attention to each other."

Jane thought she heard just the slightest frost form over his words. She had indeed sounded snarky.

"It's odd for me to be back home right now. Staying at my parents' makes me regress, I think. I'm their high school daughter again. Sorry if I sounded—"

Chuck shook his head and held up one hand. "No apologies. If you were wondering if Mary and I are more than friends, though, you could just ask me."

Now Jane was blushing and it had nothing to do with high school. That is, of course, exactly what she was wondering. Could she have been any more obvious?

Jane tried to sort through the debris flying through her mind. Does he think I'm attracted to him? Does he think I'm still trying to beat Mary Wainwright at every game in town?

"And if I did ask that . . . ?" said Jane, raising an eyebrow.

"The answer is that we date," said Chuck Havens. He shifted his feet and nodded in the opposite direction. "I've got to get going. Took the morning off because there was an assembly, but have to teach after lunch. I'll see you tonight at rehearsal?"

Jane nodded.

After taking a few long strides in the opposite direction, he turned back. "Mary and I date, but not exclusively," he said, waving.

Jane fought the urge to laugh out loud at the high school triangle being set up before her eyes . . . that she herself had put in motion . . . and watched him trot off toward home.

She had let the scene speak and tried to practice listening more than talking, just as Detective Oh had taught her, and it worked.

She knew that Mary and Chuck had said they were together in the parking lot when Marvin was hit. If they were a couple, they might be providing an alibi for each other. If Mary thought they were a couple, but Chuck did not, one of them might be persuaded to chat a little more freely about what they saw and heard last night. And, if Chuck was out running this morning, why was he wearing leather loafers instead of running shoes and why hadn't he broken a sweat before his cooldown walk?

Jane surprised herself by arriving at the Kendell place early. No Tim, Margaret, or Bruce and Claire Oh. No other cars in the driveway. Because she was there first, she decided to drive around to the back of the house and explore. It was a large piece of property, more like a country estate with city-block proportions, and so, city amenities. A serviceable city alley provided access behind the extra deep yard. Entering at the end of the block, she drove behind the property, where she had an excellent view of a six-car garage with what appeared to be an apartment built above. There was an outside staircase that led up to the second-story space. Jane pulled her car up close to the building and parked. An ironwork fence that closed off the property appeared to be sturdy enough, but Jane shook the gate and found that she could open it just enough to slip her hand through and work the inside latch. Pushing up, then moving the pin first to one side then the other, allowed her to release the gate and it swung open.

"That was way too easy," said Jane aloud. This property should be better protected. Who had advised Margaret about security?

Jane paused at the bottom of the stairs leading to the second floor. Tim had said they were not going to bother with cleaning and inventorying the coach house. Margaret had told him not to bother . . . even if there were any knickknacks in there, they would have belonged to Freddy and she would probably want to keep anything personal of Freddy's. Both Margaret and Rick had assured him there was nothing of value if, indeed, there was anything at all. Freddy had used it as a writing studio, but after his death the space hadn't been used for anything, except possibly storage of automotive or gardening equipment. Since there was a separate gardening shed as big as most two-bedroom homes, Tim had doubted that any valuable garden statuary or accessories had been carried up the stairs. That didn't mean Tim didn't want to check out the space—he and Jane both lusted after anything behind a locked door—they just hadn't yet taken the time. They were too pressed to ready the main house for the sale.

Jane, however, had a little extra time right now.

Climbing the stairs alongside the building, Jane thought about the space being used as Freddy's writing studio. On the wall that faced the alley, there were high, horizontal light-borrowing windows whose purpose would be to allow in the daylight but not to subject anyone to the alley view. On the other three sides, large, mullioned windows looked out onto the gardens in every direction. Jane could see that there were some transparent curtains hanging on the window that faced the main house, almost half a city block away across the lawn. The fabric wasn't opaque enough either to block out light or to allow anyone to forget just how magnificent the setting was.

At the top of the stairs there was a small landing with a built-in bench opposite the door. On the door was a small engraved plaque. Although it was badly tarnished, Jane rubbed the metal with her thumb and made out some letters:

A-T-E-R U-B

Jane used the corner of her shirt to rub the plaque harder until she could read all of the letters. *THEATER CLUB*. So this wasn't only Freddy's writing studio, it was also the headquarters for something called the Theater Club. Henry had mentioned the theater club in his speech about Marvin at the EZ Way Inn, but Jane had heard it in small letters—figuring it referred to a loose group to which they all belonged—not formally, not spelled out in caps, with a real clubhouse that had a metal plaque on the door.

Jane tried turning the large burnished brass knob. Locked. As much as Jane wanted to get into the space, especially now that she knew it was also the theater club, she was actually relieved the door was locked. If security had really been as loose on the coach house as it was on the back gate, she would have to advise that Margaret do a complete inventory with Tim before the sale, since a burglary seemed much too easy and inevitable. As soon as word spread that there was a house sale being prepped—and word always spread, leading pickers and dealers to ring doorbells and knock on windows days in advance of the sale—the property became even more vulnerable. Although no one could actually see the circle drive in front of the house clearly from the road, someone might be out walking his dog, glimpse a car in the driveway, creep closer, and recognize Tim's T & T Sales van. A dead giveaway that although no one was living there, objects of value were still in residence.

Jane stood on tiptoe trying to see in the small window at the top of the door. Maybe if she stood on the bench, she would . . . Hello? Jane noted hinges on the painted green seat. A storage bench just might hold a spare key. She checked her watch. She probably had a few more minutes before the rest of the group arrived. Couldn't hurt to take a peek.

"Aah," said Jane, opening the squeaking bench, jumping back and turning suddenly cold despite the sunny June morning. "You got me again."

Mr. Bumbles lay inside the bench, his demonic grin intact. This time, though, his hands were placed together to hold a block-printed sign: IT'S ABOUT TIME SOMEBODY LET ME OUT OF THIS BOX! FORGET YOUR KEY AGAIN?

Jane wanted to move the dummy to see if a spare key was placed underneath him, but as she reached out to touch him, she was struck by the dust that covered his face, hands, and clothing. Intricate cobwebs were laced over his body. Jane examined him from every angle before reaching in to touch him.

"You've been lying here quite a while, Bumby. I think you just might have a twin brother back at the house. You do, don't you?" Or, Jane thought, maybe even a triplet, since that would explain the dummy having changed clothes from dungarees into his little suit. It made sense that a performing ventriloquist would have multiple dolls, didn't it? So maybe Freddy had a set? Or Margaret? On the other hand, what made sense about being a performing ventriloquist?

Jane reached in to move Mr. Bumbles, surprised anew at how creepy it was to touch the doll and feel its wooden body beneath its clothes. These were the things bad dreams and B movies were made of—the ventriloquist's dummy that took on a life of its own and enslaved his master.

When Jane placed him into a sitting position, she was pleased to find a rectangular metal box that had been hidden beneath him. Just the type of container to hold a spare key. And since Bumby had scared her half to death, she felt she had earned the right to let herself into Freddy's studio. Inside the box were six identical keys, all strung on individual linked chains. Each chain had a silver engraved wafer attached to it in addition to a key.

Jane placed the chains over her left hand and held up the tags with her right to read the etched letters. Names. *Marvin.*

Henry. Bry. Melanie. Suzanne. Of course, these were members of the theater club. Jane picked up the last necklace and held it close to read it. In the distance she heard a car door and even from across the vast lawn, she could pick up the voice of Claire Oh talking a mile a minute. Jane put five necklaces back in the box and arranged Mr. Bumbles back in his benchlike coffin.

Although she wouldn't visit the clubhouse now, she'd hang on to this sixth key so she could visit later. It wasn't really stealing if she took this key and placed it around her own neck, feeling the cool metal against her skin as she tucked it beneath her shirt. Of course it wasn't stealing since she could just say she was returning the key to its rightful owner. And she did plan to do just that. As soon as she once again met up with its rightful owner, they would have a good heart-to-heart and she would hand her the key with her name engraved upon it.

Jane decided to leave her car parked next to the coach house. She walked the lawn, which gently sloped upward toward the main house. Once she reached the brick walkway through a slightly overgrown herb garden, she turned back and looked at the coach house. Freddy, if his desk faced out the large front window, would be able to look up from writing his play and observe life going on in the garden and, if the curtains were open, in the large living room at the rear of the house. The theater club, if they were meeting and rehearsing or whatever they did in their elegant clubhouse, would have a direct view into the rear bedrooms of the house. Jane moved to different spots in the yard, looking first at the coach house, then staring up at the main house. Looking back and forth between the two buildings was where Tim found Jane when he bounded around the house into the garden.

"You're here?"

"Where?"

"What are you doing back here? Where's your car?"

"Tim, do you think sometimes we ask the wrong questions in life?"

"Oh no, I don't have time for this right now. Claire's tearing through the house like a banshee and thought she spotted someone walking in the backyard and sent me out here. I was hoping I could tell her she was wrong," said Tim, sighing. "It would give me so much pleasure to tell her she was wrong."

"I was just looking at the view from Freddy's writing studio," said Jane, gesturing toward the coach house.

Tim looked back and forth from the coach house to the main house.

"Yeah, he could see the house. Why is that so interesting?"

Jane walked away from Tim into the garden and centered herself, her back to the coach house, and looked up at the house. The drapes were all open. The main staircase that ran through the center of the house was visible and she could see Claire walking purposefully up to the second floor.

"Come stand by me," said Jane.

"Why must I be . . ." Tim started his complaint with a weary voice, but when he stood beside Jane, looking where she had pointed, he ended with a laugh. "Wow!"

"What do you see, Mr. Director?"

"I see *Murder in the Eekaknak Valley,*" said Tim. "It's Freddy's set. Right down to the description of the drapes and the wallpaper. I thought he was precise in his set design information and stage directions, but I didn't realize he was just putting down everything he saw outside his window."

"Instead of a play, he was writing a documentary," said Jane.

In the script, Freddy had reduced this exact view of the house for his set. The stairway was placed in the same spot, even the paintings on the wall were described as the ones that were actually on the walls in the house. The doors and windows were placed in the same proportions, and the brick patio leading to the gardens was described as leading out from the house, backstage.

"It's reversed a little, so the gardens remain in the back, but it's weird how looking at this view of the house is exactly his set description," said Tim.

"And exactly the way Marvin built it," said Jane.

"He even had the wallpaper exactly right, which I'm not sure I would have gotten from the description the way Freddy wrote it," said Tim. "Freddy said the walls had a tiny gold tulip-like print, but the wallpaper is really a fleur-de-lis pattern, and that's what Marvin painted. Exactly." Tim gave a little shiver. "How did he know what Freddy wanted . . . he was using the same script as us . . ."

"Marvin wasn't using the script at all," said Jane. "He was painting from memory."

"There is work to be done, you two." Claire Oh stood on the second-floor Juliet balcony looking down at them. "What in the world are you doing staring into space?"

Jane ignored Claire and turned to Tim.

"You told me you were giving me a murder to take my mind off my troubles. You said Freddy died mysteriously?" said Jane.

"I was, you know, exaggerating, talking about the play. A murder mystery. I mean it was odd that Freddy collapsed the week before the play was supposed to go on, but he was an old man. He had a heart attack, I think, right in the garden, but he didn't . . ."

Tim stopped talking and Jane looked around where they were standing.

"On the brick path in the garden, right? Where the cousin is found murdered in the play?" asked Jane. "Where we're standing right now."

"Mrs. Wheel?"

Detective Oh had, in his usual manner, approached quietly on her blind side.

"We were just admiring the view," said Jane.

"Ah, now there is another missing painting," said Oh, immediately adopting their position and looking toward the main house.

Jane turned to Oh, knowing if she waited, he would tell her what he meant.

He pointed toward the living room, where two paintings hung on the back wall, the one facing them. "There are two there, but on your stage set, which I looked at last night . . . it is this house, right? There are three paintings on the stage walls."

Jane dug into her tote bag, which she had set down on the lawn as she had walked back and forth. Pulling out her now battered *Murder in the Eekaknak Valley* script, she turned to Act One, Scene One, where the set for the house was described: *center staircase which winds around a pillar, carved with a niche . . . wallpapered background . . . two paintings (portraits) on the left . . . one painting, a still life of fruit and wine, over the demilune hall table*. Jane looked up from the script and back to the house, Oh was correct. In the main house, the real house, there was no painting over the hall table.

Jane, Tim, and Oh tore themselves away from the living tableau of *Murder in the Eekaknak Valley* and walked around to the front door to enter the house. Margaret stood in the main foyer, looking up at the chandelier.

"Should we dust before the sale?" she asked.

Claire, standing on the landing and looking down at them all looked as if she was about to berate Margaret, was interrupted by Tim. Jane thought she saw Tim actually cast a warning look at Claire before he touched Margaret's arm and shook his head.

"Shoppers like the dust. They don't want housekeeping, they don't judge. They want old and untouched and so that's what we try to give them."

Margaret smiled. "Untouched," she repeated.

Claire swept down the stairs. She was a woman made for grand entrances. Without comment, she took Jane's arm and walked her along through the dining room, through the hallway that led to the rear of the house. Now that Jane understood the layout, she realized Claire had brought her right into the rear living room area that was actually Freddy's setting for most of the action of his play. Jane looked around and realized it really felt like she was standing on Marvin's set. She had been working in the house and working at the theater for the last few weeks, but she hadn't seen similarities. Now she couldn't *not* see them. Claire paid no attention to Jane's scrutiny of the room. If she could have gotten away with it, she might have taken Jane's head in her own hands and pointed her, eyeball-to-eyeball, into a focused, listening stance.

"Those paintings are not here," said Claire. "I didn't expect them to be, but still, I thought I'd find something that would explain or lead to what happened. I don't know why, I just . . ." Claire was whispering, fast and low. "Margaret's losing her grip. She's always been sweet, but not savvy about people. Animals, bugs she understands, but people? Way too trusting. And now she's broke. She needs the money from all this stuff, but even more important, she needs those big-ticket items."

"Broke . . . you mean low on cash or do you mean broke-broke?" asked Jane.

"Her dad was a lousy investor to begin with and it didn't help that he put most of his stuff with some Kankakee prototype of Bernie Madoff. Everybody thought the grandfather, Freddy, was a goof with all his theater stuff, but it was his son, Margaret's dad, who lost the big money. And Freddy had always said Margaret and Rick would have enough even if their dad didn't have vision. Freddy promised them that their fortune was safe, put where their dad couldn't get to it. Always told her . . . Ah what's the difference? She's got a broken heart and if we don't scrape up enough for her to pay off at least one of her mortgages, she's in trouble."

"This house has to be worth a lot . . . it's a whole block, it could be—"

"You know of any property selling for what it's worth these days? And in Kankakee? It's not like this is a great place for a housing development. The house has been on the market for over three months. I called the Realtor yesterday and there's only been two showings and she thinks those were just *curiosity* visits. Tim put the kibosh on showing while you guys have been prepping, but I asked about interest in the place, and there haven't been any calls anyway."

"Did Margaret talk to her brother?"

"He swears that he wrapped up the paintings I described. I called the auction house and it's possible, just possible that the paintings they received are close enough in subject matter. I mean, Rick could have figured those were the ones I meant for them to send, but even if he just made a mistake, where are the real ones?"

Jane noticed that even though they were whispering head to head, both of them had roving eyes. Behind Claire, Jane scanned the walls, willing the missing work to appear. Claire, Jane noticed, was staring beyond her as well.

"The paintings in this room have been here a while. Tim and I took them down to look at the backs and you can see from the fading around their frames that they haven't been switched."

"I know. These are okay. A watercolor, a print, there's an okay oil in the hall, but they aren't anything special."

"It's funny though, that they were duplicated as the prop

paintings for Freddy's play. I found the paintings for the set up on the third floor with his props and I didn't even notice that the still life and the hunt scene were copied from this room. What a weird—"

"Props?"

Jane and Claire looked at each other and headed for the kitchen staircase that would take them up into attic storage.

"I can't believe you didn't think of this earlier, Jane. Freddy could have hidden the good paintings with his props so that his idiot 'businessman' son wouldn't sell off those, too, with the rest of the family store."

"I didn't know there were any missing paintings before you showed up," said Jane. "Besides, I really don't think there's much art up there. There were the three pictures for the set that Freddy had labeled for the play. But that was . . ."

Claire, as grand a lady as she might be when making an entrance, hunkered right down into the dust and cobwebs of the attic storage room. Jane had to admit she was game when it came to a real treasure hunt. The wooden racks where Jane had found the paintings held five canvases. Claire looked through them, scanning them from corner to corner, then shook her head.

"I don't think there's any more artwork. The first trunk is empty, we used everything. The second trunk has some stuff, but nothing valuable. . . ."

Claire went through the books and candlesticks and other smalls that Jane had decided not to use for set dressing. The first trunk had held all of the essential objects that the play called for.

"You said the house is for sale," said Jane. "Already on the market . . ."

Claire nodded, slamming down the lid of the trunk in disgust.

"That means the Realtor has a key?"

"There's a lockbox on the side door. The one off the kitchen, through the pantry area. Why?"

"We've always used the front door. That's why I didn't see it. Until today, I hadn't even taken the time to walk through the backyard," said Jane. "That lockbox. Every Realtor in town can get into the house. I mean, potentially. We need to have Claire call her broker and find out who she showed the house to and when . . . and if it was before Rick came and picked up the wrong objects to send to auction."

When Claire and Jane were back in the kitchen, Claire browsed through all of the open cabinets with prices and signs taped to the doors, while Jane flipped through a small notebook she had stashed in her back pocket.

"Margaret, Rick, Tim, Bryan Kendell—those are the people who have keys to the house. Now I have to add the Realtor and . . ."

"And who?" asked Claire, turning over a crystal dish, holding it sideways to the light from the window to see if she could read a signature.

Jane decided not to mention the keys to the coach house. No reason to start a stampede. She would check it out herself this afternoon, and if there was anything to discover, it would all be done by the end of the day. Before she could think of a misdirection in which to point Claire, Claire handed her a small bowl.

"Get this out of the five-dollar cabinet. It's Orrefors."

Tim was disappointed when Jane announced she was going back to her parents' house for lunch. He had brought his usual picnic basket of surprises, and counted on feeding Jane as one of his small pleasures. Jane asked him to save a bite of whatever he had for dessert and promised to be back in an hour. She owed it to Rita, though, to at least give her a fast romp before saying good-bye again for the rest of the day and night.

Jane cut what was going to be a fast fifteen-minute walk to ten, trotting around a block and a half, then bringing the reluctant dog back in the house through the garage door. Jane refilled the dog's water, tossed a biscuit her way, then packed a canvas tote with her rehearsal notes. She rummaged on the breezeway desk, where she had set up camp, slipping the sheets of paper with everyone's measurements, the copies of individual actors' prop lists, everything she might need for reference or for tonight's rehearsal. Stepping into the house from her makeshift office, she allowed herself one glance around her parents' lair.

Had anything changed since her senior year in high school when they had moved in? It all seemed so familiar to her since most of the arrangements of furniture, the knickknacks on the lone shelf Nellie had allowed for nonessentials—all were exactly the same as they had been in their previous house, the one that Jane and Michael had considered their true childhood home. Jane scanned the bookshelves that flanked the nonworking fireplace that Nellie had never wanted to fix, since fires were dirty, and marveled at the fact that the same few books, in exactly the same order, were on those shelves that she remembered from fourth grade. The *World Book Encyclopedia,* of course, which Don had bought for his children as an essential component of their education, occupied the top two shelves. In addition, there were four brown faux leather volumes of Zane Grey that Don had from somewhere, a collection of Mark Twain essays, two Reader's Digest condensed novels from God-knows-where since there were no adult fiction readers in the house, and Jane's favorite, the large green out-of-date atlas that she had loved paging through. Jane remembered reciting the names of countries and cities and rivers and mountain ranges, asking her father what he knew about them. She never bothered to ask Nellie, since the only answer would be a "What the hell you care about Tasmania for?"

"Except for the night we found that theater program," said Jane to Rita, who was whimpering lovingly to a large bone-shaped biscuit, paying no attention to Jane's chatter. "And we didn't even realize that it was a theater program, Rita." The dog shook her body and turned herself away from Jane, who clearly didn't realize that Rita was busy with something important.

Jane approached the bookcase, letting muscle memory take over. Every book was identically placed, so perhaps they had been packed from the old house in boxes exactly in that order and placed on these shelves precisely as they had been at the old house. Jane and Michael had found the program in the atlas, so Jane removed the large book, held it in the crook of her left arm, and paged through.

Jane knew that if the program had been left and forgotten inside the book, it would still be in the same place. If Nellie had remembered it, she probably would have destroyed it or at least hidden it away from those snoopy children of hers. Jane was almost positive that she and Michael had been paging through the states and turned from Illinois to . . . and there it was. Protected in the old atlas, the proof of Nellie's life in the theater remained intact.

MURDER IN THE EEKAKNAK VALLEY

A MYSTERY IN THREE ACTS

by Frederick Kendell

The program was hand-printed on heavy paper. It was probably a prototype for the programs they had planned to print for their opening night. Closed up in the atlas, it had been protected from dust and mites and remained in good condition for a fifty-plus-year-old piece of ephemera. Jane turned to the cast list. Henry Gand played Phillip Craven, the dashing detective, and as Jane already knew, there was her mother's maiden name, Nellie Schaltis, playing the ingenue, Hermoine.

Jane knew from the last names of other people in the cast that these were people from the other side of town, the wealthier side, the educated side. These were the sons and daughters of business owners and bankers, not her mother's friends, the Lithuanian and Polish factory girls who had dropped out of high school to work long hours at the hosiery factory and bring home weekly paychecks to their mothers.

From the first time Jane had mentioned acting in a play in high school, Nellie had harassed her about it, calling it a waste of time and worse.

"Bunch of show-offs saying, "Look at me, look at me," that's what theater sounds like to me," said Nellie.

Jane smiled, fingering the program, remembering the time Nellie had come to the dressing room at the Krannert Center after seeing Jane in a college production. Don had carried a bouquet of red roses and beamed at his daughter, so proud and so impressed that there was an actual dressing room with lights around a mirror and his daughter's name taped right on top of that mirror. Nellie hung back, arms folded, and when Jane asked her if she had liked the play, Nellie had just shrugged. "It was okay."

Jane remembered now, when they had gone out to a restaurant, Nellie had leaned over and told her that she had done a good job mixing the drinks in Act Two.

"That looked real, when you measured out that scotch, and held it up, looking at it in the light. I liked that part," said Nellie.

At the time, Jane thought it was funny that Nellie picked out one unimportant moment, a bartending moment of all things, to compliment. She now remembered what Nellie said after that, though. "You got to own them things you touch. When you poured that drink, it was real, like those bottles were yours."

Jane had begun to thank her, touched at how much she had noticed. Jane also felt she had a good moment in that scene.

"Not like when you arranged those flowers," Nellie continued. "You looked like you didn't know a tulip from a begonia in that scene."

Jane remembered all of this now because the whole night came flooding back. The guy doing props hadn't shown up and they needed new flowers. The assistant director had run out to a supermarket and bought a cheap bouquet that had a few especially sharp, thorny roses in it. Jane kept pricking her fingers when she tried to select stems to put in the vase. She had let those flowers throw her in that scene but thought she covered it. Everyone, including the director, had told her she covered well. Except for Nellie.

Jane put the theater program in the tote with all of her rehearsal material and gave Rita a good rub between the ears.

"There's more to that Nellie than meets the eye, right, Rita?"

"Damn right there is."

Nellie gave a low evil chuckle while Jane tried to recover her equilibrium.

"Mom, when are you going to stop sneaking up on me?"

"You're in my house, going through my stuff, and I saw you steal something of mine and put it into your bag. Who's the sneak?"

Jane looked back and forth from Nellie to Rita. The dog was standing so close to Nellie, there was no light between them, and both, if Jane's perceptions were on target, were giving her the fish-eye.

"You were an actress. Why didn't you tell me? Why'd you always say it was a waste of time?"

"It was my business. And it was a waste of time."

"Did you like doing it?"

"It was all right. I didn't like it the way Henry and them did. They were always crazy to put on a show. Henry heard that Freddy Kendell was writing a new play and . . ."

"Were they friends? In school together or something?"

"Henry's just a few years older than me. How old do you think I am? Freddy was old. He had a bunch of people his age and his son's age to be in the play, but he needed some kids like us and all them rich people knew each other from the country club, so he told Henry to get his friends together and he'd pick some of us to be in his play."

Jane kept gathering up her things for the rest of the day while she listened to her mother. "I want to continue this conversation, but I have to get over to the Kendell place now." Jane turned back to her mother. "This is why you give Tim such a hard time at rehearsal. He's not directing it the same way Freddy did."

"It ain't the same play."

"It never is, Mom. Theater is a living art—every production is different. Every actor, every director brings something new. . . . At least that's what you hope for."

The strumming of a harp interrupted Jane.

"Where's the damn angel coming from?" asked Nellie, looking around.

Jane held up her phone. She answered Tim and promised she was leaving immediately.

"To be continued," said Jane.

Jane ran into her bedroom to grab her phone charger, threw it in her bag, and yelled good-bye to Nellie and Rita. When she got to her car, she found Nellie slumped down in the front seat.

"What?"

"You're the one wanted to *continue* everything, Mrs. Drama Queen. Besides, Tim called me at the tavern this morning and asked me to come over when I could and help out at the Kendells'. That Margaret's a little crazy about the dust, so Tim asked me if I'd do some washing up of stuff for the sale. Dad sure as hell didn't need me at the tavern. Place is as dead as a doornail today."

"But after Marvin and everything, don't you want to . . . ?"

"What? Lay around and think about the poor old guy all day? Nope. I'd rather wash dishes and see if Margaret knows something about who clobbered Marvin. Nobody died until she showed up, right?"

"No, Mom, I don't want you—"

"You said 'to be continued,' like a damn TV announcer, and I'm continuing. No time like the present."

"Okay, fine," said Jane, starting the car. Before backing out of the driveway, she reached up and removed the silver necklace she had been wearing all morning. "I guess you can start by telling me all about this."

Nellie took the chain from Jane and studied the key that hung from it. Then she picked up the tiny disk and tromboned it back and forth in front of her eyes, squinting to read the engraving. Aloud she said, "How about that?"

Jane raised her eyebrows and echoed, "Yeah, how about that?"

Shifting into reverse, Jane kept one eye on her mother, who carefully slipped the chain around her own neck.

"What are you doing?" asked Jane.

"It's mine, ain't it? It's got my name on it. I guess I can wear it if I want to."

"Old Freddy Kendell was a weirdo, but he was a nice enough guy. Always throwing in new things when we practiced the play, making jokes, hiding things on the set. He had a rubber chicken he used to stick in a desk drawer," Nellie said.

Jane heard what sounded like ice breaking up on a pond. Had she driven over a carton of bubble wrap? No . . . it was Nellie laughing. Who knew that Nellie was a sucker for prop comedy?

"He loved his grandkids, always talked about them. Thought his son was a complete dope. Funny, though . . ."

"What?" Jane drove slowly back to the Kendells'. Might as well let Nellie talk as long as she was in the mood. Jane was afraid once they arrived at the house and Nellie went on duty washing dishes and cleaning up the place, the rare talkative mood she was in right now would pass for good.

"Everybody thinks just because somebody wears a suit and ties their tie, they're one of the sensible people in this world. The ones like Freddy who act like nuts? Everybody thinks they're nuts, but . . ." Nellie fingered the chain she had slipped around her neck. "Freddy was just his own guy, that's all. He wore crazy clothes and sang and danced and made that dummy talk for him. One time, he had the dummy direct the whole rehearsal. It was creepy as hell. But with Freddy, you knew what you got. He was nuts, but he was honest nuts."

Jane nodded and pulled over before reaching the driveway leading to the Kendell place. She didn't want to pull into the circle in plain sight of the house and have Claire Oh come bustling outside. She did want to hear the rest of what Nellie had to say.

"But Fred, Margaret and Rick's dad? He was the real nut. Quiet. Mean as hell to his wife. I don't think he ever let her say more than three words in front of company. Freddy hated him—his own son, too. But he loved those children, Margie and Rick, and was always talking about how he'd take care of them. How he had to provide for them. He worried about Fred investing away the family money. He said he'd write the plays that would be their fortune. I was just a kid when Henry brought me here to be in Freddy's play, and I had never read a play let alone acted in one. But I'll tell you one thing for sure. Even though I didn't know anything about plays, I knew this one sure as hell wasn't going to make a fortune for anybody."

Jane laughed. Nellie had taste. She knew what she was talking about.

"We did the best we could to make it sound right, but the play was corny as hell."

"It is corny," agreed Jane.

Nellie gestured that Jane should drive on. Jane could tell she was winding down. This had been more talking in one sitting than Jane had ever heard from her mother. Detective Oh would tell her to fight all her instincts to draw her out even more and just quietly let her keep going. Jane bit her tongue to keep from asking any questions.

"Yeah, this one's corny, too," said Nellie with a sigh.

Jane parked her car behind Tim's truck.

"What do you mean, this one?" Jane asked, forgetting all about the tongue-biting.

"This play we're doing with Tim. It's just as corny as the first one," said Nellie.

"I have the program from the play you were going to be in from before, Mom. *Murder in the Eekaknak Valley.* Same play, same characters. But you were playing Hermione, the young girl, not Marguerite. Maybe you're just confusing the lines because you're playing a different part?"

Too much. Jane could hear Detective Oh now in her ear, telling her she had said too much, offered too much of her own opinion. She had made a judgment, and that was guaranteed to make the other person defensive. Or, in Nellie's case, shut down for another decade or two. The seventeen-year cicada had nothing on Nellie.

"Oh, that's it, huh? I'm just senile."

Nellie got out of the car and slammed the door.

Jane watched her mother march up the front steps of the house and walk right in the door without hesitation. Nellie might claim to have felt like she was from the wrong side of the tracks when she was young, but she sure as hell wasn't intimidated by a big fancy house anymore.

Jane pulled the old program from her bag. The small block printing was the same as that on the Mr. Bumbles notes she had seen. Except for the one that was written in wobbly cursive, the others were all written in these boxy capitals. The name of the play was the same, *Murder in the Eekaknak Valley.* Character names were the same. Jane read the author's note.

> I hope this entertainment provides you, the audience, with a delightful evening. I dedicate this play to my grandchildren, Margaret and Ricky. Dear children, may this play have a long life and provide you with years of pleasure.

Jane slipped the program back into her bag. Freddy might have been a nut, but this program note didn't give off the kind of nuttiness Nellie had described. He simply wanted his play to go on forever. Didn't every writer seek immortality for his work?

By the time Jane got into the house, Nellie was already at the kitchen sink. Margaret looked happier than she had earlier, handing Nellie dusty bits and bobs of pink and green Depression and creamy white milk glass that she was pulling randomly out of the cupboards. Nellie looked perfectly at home and Margaret looked content. What was wrong with this picture?

In the front parlor, Claire was going through boxes of jewelry with a loupe, checking hallmarks and sorting the good from the better under a bright light Tim had rigged up for her. She, too, seemed content with her work and barely looked up when Jane peeked in.

Tim was in the rear parlor—the stage set—going through a heavy oak cupboard, pulling out boxes of poker chips, old boxed games, cribbage and euchre scoreboards. "We're in good shape, honey. Better than I thought. Claire is fast with that label gun and she got all the good vintage clothes upstairs priced. If we can get anyone to buy good furs in June or— Just in general, the closets will offer some cash. And as long as Margaret has something to do with her hands, like washing up, she's okay," said Tim.

He was talking in that faraway rambling voice he slipped into when he was captivated by the stuff in front of him. Jane knew that the board games were something he no longer cared deeply about, but in the old days, when he and Jane used to hit all the Saturday-morning sales, vintage board games were one of their favorite finds. Tim would scoop up the good ones, the ones that had been barely touched, the corners of the boxes still strong and unbent, not mended with tape. Jane always chose the ones Tim rejected—a broken-down box with the Clue board and a lone surviving Mrs. Peacock, or an early Monopoly without the game tokens and missing the hotels and houses—that way she wouldn't feel guilty about buying the game for a song and deconstructing it even further. She'd flip through the Chance and Community Chest cards and stack them on her desk at work. If someone on her creative team asked her a question, she'd instruct him or her to draw a card. Get Out of Jail Free was the best pick—if they flashed that one, Jane would say yes to whatever they asked.

"Detective Oh?" Jane asked Tim.

"In the library," said Tim.

"With the candlestick," Jane muttered under her breath.

Jane walked to the opposite end of the house where there was a small office and library set off from the rest of the first floor. A hallway and bathroom separated these rooms from the living space. Once one entered the library, it was easy to forget that there was a "rest of the house."

The bookshelves were floor to ceiling with sliding library ladders on both sides of the room. Earlier in the week, Jane had climbed the ladder and asked Tim for a push so she could play out the Marian the Librarian scene from *The Music Man* in her head.

Get Out of Jail Free cards . . . *Marian the Librarian?* Jane wondered what exactly made Freddy any more outwardly nutty than anyone else.

"Mrs. Wheel," said Oh. He was carefully paging through what appeared to be a very old volume of Shakespeare. "Nice edition. Many good books here. Valuable, but perhaps not valuable enough to really help Margaret, I'm afraid."

"But there are a lot. The good news about this sale is that the sheer volume of stuff will, if we get enough people in here, really add up."

"Yes. I've been to these sales, though. With Claire, with

you, and there is always so much left. At the end of the day, won't you be asking people to fill up boxes and just take things? For very little money?"

Oh was right. If every item in the house sold, it would be good news for Margaret and her brother. But with every sale, so much did not sell. Then things had to be boxed and bagged and hauled and driven and donated and dumped.

"Mrs. Wheel, have you had a chance to reflect on the events? Do you think Mr. Marvin was murdered?" Oh closed the book and replaced it on the shelf.

Jane had become so enmeshed in Freddy's world of the play and the theater club and linking Nellie to the first production that she hadn't really thought about Marvin since her visit to the cultural center property with Rita that morning. There was nothing that the scene in daylight had told her that differed from the scene at night. The boards were stacked neatly and safely against the tree, and if one came loose, it seemed highly unlikely that it was an accident. On the other hand, no one had seen anyone come in or out of the woods, although Nellie claimed that some shadowy figure had been over in Marvin's work area—although couldn't that have been Marvin himself? Moving around, beginning to cover his equipment for the night, and perhaps, just perhaps, replacing one of the beams because it was getting too dark to cut it and failing to secure it against the tree while he bent to tie the tarp? Nothing was stolen. No one came up with any reason someone would want to kill Marvin, a retired widowed stage carpenter who had returned to his hometown where he had a few cousins and old friends and who volunteered in the community theater. It certainly appeared to be nothing more than an accident.

"Yes, I think he was murdered."

Oh almost smiled. "Should I ask why?"

"Not yet," said Jane.

Jane walked to the opposite end of the room. A set of French doors at the rear of the library opened onto the back lawn. If Tim, Claire, Margaret, and Nellie were still working away where she last saw each of them, they could cut across the lawn and get to the coach house completely unnoticed. A big if, but worth the effort. Jane asked Oh if he wanted to visit Freddy's writing studio with her, filling him in on what she had learned about Freddy's theater club and some of its members.

"Since Marvin was a member, it seems like a visit is in order," said Jane.

"Shall we ask your mother for her key?" asked Oh.

"No need," said Jane. "Mr. Bumbles is guarding others."

Jane and Oh opened the French doors, allowing a breeze to rifle a small stack of papers on the walnut partners desk regally placed at what Jane saw as the head of the room. She loved the fact that it was a manageable size, more manageable than her desk at home, but still, a double workspace. If one wanted to dream, one could sit and gaze out of the window, watching the birds swoop and dive through the gardens. If one had columns of figures to add and correspondence to attend to, one could sit facing the interior, all business. Jane allowed herself a personal moment, a want and a need. She would soon be divorced from Charley, maybe even by the end of this summer. If she sold her house and most of her things and moved to an apartment, perhaps Tim could find her a desk like this she could afford. She could sit on one side as Jane, the picker, toting up her purchases and writing her invoices for Miriam and Tim, and then, on days when she was Mrs. Wheel, sorting out clues with Oh, she could sit on the other side, studying the patterns of cardinals in flight. What was the price tag on this desk?

". . . isn't that right, Mrs. Wheel?" said Oh, closing the French doors behind them.

"Sorry. I was furnishing my new apartment with that desk

in there," Jane said. "Charley and I, you know, we're . . ." Jane had to figure out her language on this. Were they splitting up? Splitsville? Would she be all slangy and flippant? No. At least not with Oh. "As you know, Charley and I are getting divorced," said Jane. "It will be finalized soon. At the oddest moments, I am struck with something I need to do . . . or will need to do. Most of the time, I don't think about it at all. Seeing that partners desk, it struck me how much I liked it, how it was better than the desk I already have that Charley might want anyway. I could build a home around that desk, but all the time I was married to Charley, I never thought of us needing pieces of furniture like that. So does that mean we were never partners?"

Jane stopped abruptly and cleared her throat. She had not talked this out to anyone, not even Tim, so why was she babbling away to Oh? They were halfway across the lawn to the coach house when she allowed herself to glance at him. He was looking at her, waiting.

"I'm sentimental about stuff, you know. Literally. About stuff. Things. But I don't like to talk about myself . . . about my own—"

"Yes, Mrs. Wheel. I understand. We are all our mothers' children."

They had climbed the stairs and Jane opened the bench, hoping to see Oh flinch just a little when Mr. Bumbles was revealed, but she was the one who winced. Had he just implied she was like Nellie?

"This Mr. Bumbles is a fellow who gets around," said Oh. "This is the third one, yes?"

"Two in the house, one in a suit and one in dungarees and plaid shirt, and now this dusty fellow," said Jane, nodding. She would have to disabuse Oh of the notion she was anything like Nellie, but it would have to wait until they were not in the middle of work. Jane chose Marvin's key from the box and unlocked the coach house door. She slipped the chain around her neck and together, she and Oh entered the space.

The wall of windows that faced the house allowed so much light into the room that at first they had to blink and adjust. Dust motes made for a kind of glaze and shimmer, but once they adjusted to the brightness, they saw an enormous space. The dimensions, after all, were that of the six-car garage below, so the undivided space was vast.

Centered in front of the windows was a desk and chair facing the house. As Jane had learned from standing in the yard, Freddy wrote his play facing the house and describing exactly what he saw. Being on the second floor, he could see into the house much as one could view a dollhouse with a cutaway wall revealing the rooms and furnishings and people inside. This work area was defined by an intricate old Persian rug, the desk and chair, and a stuffed chair and ottoman with a side table. All that was missing was Freddy, the Noël Coward of Kankakee, dressed in a smoking jacket, pacing between desk and chair, composing lines of dialogue for those characters in his dollhouse across the lawn.

This studio area comprised only a fraction of the space. It was a beautiful jewel-like workspace, made all the more elegant by being placed in the center of a pristine loft. A giant expanse of wood floor, bookshelves built into the side wall, and the ceiling hung with—Jane walked farther into the center of the room to get a closer look—track lights? No, the ceiling was a grid of pipes on which stage lights hung. Jane saw a box of gels pushed into the corner by the bookcase.

"Why is there tape?" asked Oh, kneeling to touch the tan strips placed all over the floor in a seemingly random pattern.

Jane stood by Freddy's desk, facing Oh and the back wall.

"It's the set. It's Freddy's play. He's taped off all of the walls and doors. See . . . that tape defines the couch and there's the bar. This wasn't just a clubhouse. It was a rehearsal space. Look," said Jane, gesturing to the sides of the wall of windows, "those heavy draperies are blackout curtains. This space is actually outfitted to be a theater. With risers for chairs or with platforms for the stage area. This place is bigger and better equipped than half of the little black box theaters in Chicago."

When Jane first walked through the door, she thought she was seeing the entire space, undivided by any walls, but looking closer, she realized the space was divided . . . but lengthwise . . . into a front and back. The alley side of the coach house had a wall running the entire length of the room. It was one giant backstage area. Doors were located on either side. Jane walked over and flipped a switch before opening the door, since it appeared, with no windows, as if she'd be entering a giant closet.

"Holy Moses," said Jane, realizing that her promise to quit swearing, made years ago for Nick's sake, had caused her to revert to the most archaic expressions imaginable. Wasn't Nick old enough now to hear the real stuff? Could she remember the real stuff? "Jeezy Petes!" Maybe not.

"What is it, Mrs. Wheel?" Oh walked over from where he had been studying the taped-out set, walking through the imaginary doors, gazing out the imaginary window.

"Backstage stuff," said Jane. "Tons of it."

Several racks of costumes stood in one corner. An open trunk had long skirts and a few hoops and crinolines sticking out of it. "Rehearsal skirts," said Jane, pointing to the pile. "Before you have your costumes, you have to get used to walking and sitting and moving in whatever you're going to be wearing for a period play."

Jane waved her arms in front of the roughed-in shelves, filled with candlesticks and serving trays, crystal stemware and vases. "These are all rehearsal props . . . and stuff to dress a set."

Freddy's theater club, defunct, was probably better outfitted than most small theaters that were fully "funct" and producing shows every weekend. There was plenty of dust and cobwebs, but the place was well insulated and sealed, so everything was in good shape. Give a housekeeping crew a broom and a mop and a day or two—hell, give Nellie one good bar rag and a bucket—and they could open a show that night.

"If Freddy died fifty years ago . . . who's been here?" said Jane. "This is not fifty years of dust."

Oh looked up from the shelf where he was studying silver candlesticks, weighing them in his hand.

"Who told you Freddy died fifty years ago?" asked Oh.

"He collapsed before the opening night of the first production of *Murder in the Eekaknak Valley.* Tim told me he died under mysterious circumstances, but he was exaggerating, just trying to draw me in. But he did—"

"My grandfather did not die under mysterious circumstances," said Margaret.

"Who the hell told you that?" said Nellie.

"I never actually said Freddy died," said Tim, "I said he—"

"What in the world is everyone doing out here when we have a sale in one week?" said Claire. "And what's all this talk about dear Freddy?"

From the way they lined up, entering the coach house, each responding to the other, Jane pictured them, one by one, sneaking across the lawn on tiptoes, following Jane and Oh.

Jane faced them, wishing desperately she were better at math. If Freddy was Margaret's grandfather and she was a child when Nellie was in her twenties in the theater club, that would make him . . .

"Freddy is alive?" Jane asked.

"Of course not," said Margaret.

"Don't be ridiculous," said Claire.

"How old does she think anyone is?" asked Nellie.

Tim shook his head. "I'm responsible. I told you Freddy collapsed before the play went on and he did. He had a mild heart attack and the play was canceled."

"So he didn't die under mysterious circumstances?" asked Jane.

"Of course not. He died in hospice care. I was with him. He . . . he died the same year as my father . . . a few months apart . . . my mother died around the same time as my father," said Margaret. She began to get that same faraway look in her eye as she did when she studied the filmy crystal in the house earlier. Jane watched her wander over to Freddy's desk and run her hand over the surface. She was once again thinking about dust.

Claire walked over to her old friend and spoke quietly into her ear.

"Was there a connection between Margaret's father and Freddy's death?" asked Jane.

"Freddy was an old man," said Nellie. "And from what I heard, he died a peaceful old man's death." Jane saw Nellie give both Tim and Oh a hard look, as if defying them to argue with her.

Tim shrugged. He had used Freddy's fifty-some-year-old heart attack to pique Jane's interest about the play and the household, but he clearly didn't know any more recent history. "I just know the estate's been tied up for about four, five years and now Margaret and Rick have taken possession and they can sell stuff. That's all I know."

"Damn right that's all you know," said Nellie, turning to look at Detective Oh. Jane could see that her mother was much more interested in what Oh knew about the family.

"Your mother is correct. Freddy died of old age. He was like a father to Margaret . . . and perhaps like a mother, too. Margaret's parents were fragile people. I met them once years ago and I think that's the best way to describe them. Her father, as you know, lost the family money. Freddy had protected some assets and as long as he was alive, they were able to carry on. But once notes came due . . . Margaret's father was . . . he tried to resign himself to it all being gone. And her mother . . . once there was no more money to spend . . . grew depressed."

"I told you rich people aren't all there," said Nellie.

"Margaret's father had not only lost his money, he had advised acquaintances and distant relatives and his wife's family to follow him down the same path, and when they knew everything was gone, everything except the property here and their house in Florida, which Rick got his mother to put into his name long ago, Fred confessed to his wife that their lives would have to change. They were broke and they were disgraced."

Oh stopped talking and looked at Nellie.

She shrugged. "I only know what I read in the paper. The *Journal* said they both died of food poisoning."

"The last vestiges of what the memory of old money can buy. A certain amount of privacy and discretion," said Oh.

Jane looked over at Margaret. She was opening the drawers of Freddy's desk, showing Claire folders and holding up a silver-handled, ivory paper knife.

"Suicide?" Jane asked.

"It appeared that Mrs. Kendell prepared a last meal. She poisoned her husband and herself. There was no real investigation, but ample evidence. Mrs. Kendell relied on her husband's love for spicy food and served him a curry laced with rat poison. She tried to eat enough herself to follow him, but couldn't manage it, so settled for a bottle of sleeping pills."

"And Margaret and her brother know what happened?"

"Yes. There was no real police involvement to speak of, after the initial discovery, but there was an extensive insurance investigation. The substantial life insurance policies that Mrs.

Kendell believed would go to her children were, of course, never paid."

"A suicide clause," said Jane.

Oh nodded.

Nellie had wandered away to explore the taped-off set while Oh had quietly told the story. Jane had the feeling that Nellie had heard several versions before, despite claiming to know only what she read in the paper. Jane had witnessed her mother's refusal to gossip at the EZ Way Inn. Nellie listened to the stories and ramblings of customers and whiskey salesmen, but never chimed in or repeated what she heard. It wasn't that Nellie was above pronouncing her own judgments on all things, it's just that they were exactly that—judgments, articles of faith, and hocus-pocus that had little to do with snarky speculation and everything to do with the world according to Nellie. Nellie might believe that the Kendells were a few bricks shy of a load—that was a tenet in the world of rich people according to Nellie—but what Mrs. Kendell did or didn't put into her husband's last curry remained the personal business of the Kendells.

Jane accepted this horrible story for what it was: the background she had sorely needed to put this puzzle together. Or were these facts just more random pieces that belonged to an altogether different puzzle?

"I still don't understand, though, about the play," said Jane. "Was it ever put on?"

Four different answers in unison.

"No," said Tim.

"Yes," said Margaret.

"What's the difference?" asked Claire.

"What play?" asked Nellie.

"And why is Mr. Bumbles trying to stop this production?" continued Jane.

Margaret was standing between her grandfather Freddy's

desk and the giant wall of windows. She held a book and the paper knife and at the mention of Mr. Bumbles, she dropped both. Claire clutched Margaret's arm as she appeared to be falling, and Oh sprang to her side with the desk chair, giving her a seat before she could fall.

As pale as she looked, she wasn't out for the count. She looked directly at Jane and shook her head.

"Who told you about Mr. Bumbles?" she asked.

"I met him the first day Tim brought me to the house to work," said Jane. "He was just . . . hanging around." *If there are gods of puns, please forgive me,* thought Jane. "And when Penny Kendell had an accident, she received a note signed Bumby, and there's a Mr. Bumbles in the storage bench just outside that door," said Jane.

"And there were some notes in the scripts of *Murder in the Eekaknak Valley* that warned us that the play was bad luck," said Tim. "They were signed by Mr."—Tim caught himself—"by someone who claimed to be Bumby."

"You should pay attention to the notes," said Margaret. "'The play is bad luck.'" Margaret shifted in her seat, sitting up a little straighter. "Besides, Mr. Bumbles never lies."

Jane made the mistake of looking at Nellie, who was on her way from the small bathroom backstage where she had found a clean towel and soaked it in cool water to revive Margaret. When Nellie heard Margaret's remark about Bumbles, she stopped in her tracks and twirled her finger around her temple, nodding toward Margaret, and cleared her throat. Jane looked away from her mother immediately.

Although Margaret looked dead serious, Claire burst out laughing. Jane had never heard Claire Oh laugh. In fact, she wasn't sure she had ever seen evidence that she had a fully hinged jaw.

"Ah, you think I kid," said Margaret, barely changing expression, giving a sideways glance at Claire, but I—"

"Let me out."

Jane looked at Nellie, since the cranky, half-strangled voice sounded more like her mother than anyone else in the room. Nellie, however, was looking around behind her, trying to find the source of the cry.

"I said to let me out now."

There was a loud knocking and although Jane thought the voice came from near the backstage area, she couldn't pinpoint the banging.

Tim had grown so white he was tinged with blue.

Where was Detective Oh? Jane turned around and saw him on the other side of the space, stationed near Nellie, looking ready to assist her if she got frightened. Nellie, however, just looked, in equal parts, mad and frustrated. Jane thought Oh might do better to station himself next to Tim, who could be going down at any minute.

"That knocking has to be coming from there," said Nellie. She pointed to double doors that adjoined the backstage area. Jane had opened the single door that led directly backstage while exploring but had not opened the bifold doors that were almost hidden along the side of this area between the front of the house and backstage area. Jane looked up, noting that the heavy draperies which would block out light in the event that the space was used for performances would also cover these doors. More backstage storage? Side-stage storage? Lighting cabinets?

Nellie was already heading for the doors, but Jane beat her to them.

"Stand back, Mom," said Jane, grabbing one of the door handles and giving it a sideways pull.

The hinged door folded in on itself in the middle and then swung open wide from the main door frame, revealing a multi-shelved storage space about six feet wide. Nellie, right behind

Jane, imitated the way Jane opened the door and with a Nellie-ish flourish—part anger, part impatience—did the same on the other side, yanking the door to the side, then out.

Jane had fully expected to find something grotesque—backstage props lined up in a row often have the look of the unworldly. Taxidermy, grimacing masks, menacing sculptures, bloody skulls, severed limbs. She had not, however, expected to see twenty-four versions of maniacally grinning Mr. Bumbles in various postures, sitting and standing, inside the giant cupboards.

Tim squeaked out a mild "Yikes," but the rest of the observers took in the surreal gallery in silence.

There were several Mr. Bumbles dolls dressed as the boy in plaid and denim, the way Jane had originally met him. There were also versions of Bumbles in top hat and tails. He was dressed, as if for Halloween, as both a pirate and a hobo. And there were some in which he was attired in business casual circa 1958, with slacks and a V-neck sweater over a button-down shirt, looking as if he were preparing to sing a Christmas duet with Perry Como or Bing Crosby.

"Well," said Nellie, after scanning the four long shelves, left to right, "which one of you wanted out?"

"I would say the one who's already been out running around doing mischief," said Jane, stepping back from the closet and looking over the rows.

"Are they serious? Do they believe one of them talked?" asked Claire in a loud whisper.

Margaret, in a soft stutter, started to explain, "It was . . . I was just . . . I am a . . . my Grandpa Freddy taught me to . . ."

"Yes," said Jane, "I know your special talent. I saw your yearbook."

Tim began to breathe more normally.

"But even if you were playing a joke on us, Margaret," said

Jane, "I think your instincts were right. One of these guys has been out recently and probably has more of a taste for mischief than the others."

Jane now stepped forward and pointed to Mr. Bumbles wearing a brown tweed suit. His shiny black shoes weren't streaked with dust like those of the other Bumbles dummies lined up in the closet. His jacket was rumpled and his overall appearance, if one compared him to his fellow Bumbles, was disheveled. Most interesting to Jane, however, was his neckwear. Or lack thereof. She reached into her pocket and pulled out the polka-dotted bow and clip she had picked up behind the theater that morning, thinking a child had lost it on a jaunt along the walking path. Around Bumbles's neck was the remnant of polka-dotted ribbon which comprised only half of what had been a sporty bow tie.

"I think Mr. Bumbles wanted to get out and find his lost tie, don't you?" asked Jane.

Nellie nodded and grabbed the fabric from Jane and held it up to Mr. Bumbles's neck. "You find this last night?" she asked.

Jane shook her head and explained how she and Rita had found it on their walk that morning.

"That little sonofabitch was there," said Nellie, pointing at Bumbles. "That's who I saw. That little dummy killed Marvin."

16

Jane could wrap up the case now.

After fingering Mr. Bumbles for Marvin's murder, Nellie stared at the row upon row of Mr. Bumbles in the cabinet, then shrugged, brushed her hands together as if to say that's that, and motioned to Margaret to come with her so they could get back to the dishwashing waiting in the house.

Case closed.

Except for a few problems.

First? Mr. Bumbles was a ventriloquist's dummy.

Last? Mr. Bumbles was a ventriloquist's dummy.

Claire and Tim had followed Nellie and Margaret back to the house, leaving Jane and Oh alone in Freddy's Theater Club. Jane continued to stare at all of the Bumbles, who, perhaps not so oddly, stared right back.

"Freddy must have single-handedly kept a toy company in business. I wonder where he bought these?" said Jane.

Oh crossed over to Freddy's desk and opened a drawer.

"If you think it's important, Mrs. Wheel, we could probably find out."

If she thought it was important? What was important about any of this? Mr. Bumbles seemed to be at the heart of everything—he had tried to warn Jane and Tim away from the house, away from the play. He had played havoc—or, at the least, a game of marbles—with Bryan and Penny Kendell, sending Penny to the emergency room. He had left a note in Rica Evans's script . . . in several scripts according to Tim. And now, according to Nellie, he had clobbered Marvin with one of Marvin's own four-by-fours.

"I guess if we hang Marvin's death on Mr. Bumbles, everything about him is important. I mean, what was his motivation?"

Oh looked as if he wanted to say something, then thought better of it.

"I do know that it isn't Mr. Bumbles himself," said Jane. "But instead of trying to say whoever the person is dragging around Mr. Bumbles, or one of the Bumbles, I just think it's easier to . . ." Jane paused, considering how to put this in the most professional manner. "I'm just naming our perpetrator Mr. Bumbles."

Oh nodded. "That's a good idea; however, it's not what troubles me. Mr. Bumbles as a mischief-maker, one who left notes in the scripts? That could have been Freddy. He was a prankster and Margaret often told us of his antics with Mr. Bumbles. But the more serious offenses? The accident with Penny Kendell, Mr. Marvin's accident or worse . . . those are the work of an unsound mind. Using the doll as a surrogate? And if this person has access to this house as evidenced by his access to the dummies, he could be in a position to harm you or Mr. Lowry when you are here working. You mustn't continue to work here alone as you did last week."

Jane couldn't say exactly what she was thinking. Now that Claire Oh had her friend Margaret's ear and now that she had seen the treasure trove in this house? No chance Jane and Tim would ever be here without Claire latching on. So if the old saw "safety in numbers" had any validity, the Kendell mansion had just become a much more protected site.

"Do you really think trying to scare us is the work of an unsound mind? Or is it someone who wants us to think he or she is just some creepy psychopath? What's scarier than a ventriloquist's dummy? Why not try to scare someone or distract them if what you really want to do is have access to this house? That would explain trying to scare Tim and me away from the sale," said Jane. "Bumbles doesn't want to hurt us, just wants to keep us, and possibly Bryan and Penny Kendell, who have a key, away from the house so he or she has more time to hunt for valuables. Makes sense to me that it was Bumbles who took the artwork, made the switch for the auction house."

"Bumbles, not brother Rick?" said Oh.

"Unless Bumbles *is* brother Rick," said Jane.

Feeling more like an amateur psychiatrist than a detective, Jane tried to put things in order. Jane walked over to the closet and picked up the wandering Mr. Bumbles, the one Nellie had accused of Marvin's murder. When Jane picked him up, his right leg slipped out of his body and hung lower than the left. She realized it wasn't just his tie that was torn away, he also had a broken leg. He had been up to something all right.

"What does the other guy look like?" Jane asked Mr. Bumbles.

"It wasn't a toy company, Mrs. Wheel," said Oh, studying a page from Freddy's desk drawer. "The Bumbles, at least the more recent acquisitions, last twenty years, were made and maintained by a private woodworking firm here. Looks like the last new Bumbles was made nine years ago. The company did repair work. This is an invoice from six years ago for repairs on Bumble number seventeen. His neck was rehinged," said Oh.

"Yikes," said Jane.

Jane closed up the cupboard but took the Bumbles with the broken leg down before latching the doors. Why not take him into protective custody for the time being? Besides, he had a broken leg. Perhaps Margaret would want them to leave him at the woodworker's for repairs. Then again, if she felt the need to resurrect one of her ventriloquism routines, she did have about twenty other dummies to choose from.

Jane locked the door to the theater club but decided to hold on to Marvin's key. She fingered the cold silver of the key and name tag, slipping them underneath her shirt.

Oh reached into the storage bench and pocketed the other keys as well. "No reason to make it even easier for our Bumbles to come and go at will," said Oh. "I'm sure Margaret would agree."

Margaret, after her earlier comeback as the ventriloquist, had once again become the protégé of puppetmaster Nellie, who was instructing her on the finer points of dishwashing. Margaret, every bit the grateful student being trained in the ways of an important art, was properly respectful, carefully imitating the way Nellie dried a glass, rubbing the rim so hard it threatened to break apart in her bare hands.

"You don't want spots," said Nellie, a pronouncement so fierce that any pupil had no choice but to shake her head, agreeing that *no, she certainly did not want spots.*

Jane studied Margaret from the doorway. Could she be fooling them all with her shy and confused demeanor? She had access to the house. She could throw her voice. She knew her way around the Bumbles family. Maybe she had taken the valuable articles, then used her mighty acting skills to convince Claire that her brother or someone was taking advantage.

Nellie handed Margaret a new towel. "Can't get 'em dry with a wet towel," said Nellie.

Why did everything Nellie say sound like it should be embroidered on a pillow or scrawled on a public bathroom wall?

Margaret reached out a shaky hand for the clean towel. If she was faking her fragile state and was good enough to fool

Nellie, who had X-ray vision for phonies and liars, Jane would be shocked.

Margaret is as needy as a dry sponge, thought Jane, almost satisfied that she could hold her own with embroidery-worthy thoughts.

The plan was for Jane and Oh to run over to the woodworking studio with the damaged and tieless Bumbles in tow and see if there was anything to learn about the dummies. Jane knew that it might be a wasted errand—after all, what could the woodcarver/repairman tell them about a dummy that would be helpful in terms of solving either a murder or a theft? Then again, Jane pointed out to Oh that a repair on a dummy had been done six years ago according to one of the receipts, and Freddy had been in ill health at the end of his life around then. Who was maintaining this collection?

Besides, who wouldn't want to visit a business named Geppetto Studios?

While Jane and Oh were off *detecting,* as Claire Oh characterized their errand, she and Margaret would stick with Tim and Nellie, organizing and prepping for the sale at the house, then everyone would grab dinner and meet at the theater for rehearsal. Although there had been some lip service paid to canceling the show because of Marvin's death, the talk seemed to have faded. Jane was gathering up her bag of tricks when she heard Tim on his cell phone telling someone that rehearsal would begin at seven thirty, as originally scheduled.

"Interesting," Jane said to Oh. "We are always here if we're not at rehearsal, and still someone manages to get in and out, taking out and replacing one of the Bumbles? Pretty lucky timing, wouldn't you say?"

Oh drove Jane's car so she could respond to a text message from Nick. Although she had never met a short story she couldn't make into a novel, and did not feel that tiny keyboarded messages were her forte, she was trying to keep in touch as best she could with Nick in his preferred means of communication. Jane smiled to herself—today was the communication trifecta. She had seen new photos on Facebook, read a tweet, and now had a text. Since she had sent Nick an e-mail, he might return that, too, and that would mean they had covered all the electronic ground available to them for the day. After hitting send, she stretched out her fingers and arms and picked up broken-legged Bumbles and sat him on her lap.

According to the receipt that Oh had found, one of the Bumbles had needed rehinging. How many times a day did she feel that she could use rehinging? Jane was pretty sure the Geppetto woodworkers would not have help for the wearing out of her own joints and hinges, but they might be able to say who had been bringing the dummies in for repair and refurbishing. Margaret, in London for half the year, said she hadn't visited the Bumbles collection in years. When she had come to the house to assess the property, she hadn't even gone into Freddy's studio.

If Jane hadn't met Margaret, watched her shake and falter, she wouldn't have believed that there was any part of the property she hadn't visited. An heir to the estate, one who needed to wring all the profit from it that she could? Why in the world wouldn't she visit the old theater club? Claire, speaking for her, said that Margaret had told her she wouldn't want to sell anything that had a close personal connection to Freddy. She knew there was nothing particularly valuable, and until she had to clear the house, she was putting off going through the detritus of Freddy's life. Claire said Margaret knew all of it would be painful, and she was taking on what she could, when she could.

"But Freddy had told her that it was his play that would provide for her," said Jane aloud to Oh. "Why wouldn't she think that some clue to what he meant would be in his studio?"

"Mrs. Wheel," said Oh, following her directions to Geppetto Studios. "I'm afraid you're asking aloud the question provoked by a long chain of your silent thoughts."

"Sorry," said Jane, fingering the key she now wore around her neck. If Nellie kept wearing hers, too, people would think they were going steady. "This is the place."

Oh parked in front of the shop with no problem. It appeared to be a simple storefront office on a side street just southeast of Kankakee's downtown area. Jane noted that although the office had a stenciled GEPPETTO STUDIOS on the window, there was no visible light, no posted office hours, no other information on the outside of the building. There was, however, a buzzer next to the door. Jane, just for good measure, tried the door first, found it locked, then pushed the button. She could hear the buzzer sound and thought she heard a faint rustle from inside, although neither she nor Oh, noses pressed against the window, saw anyone moving.

They did, however, at the same time, see someone sitting at the desk, shoulders slumped, head down, looking ominously crumpled over his work.

"Is he sleeping?" said Jane.

Oh knocked on the window, trying to rouse him.

Jane slid her phone out of her pocket, ready to dial 911.

So fixed were they on the dark corner of the office, they didn't see a figure come out of the shadows and open the front door. An older woman peeked out from around the door frame.

"Are you looking for someone?" she whispered.

Although Oh did not jump or startle as obviously as Jane

did at the sound of the woman's voice, she was sure she sensed a twitch next to her.

"The gentleman at the desk," said Oh. "We were concerned."

The woman nodded.

"Come in and see for yourself."

She moved out of the doorway to allow them to enter, then closed the door behind them. Jane heard what sounded like the click of a lock being turned.

Once inside the shop, they realized the small storefront was an optical illusion of sorts. Indeed they entered through an outside door directly into an office, but the back wall was actually only a partial wall with a tromp l'oeil bookcase painted on it. From the outside, the office looked small and cramped, all dark wood and thirties- or forties-era office furniture. Once inside, it was clear that the office itself was dressed like a stage set and behind the partial wall was a factory-sized workspace.

"Doesn't this cause a daily problem with passersby?" asked Oh, examining the life-sized mannequin dressed in suit, tie, and fedora, artfully arranged as a possible victim of foul play, slumped over a vintage Royal typewriter.

"Not much foot traffic," said the woman, again whispering. The combination of her whispers and the sleeping—or dead—mannequin definitely set a scene.

"What is this place?" asked Jane.

"Who wants to know?" asked the woman, barely audible.

Oh produced a card and explained the receipt they found at Freddy's.

Although the woman did not raise her voice, Jane thought she saw signs of agitation. Her hands, calloused and work-worn, clenched and unclenched at her side. Jane could tell she was unused to dealing with people in the front office.

"Is there someone else we should speak to?" asked Jane in the same quiet voice in which the woman spoke.

"It's not a good time," she said. "We're closed today for a memorial. I came to the door because we're still expecting people, and there are those who might not know to come to the back—" She broke off, actually looking back over her shoulder. Jane thought she looked like she was expecting someone, anyone, to come from the back and help her speak to the interlopers.

Jane peeked around the partial painted wall and could see a grand space, a carpentry shop that went on for a block behind this tiny office space in which they stood. There was a giant table saw and several workbenches. The walls were hung with more tools than Jane could identify. It also appeared that there were industrial steel doors at the rear of the building. The space was so massive that Jane had to squint to see all the way back. Those masses of corrugated steel were closed now, but Jane assumed they could be opened so that large pieces could be fabricated inside, then loaded on waiting trucks through the back. Geppetto Studios might be named after the humble little woodcarver father of Pinocchio, but clearly the craftsmen here were makers of far grander objects than wooden toys.

Jane unfolded broken-legged Bumbles from under her sweater and held him up in front of her. "We were hoping you could tell us—"

The woman who Jane thought might not be able to speak above a whisper found her voice. Her full voice and more.

"You bring that in here now? Today? Who the f—"

"What's the problem, Suzanne?"

Someone else had walked in from the back so quietly that neither Jane nor Oh had noticed. And although she seemed a little startled to come face-to-face with Mr. Bumbles, she held on to her composure as Jane remembered she always did . . . even in high school.

"We didn't expect you to attend, Jane," said Mary Wainwright. "Or to bring a guest."

Jane began to explain that Mr. Bumbles had been repaired previously at the shop but stopped when she saw Mary offer her hand to Detective Oh, telling him they weren't properly introduced at the theater previously. Of course she was referring to Oh, not Bumbles, as her guest.

"Although this is a private service, impromptu really, just for friends, you're welcome here, Jane," said Mary, never taking her eyes off Oh. "And I would love to get to know this distinguished gentleman a little better."

Was it Jane's imagination or did Mary actually break into a kind of flirtatious southern accent?

Suzanne, formerly the whisperer, was having none of Mary's nonsense.

"You are not welcome here. This is a private gathering. And to bring that thing in here is just cruel."

Jane apologized and covered Bumbles up with her sweater again, since the mere sight of the dummy caused the woman such agitation.

"We didn't mean to interrupt anything. We found a Geppetto Studios receipt for repairs on several of these Mr. Bumbles dummies and we're trying to find out who brought the doll into your shop," said Jane. "If you're the owner, perhaps—"

"In ten minutes we're having a memorial service for the owner. My partner, really. It's a little up in the air what's going to happen to the business," said Suzanne. "We're grieving, you see."

Although the woman, Suzanne, according to Mary Wainwright, did not exactly warm, she seemed to thaw slightly. She put her hand up to her temple and glanced back. When no help came from Mary Wainwright, who had taken Oh's arm and led him to the other side of the office, chatting as if she had found an old friend, and no one else seemed to be arriving from the back of the workspace, she shrugged and gave in to her need to say something about what was going on.

"That dummy you have," she said, shivering, "whenever it was in our shop, it was bad luck. We knew it was bad luck, the Bumbles have always been bad luck, but Marvin said everything would be okay and now he's—"

"Marvin? Marvin the carpenter?" said Jane.

"Marvin was so much more than a carpenter," said Suzanne, too sad to be insulted by Jane's characterization. "Marvin was a wonderful set designer and an amazing artist. He could do big projects and he could carve the most exquisite miniatures. And he was a wonderful man. He never forgot us. He could have gone to New York or anywhere. He was asked. But he liked Chicago so he could come here and make things and give us work, pay us to make things. He never let any of us go, even when times were tough. He found work for everyone and he . . ." Suzanne, whose age Jane couldn't have determined when she first came to the door whispering at them, now seemed to be very old. Her hair was a short tight mass of steel wool curls, and her face was crumpled tissue paper. When she had first emerged from the back, her erect posture and masklike expression hid her age, but now she looked like a woman who had nothing left to hide.

"Without Marvin, I don't know what will become of me," she said. "I was prepared when Freddy died, but not for Marvin. Not this way."

"Mrs. Wheel," Oh said, waving at her from across the small office. Mary had backed him into a corner and seemed to finally take a breather from her one-way conversation with him. Jane wanted to pursue the conversation with Suzanne. Now that the door had opened and included Freddy, Jane knew she had something to learn from Suzanne.

But Oh was a drowning man and he was her partner. She had to help. She took Suzanne's arm and apologized again for intruding, walking her over to Oh, not wanting to let her drift to the back of the shop while she went over to throw out a life preserver to Detective Oh.

But Mary was not finished with her end, the only end of the conversation. She was, indeed, only taking a breather and now that she had had a chance to inhale and exhale, she was back into action.

"We've all known Marv for years, of course, all of us who worked in the theater, and he was always so generous with his time and his talents. I mean, I thought everyone knew how he was the backbone of the theater here . . . Of course, Janie and her mother have never participated until now, so of course they wouldn't know anything about Marvin. . . ." Jane touched the key hanging at her throat, tucked under her shirt. Marvin's key.

"No, Mary, you're wrong. Nellie's been involved since before you were born," said Jane.

"You know Nellie?" asked Suzanne.

Now Mary looked confused. Jane had taken a stab, not entirely in the dark. Since Suzanne had talked about Freddy and Marvin in the same breath and since Jane knew that one of the keys to Freddy's Theater Club was inscribed with the name Suzanne, she had a strong feeling that this Suzanne had to be part of that early group which included Nellie and Henry Gand. Freddy's Theater Club. In fact, Jane would bet all the money in her wallet that Henry Gand was also sitting in back with the mourners.

"Nellie is my mother," said Jane.

Suzanne gave her a quick and awkward hug. "I haven't seen your mother for at least forty years. Whatever happened to her?"

It wasn't as if Jane believed everyone in the world had heard of the EZ Way Inn, but in Kankakee? It was fairly well known, and if Suzanne and Nellie had been old friends, and both still lived in town, wouldn't they all have kept track of each other?

"Nothing," said Jane. "I mean, she and my dad run a tavern on the west side."

Suzanne's face was blank. She shook her head. "I don't really get out much. I live in the back, in one of the apartments at the very back of the shop. I just do the work Marvin brings in. When Nellie left Freddy's club, I never saw her again. I just figured she went away and changed her name and became a great actress, forgetting all about us back here. I mean, Henry left, too, but he always came back summers and kept in touch, but when Nellie left the play, nobody ever mentioned her again."

Jane thought this seemed hard to believe. Most people met Nellie once and never stopped talking about her.

"She was a heartbreaker, your mom," said Suzanne.

"Shouldn't we be getting back for the service?" asked Mary. She wasn't happy about having Jane take center stage, but she seemed to grow even more agitated when Nellie, not even present, began to upstage her.

Suzanne ignored Mary's question, now lost in the memories of the theater club. "Nellie was one of the original members along with Marv and me and Henry and Bryan and—"

"Bryan Kendell? Bry?" asked Jane, trying to remember the rest of the names on the keys. Nellie, Marvin, Henry, Suzanne, Bry had to be Bryan Kendell, and what was the other name?

"Yes, Bryan's here with his new wife," said Suzanne. Jane must have looked puzzled because Suzanne smiled and shook her head. "Not that new, I guess. Melanie died twenty years ago, but like I said, I'm just an old lady who doesn't go outside and I just can't get used to Bry's new girl."

Melanie. That was the name on the last key.

Jane realized that although Suzanne looked her age, there was something childlike in her behavior. If she were rich, Nellie would say she had a screw loose, but because she was sad, needy, and more than a little lost, Jane thought Nellie might be kinder and describe the woman as no more out to lunch than most.

Mary looked out the window at a passing car that slowed. "That might be . . . nope. Guess he couldn't make it. We ought to get started, Suzanne," said Mary. She took a blank piece of paper and a marker from the desk drawer and printed out in all caps: CLOSED. DELIVERIES CAN BE LEFT AT THE REAR ENTRANCE. Mary grabbed a roll of tape and handed it to Suzanne along with the sign.

Suzanne recoiled, clenching her fists and putting her hands behind her back. "You know I can't . . ."

"You can tape it from the inside, Suzanne. Just tape it facing out from the inside."

Suzanne nodded and took the paper, crossing to the front door and centering the sign on the glass of the center panel.

Mary leaned in toward Oh and whispered, "Eccentric. Never steps foot outside. Lives and works in the back. Marvin made her shop manager and guaranteed her a home for life, but now . . . who knows. No close relatives that we know of, but if he didn't leave a will . . ." Mary shrugged and repeated. "Who knows?"

"You can come with us to the service," said Suzanne. "Nice to have someone representing Nellie. But," she said, gesturing to the bundle Jane still carried wrapped in her sweater. "Not him. He can't come."

Suzanne might be an oddball character, confused and grieving, but Jane didn't think her at all strange for insisting Mr. Bumbles *not* attend the service.

Jane nodded and laid Bumbles down on the desk. She then followed Suzanne, who motioned for Jane to follow her into the back of the shop, and watched with an odd mixture of amusement and resentment as Mary Wainwright took Oh's arm, claiming him as her escort. When the four of them had crossed the shop, they stepped around another partial wall where folding chairs were set up facing a sturdy, well-oiled workbench, laid with the most beautiful antique planes and woodworking tools Jane had ever seen.

If Henry Gand was upset at seeing outsiders join the group of twenty or so men and women talking quietly, he didn't show it. He got up gracefully and crossed to them, thanking Jane for coming. She introduced him to Oh and mentioned that he, too, had been at the theater the night of Marvin's death. She was about to offer more, explain that Oh and his wife were friends of Margaret Kendell, but she caught herself. She hadn't been asked for further information so why should she give any more away?

"And I heard your eloquent toast at the EZ Way Inn, as well," said Oh. "I am sorry for your loss."

Henry bowed his head in a small nod. Bryan and Penny Kendell gave a small wave but didn't get up. Rica Evans nodded, but she remained seated as well.

When Oh and Jane were seated, there was a rustling in the back of the area as someone got up and slipped an iPod into a dock with speakers and music began to play. Jane almost recognized it—she thought it might be Bach, measured and mathematical, but she wouldn't bet on it. She was never positive with classical music.

"Oh my," said Oh, in what for anyone else would have been an even tone. Jane, though, heard the utter surprise in his voice. Was the music not Bach? Was it something inappropriate for the occasion? A tanned overweight man wearing a light-colored suit more suited to a tropical climate than early spring in Kankakee stood up and moved to the workbench, preparing to speak. He cleared his throat and smiled, looking benevolently out at the group gathered in front of him. He looked vaguely familiar, but Jane couldn't place him. Someone she knew from when she lived in Kankakee? A customer from the EZ Way Inn?

"Although I am happy to once again be home in Kankakee, I am so sad that I arrive in town on this sad occasion. I planned this trip with a light heart, never dreaming that an event such as this would be my first stop. For those whom I have not yet met, I am Rick Kendell."

17

Rick Kendell gave a bland recitation of what a wonderful craftsman and gentleman Marvin had been. Marvin was one of his grandfather Freddy's young protégés and Rick characterized himself as just a kid, hanging around gawking at everyone. When he said that, there were a few rueful chuckles, since Henry, Suzanne, and Bryan were now part of a much older generation and Rick, a few years older than Jane, was certainly no longer the pesky little grandson he owned up to being.

Now he was the pesky adult. Jane had never heard a more self-serving eulogy, if that was what Rick Kendell's speech was supposed to be. Since he said he had just arrived in town that morning and heard of Marvin's death, an impromptu speech would not be surprising. Kendell's words, however, were not offensive because they were hastily composed; they were upsetting because they were not at all elegiac and they were far from comforting.

"As some of you may know, Freddy gave Marvin the seed money to start Geppetto Studios and also helped him pay for the conversion of this building, one of my great-grandfather's original factories, into this lovely scenery-building workshop. I know that many of you have benefited from Marvin's guidance and Freddy's generosity. Those of you who were not techies employed by Marvin either enjoyed his beautiful sets as audience members or worked on them as actors. You probably don't know that Freddy retained ownership of this property. Although Marvin was in the process of negotiating with the estate to actually buy this wonderful building that houses Geppetto Studios, his unfortunate accident means that this transaction cannot be completed. This leaves the fate of this building to me."

Jane watched the people around her react to this news. Suzanne was too horrified to weep. She sat unmoving with her mouth open in a tiny ring. Even Mary Wainwright, who always looked as if her smile was surgically implanted, allowed her mouth to relax into a straight line. Henry fought a battle that showed in his eyes, allowing them to narrow, then widen, then narrow—moving from puzzlement to astonishment to determination. Rica held a handkerchief over her mouth, as if the air had grown too foul to breathe. Bryan stayed cool, although Penny wept, adjusting her wrapped ankle so often that Jane thought the weeping might have more to do with personal discomfort than reaction to Marvin's death and Rick's pronouncements.

It was the reaction of Detective Oh, however, that Jane found most surprising. Jane had grown used to his unflappable demeanor. She had studied him, feeling that even the slightest movement of an eyebrow or smallest twitch of his lips had something to teach her. Jane would not be able to say whether she found his face handsome. She only knew that she was drawn to its complexity, that his minimalist expressions held humor and intelligence and honesty and curiosity, and greatest of all, compassion. Now when Jane looked at Oh, mostly to see if he, too, was observing the people around her, she saw an expression he had not shown her before. And when Rick Kendell claimed that the fate of the building was in his hands, Oh did something most unusual.

He cleared his throat.

Jane had never seen her mentor call attention to himself. In the stunned silence that greeted Rick Kendell's words, Oh's loud "ahem" was enough to prompt Rick, who had not paid any attention to Jane and Oh when they first took their seats, to turn now to look at them.

Rick's face reddened immediately and his next sentence came out in a faltering manner, almost identical to Margaret's nervous speech pattern.

"The fate of the . . . the building's future . . . I mean, of course, that it will be up to me and . . . my sister, Margie, Margaret, of course, and me . . . to decide the next step."

He quickly closed by saying that Marvin was a kind and talented man and they would all miss him. The workbench, which served as a podium, was a large, sturdy affair, but Rick's heft was a match for the table, and when he leaned on it, Jane thought she saw a few of the tools shift slightly. She knew it was only her imagination, but perhaps the perceived movement of the solid objects was some kind of metaphor. Before Rick had spoken, the room had been full of sad individuals who were saying good-bye to a friend. Now there was a seismic shift in mood. The friends were angry and unsettled, whispering furiously to each other as Rick struggled out from behind the work area to shake hands with Detective Oh.

"Whatever brings you to Kankakee, Bruce, and to the . . . to Marvin's . . . is Margie here? I thought she was in London, but . . ."

Oh might have let him babble on for days, and although Jane usually enjoyed Oh's capacity to remain quiet while others filled in all the spaces, she couldn't stand the high tension of this moment. Rick Kendell's anxiety, which was amusing and informative, she could take, of course, but Oh seemed not so much the silent beacon of calm resolve as much as he looked like someone who was about to punch someone.

"I'm Jane Wheel, Rick. I work with Tim Lowry," she said, extending her hand.

Her gesture, at least, stopped the flop sweat in which Kendell had broken out, threatening to drown them all.

"Tim? Oh, T and T Sales," said Rick. "Right. I just came in from Florida to check out the progress on that. Lowry told me he thought the sale could go on in a few weeks and I came in to see if we could hustle it up a bit."

"Now that Claire and Margaret are here helping, that might be possible," said Jane, "although Tim has the final word—"

"When, Rick?" said Oh.

"When what?"

"When did you get in?"

"Last night," said Kendell. "Late. I didn't go to the house or anything. Checked into a motel and went right to sleep. Then came here this morning to check on the building. My lawyer suggested I come over and talk to Marvin. You know, see what his intentions were, see if he wanted to buy the property since that silly lease expires in a few months. Thought I'd give Marv first crack at it. Then I found out . . . you know. And Suzanne thought maybe I'd want to, you know, in memory of Freddy . . . and I—"

"What time? Exactly?" said Oh.

"I don't know. Eight? Nine? I found a restaurant downtown that was open and ate and had a few drinks, then went to the motel, and by the time I checked in there, it might have been ten or eleven. Why?"

Instead of answering Rick, Oh took a deep breath and composed his face into what Jane recognized as Oh's face.

"Your sister will be surprised to see you," said Oh. "She thought you were remaining in Florida."

"I didn't think I should leave it all up to her. She gets nervous. Didn't seem right to make her go into the house alone. I don't know—"

"She's not alone," said Jane. "She's got Tim and me and my mother, Nellie, and of course Detective Oh and Claire," said Jane.

"Nellie?" said Rick. "Nellie from Freddy's club? You're Henry's daughter?"

"Nellie is my mother. She and Henry didn't . . . I mean . . . she married my father, Don, not Henry. She hasn't been a part of the theater club for—"

Jane stopped. She really didn't know how long her mother had hung with the theater club. Jane had thought it was only for one play—*Murder in the Eekaknak Valley*—and when that was canceled Jane thought Nellie probably quit. But maybe not. She did rank high enough in the membership to have her own key.

"I had such a crush on Nellie," said Rick. "She was so beautiful."

Okay, thought Jane, *I've seen photos and she was a looker. I can accept this.*

"And she was so sweet," said Rick, a faraway look in his eye. "I was home from school, between schools actually, and I hung around watching rehearsals, and that Nellie was an angel, so sweet and so funny."

Okay, thought Jane, *now we've entered fantasyland.*

"I can't believe Henry let her get away," said Rick. "He's so old now," he added, sounding surprised.

For a moment, Rick, with his smooth round face wreathed in what still could be considered baby fat, did look like a kid, shocked that everything around him had changed. The moment passed, though, and his shock over seeing Detective Oh also passed.

"I suppose you think it's rough of me to come in here and

talk about the building and all, but hell, I didn't know Marvin had died. I just showed up to talk over the sale with him."

"Margaret didn't mention that this property was to be sold," said Oh. "And she usually shares everything with Claire. Everything," he repeated softly.

"I haven't talked to my sister face-to-face in years. She's always on her way to London or marrying someone or divorcing someone. I've always handled more of the business. Mother always wanted me to handle this stuff, and Margaret and I both have bills to pay. This factory is a great property and Freddy gave Marvin one of those dollar-a-year leases so he could employ these misfits—hell, he even houses Suzanne here. When's the last time old Vampira had a dose of vitamin D?"

"So you decide that Marvin's funeral is the right time to play landlord?" asked Jane.

"Did you say you worked for Tim Lowry? That means you work for me, too, right?" Rick smiled, showing pointy little teeth in the center of that big round face.

Jane opened her mouth to reply, but Mary Wainwright pulled her away with a question about the set. As Jane half listened to Mary and Suzanne's questions, she heard Oh's response to Rick Kendell.

"Mrs. Wheel works with me, Rick. She's my partner. And I can assure you she won't be bullied. Margaret will have to agree about the sale of this property and she might feel that honoring Freddy's wishes is more important than any money you might get for this place."

"Maybe I've already got an offer," said Rick. "And Margaret needs money even worse than I do."

Rick walked away from Oh, who regained his composure. So subtle were the changes in her friend's demeanor, Jane realized that she might be the only one in the room who noticed that he had momentarily lost it.

"Isn't that right, Jane?" asked Mary, assuming that Jane had been paying attention to the questions about finishing the work on the play. Jane realized that she would now have to assume Marvin's role as set designer. The play was opening on Friday and there was no one else to step in.

"We'll just go with the staircase that's there. I can help Tim account for that entrance—we'll just make it so Rica comes in from the garden. Marvin had finished everything major. I can do the final touch-up painting in a day if I have a little help," said Jane.

Henry had been standing at the edge of the little group and he nodded when Jane spoke. "I'll help you finish. I was Marvin's assistant on this anyway. He and I couldn't move around like young men anymore, but between the two of us, we did okay. I can still be a help to you. And we've got some other youngsters here who can help."

Jane looked at the youngsters to whom Henry pointed. Three middle-aged men, probably a few years older than Jane herself, were helping Suzanne carry out a large coffeepot and trays filled with cups and coffee cakes.

"Suzanne always finds good people down on their luck. She learned how to do that from Freddy. Freddy found every misfit and oddball in town and gave them a key to his theater club so they'd have a place to belong," said Henry.

"A key?" asked Jane, fingering Marvin's key under her shirt.

"Not literally," said Henry, with a little laugh. "Freddy just thought there wasn't enough art around, that kids and adults, too, for that matter, didn't have enough places to go or things to do in Kankakee, and he thought theater was a wonderful place to express yourself. He hated business even though he was good at it. It's because Freddy retained ownership of some of the property that the whole family didn't end up on the street when his idiot son lost all their money. You'd think

Rick would remember that it was his grandfather who took care of them and his wishes should— Freddy always said if there was a kid who couldn't fit in at school or find a job that made him happy, he could find a place in Freddy's theater club. He said any kid could go through a door if he had a key."

Jane looked over at Oh, who had accepted a cup of coffee from Suzanne, which Jane knew he did not drink. He was nodding and listening to her speak rapidly, glancing over her shoulder at Rick Kendell as she talked. Jane remembered why she and Oh had come to Geppetto Studios.

"Henry," asked Jane, "do you know who brought Mr. Bumbles in to Marvin for repairs?"

Henry shook his head. "Marv would be the only person who could answer that. Suzanne might know, but then again, she didn't always go up front to meet people. None of the people around here except Marv would want to work on a Bumbles, that's for sure."

"Why?" asked Jane, leaving out any speculation about the general creepiness of the Bumbles.

"Marvin said once that every time one of those dolls was sitting on a shelf, something bad happened in the shop. Teddy over there, who has as steady a hand with tools as you could ever imagine, cut himself and had to get forty stitches when a Bumbles was looking at him. That's what he said, anyway. Bumbles was looking at him, laughing when the saw blade jumped. And another time when there was a Bumbles here, there was a break-in at the front of the shop, in the office. Nearly scared Suzanne to death. Electrical shorted out once. Stuff like that. And now Marvin . . ." said Henry, his voice breaking.

"But Bumbles wasn't here," said Jane.

"What?" asked Henry, wiping his reading glasses on his handkerchief.

"You said all the bad luck happened when Bumbles was in

the shop for repairs, but there wasn't a Bumbles here in the shop when Marvin . . . and Marvin wasn't here when it happened. I brought the Bumbles . . ."

Henry looked at Jane with wide-open eyes, but she had the feeling he wasn't following her out-loud thinking, and she wasn't sure what there was to follow anyway. She shook her head and stopped talking, giving Henry an awkward pat on the shoulder.

People were leaving after their obligatory coffee and bite of cake, except for the resident carpenters of Geppetto Studios. Once people had stopped milling around the actual work area, a few of the workers had begun painting in a corner of the workspace. Jane was pleased to see them working, since she noted it was the last window frame they needed to complete the set over at the theater. It probably could be placed tomorrow and they would be done with all the work needed to be finished up at the studio. Jane felt vaguely guilty that she had seen Marvin drive up and unload his truck night after night and hadn't been even the least bit curious about where he was getting all of this work done. She had this achy sense that she would have liked Marvin, liked working side by side with him in this magnificent space. There were little things about the space, like the niches in the original brick factory walls that Marvin or Suzanne or one of the Geppettos, as Jane was beginning to think of the carpenters under Suzanne's supervision, had filled with tiny carved figures or miniature books or small beeswax candles and vintage candle molds. As utilitarian as the space was, it had been warmed and charmed into something else. It reminded her of Freddy's theater club space. It had character and personality . . . it was a home.

Everyone Jane had recognized—Penny and Bryan Kendell, Rica Evans, Mary Wainwright—and all the rest of the guests had left when Jane finished up checking out the window frame and chatting about other touch-ups that could be done on the set. Even Suzanne was nowhere in sight. Detective Oh was tapping furiously on his phone. Jane guessed he was texting to Claire, advising her to prepare Margaret for a visit from Brother Rick.

Just then Suzanne came up behind Jane and asked if there was anything else they were going to need before opening night. Her eyes were red-rimmed but dry.

"Might be corny, but Marv really would say that the show must go on. So would Freddy," said Suzanne.

"I've been wanting to ask someone, Suzanne, why didn't the show go on the first time? Forty years ago. I mean, Freddy had a heart attack, I know that much, but when he got better, why wasn't *Murder in the Eekaknak Valley* ever produced?"

"Oh, Freddy just kept rewriting it and rewriting it. He said he wanted it to be perfect so it would live on as a legacy for the kids, his grandkids. Margie and—" Jane could see that Suzanne had a hard time even saying the name. The old woman swallowed hard and added, "Rick."

Oh looked up from the phone and nodded at Jane. She nodded back. It was time to grab a sandwich, then head over to the theater.

"I'm sorry we barged in here today and so sorry about Marvin. I wish I had known him better," said Jane.

Suzanne nodded. "He was a loyal man, a good friend," said Suzanne.

Suzanne suggested they leave by the side door, which had a lighted, covered walkway leading to the front of the building, where they had parked. One row of folding chairs remained and Suzanne started putting them away. Oh and Jane both began to help her, but she waved them off, claiming she didn't need any help. Jane picked up her bag and started for the side door, thinking about where they might grab a bite before heading to the theater, but then she remembered what they had come for. And *who* they had come with.

She held up a hand to Oh, jerking her thumb back at the office, making what she thought was a kind of Mr. Bumbles face, and since it almost made Oh smile, she figured she had done a decent impression. She ran back toward the office to grab the dummy. All the vintage desk lamps were turned off, and although it was still light outside, the shades had been pulled, leaving only a narrow frame of light around the window.

Jane loved the setup. There was nothing as atmospheric as an old office from the forties, maybe even the thirties. Jane had noted when they entered the similar desks in opposite corners, quarter-sawn oak, substantial workspaces, one with a built-in typewriter that was unfolded into the work position. On the desk where the fake victim or sleeping private eye—depending on your point of view—slumped over his typewriter, was a black Bakelite rotary telephone. Jane felt a small lustful stirring for that phone. She loved the way it looked, of course, all curvy and shiny and heavy and real. It was the opposite of the skinny little rectangle that passed for a phone that she kept in her own pocket. This beautiful Bakelite piece of equipment was as substantial and well-designed for its day—utilitarian, of course, but also clean and modern. What the hell—Jane had to pick up that receiver, feel it in her hand, cradle it between her ear and shoulder.

Mr. Bumbles was perched on the shelf above the desk. His legs were crossed, and he was smiling down at Jane as if he approved of her trying out the phone.

Jane picked up the receiver, so heavy and satisfyingly smooth in her hand, and hugged it into her shoulder. She looked down at the base, thinking about dialing the number of the EZ Way Inn—the way she remembered it from her childhood,

Wells 9-9129. The private eye's fedora was still tumbled to the side on the desk, half covering his face.

He's huge, this guy, thought Jane. He was much bigger up close than he had appeared when they had seen him from outside the window. *And fully to scale,* thought Jane, glancing down at the meaty paw on the desk. The hand was clenched around a letter opener, which also looked like it might be Bakelite. Wanting a closer look at the piece, Jane touched the hand of the mannequin. Unlike the carved wood of Mr. Bumbles's features, which was always warm to the touch, this hand was cold. Jane felt herself go rigid with revulsion, then just as quickly go limp. To anyone looking in the window, if he could see around those heavy shades, Jane Wheel would appear to be a forties-era secretary screaming into the office telephone that someone had just murdered her boss.

Close.

It was modern-day Jane Wheel, screaming into the forties telephone that someone had just murdered Rick Kendell.

Jane hadn't ever met the police officer who questioned her about finding Rick Kendell sprawled across the desk in the office. It was just as well. Jane didn't really want to explain herself to any local law enforcement officer who might already be familiar with her penchant for finding bodies, who would be reminded that Jane Wheel was often at the right place at the right time when it came to murder in Kankakee. No. Stop. Reverse that. Think like a normal person. If one was at the scene of a murder, it must be the wrong place, wrong time.

She found the most difficult part of the question-and-answer session came when she tried to explain that Bumbles had been moved to the shelf and had his legs crossed. Detective Randy Ramey seemed to brush this part of her answer aside and moved on to the next question when Jane repeated it for him.

"Look at him there, watching and grinning, sitting there all smug with his legs crossed," said Jane. "I did not put him there."

Detective Ramey looked up from the small notebook in which he had been writing.

"Mrs. Wheel, I don't follow why—"

"Someone, whoever killed Rick Kendell, wanted us to notice that Bumbles approved," said Jane.

"Would you like us to get you a cup of tea or coffee or something, Mrs. Wheel?" asked Ramey.

Jane looked around for Bruce Oh, who had been consulting with the team examining the site from which Rick Kendell's body had just been removed.

Suzanne and the rest of the Geppettos, those who worked here, belonged here, were the only people, aside from Jane and Oh, left in the building. All of those who had attended Marvin's memorial had gone, one by one, or in groups, and one of the police officers was now looking through the memorial guest book with Suzanne. Jane had heard her tell the officer that she couldn't think of anyone else who had attended who hadn't signed.

"Rick," Jane heard her finally say. "Rick was here and he didn't sign. And those two over there," she added, pointing to Jane and Oh.

Jane and Oh, the other unexpected guests who hadn't signed the book and who ended up being the last people to leave the memorial service, explained their presence at Geppetto Studios, if not their entire mission. They had come to meet the carpenter who repaired equipment for Freddy Kendell—to ask a few questions concerning the Kendell estate. They had decided to stay for the memorial service for Marvin, with whom they had been acquainted through the theater. Jane had only to look at Oh to know that she should say as little as possible. This was because of his always cautious, *never say more than is absolutely necessary* manner, but also, this time, because Jane knew that the only person she had seen who looked like he wanted to murder Rick Kendell was her partner, Bruce Oh. Most of the people in the building had a reason for wanting Rick Kendell dead, but Detective Oh was the only one who had, so uncharacteristically, actually shown his hand.

Jane knew, of course, that she and Bruce were also the only two people who had constant alibis, since they had been in the back of the building the entire time, in conversation with or in full sight of others. Each of them had been in contact with at least one of the Geppettos or Suzanne, asking questions about Marvin, the business, or, in Jane's case, consulting about the set of *Murder in the Eekaknak Valley*. All of the other mourners had disappeared, and any of them could have left by the front office, stopping first to ask Rick to sit down for a little chat, planning all along to kill the new landlord-in-waiting.

"Where's the dummy?" asked Jane, reconstructing the office in her head.

"As you pointed out, Mrs. Wheel, he is sitting right there on the shelf," said Ramey, trying to gesture to one of his female officers, possibly hoping for some help with the crazy lady.

"The other dummy," said Jane. "The one who was there in that chair when we came in." Jane managed to explain that there had been a tableau set up with a mannequin in what was now the death seat.

Ramey excused himself to speak with a subordinate who came over with a small pad of paper. The younger officer whispered something to Ramey, who nodded. Jane was only able to hear a disjointed phrase or two, one of them being "nail gun," and she shuddered. There were dozens of tools in the workroom behind the office, many of them perfectly usable as a murder weapon, but a nail gun seemed particularly ominous. Whoever the Bumble was in Rick's murder, he or she hadn't made the effort or taken the time to make the death look like an accident—no falling beam available anyway, as there was in Marvin's death.

Jane knew how convoluted this whole story would seem to Ramey if she tried now to explain the connection between Marvin's alleged accident and today's murder, and she knew the police would get there soon enough on their own anyway, so why hurry this process along? If she convinced the police to treat Marvin's death as a murder, the entire theater area would be closed down and the show would most certainly not go on. Jane was beginning to think the only chance she would have to figure things out was to see the play through. Somehow, the production of this play, with all of its prankish warnings and ominous allusions, was key to everything that was going on.

Detective Oh, as always, had made a fine impression on the police. He was always knowledgeable and yet respectfully curious. Even if he'd told the police exactly what to look for and where, they'd somehow walk away thinking it was their own idea.

"Think about the game show your son, Nick, loves so much, Mrs. Wheel, that's the key to dealing with others in a case." Oh had told Jane.

"*The Price Is Right?*" asked Jane. Nick loved all game shows and was weirdly good at guessing the price of a box of fabric softener.

"*Jeopardy,* Mrs. Wheel. If you put your thoughts in the form of a question, the police will not feel like you are trying to outsmart them or do their job. It can be helpful to remember that you don't ever want to know too much about a murder before the police do. Rather than seeing you as a helper, the more you know, the more likely they are to see you as a suspect."

Jane tried to figure out how to put her thoughts into the form of an innocent question—wouldn't someone have to move the mannequin out of sight and get Rick Kendell seated in the chair in order to come up behind him with a nail gun? He was too big to drag into the chair and position so perfectly. And where was the blood? There were just too many questions ricocheting inside of her head, and Jane knew giving voice to them would not make her seem merely curious. Instead, while she waited for Ramey to get his report, she tried to think herself where that life-sized mannequin that had so startled her and Oh could be stashed. She scanned the now well-lit corner of the office, looking to see if that tromp l'oeil wall might conceal a closet door. It had been such a realistic figure . . . tricked out like a forties private eye, yes, but aside from the vintage clothes, if it were just sitting . . . and then she knew. Just as sure as she knew how to spot the one Bakelite button out of hundreds in a vintage tin, a McCoy flowerpot on a table full of Morton and Haeger, and a tarnished sterling silver brooch in a bowl of pot metal pins. They were always hiding in plain sight.

Jane had been so focused on the corner of the office where Kendell had been slumped over the desk, she only now remembered that the other corner of the space held the other half of the vintage office. There was also an oak desk there with a typewriter and an adding machine. That other oak swivel chair had been empty when Suzanne barely opened the door for them. Now, Jane turned around, knowing what she would find in the still barely lit corner.

The mannequin, the same one—Jane recognized his navy blue tie peppered with red-and-white bowling pins—was now sitting up in the other chair, his arms placed on the keys of the vintage typewriter, a page of white onionskin gracefully draped over the carriage. No fedora—his hat remained on the other desk to conceal Rick's face. Someone had moved the mannequin over to the other desk, probably before asking Rick Kendell to step out front for a chat. The murderer, or possibly murderers, would tell him to have a seat, then move behind him to point out something, perhaps, some paper on the desk, a document, a contract. He or she could then take the nail gun, which could have been stashed right on top of the bookshelf, and boom. The front office was half a block away from the back of the factory space where they had held the memorial. All of the remaining guests were still congregated in the back, some of the Geppettos had even gone back to work so there might have been carpentry noise as well as conversation to mask anything going on up front. After killing Rick, the murderer could either walk back and mingle with the guests a bit more and leave by the side or back, or the murderer could have simply left by the front office door. Anyone who walked by the place on a regular basis would be used to the practical joke—the mannequin slumped over the desk—and even Suzanne, if she had come up front to lower the shades and check the door locks, might not notice that the dead private eye had put on about one hundred pounds. Hidden in plain sight—victim and mannequin. If Jane hadn't come up to fetch Bumbles and been drawn to the desk by the vintage Bakelite phone, Rick Kendell might have remained part of the vintage office tableau for the rest of the evening.

Oh came over to Jane and told her that they were free to go. Jane pointed out the other desk where the mannequin now typed a letter. It was the kind of office where two private eyes might work side by side in the same space with no secretary. The mannequin looked perfectly at home at the typewriter.

Oh looked over at Ramey, still in consultation with one of his officers, and raised one shoulder almost imperceptibly.

"I'll call him with the rest of our information later," said Oh.

"I'm not sure I'm excused," said Jane. "We were right in the middle of things."

Detective Ramey told Jane they would be in touch. Soon. Despite his disinterest in what she had to say earlier about the importance of Mr. Bumbles, he would not let her take the dummy with them.

"So far, he's my only witness, Mrs. Wheel," said Ramey. "Perhaps my only suspect." Although he didn't have the complete neutrality of Oh's face, Jane could see that Ramey had a fair poker face. Was he making fun of her or simply trying to lighten the moment, to show friendliness?

Since they were not allowed to leave by the office front door, where technicians were still working, Jane and Oh walked through the workspace toward the side door. Jane noted that

Suzanne was sitting with a female officer, pale, but otherwise not visibly distraught.

"Can we go over to her and say good-bye?"

Oh didn't answer. Instead, he took her elbow and guided her over to where Suzanne was in the middle of what seemed like an inventory list. Jane realized that the police were loading up nail guns as well as other tools from the work area and Suzanne was signing off on them.

"We're leaving, Suzanne. Will you let us know if we can help?" said Jane, searching in her bag for a "Jane Wheel, PPI, Picker and Private Investigator" card.

"This has both of our numbers," said Oh, putting his own card into her hand. It simply said "OH" with two phone numbers below. "You can phone us at any hour."

"When Marvin and I set up the front office as a double office for two private eyes, it was just for fun, like a stage set for Marlowe and Spade, Marvin said. I never dreamed I'd meet two real investigators or that there would be a . . ." Suzanne looked over at the police officer who had stepped away, then whispered, "murder."

"Whose idea was it to decorate the office like that?" asked Jane.

"Marvin knew somebody in Chicago who was tearing out some old downtown offices and he just grabbed a bunch of the stuff, said it would be fun to set up the front like that. Said we'd use it if the theater ever did *The Front Page*. He got a lot of stuff that way, for sets and all. Just went to the demo sales and cleaned them out. He said our two private eyes weren't that successful—no secretary—so sometimes he'd put one partner to work and sometimes he'd make him a victim and now . . ."

"Did you move the mannequin today?" Jane whispered. "Set him up at the other desk typing?"

Suzanne shook her head.

"Typing," Jane repeated. She handed her large leather tote to Oh. "I'll be right back."

Oh nodded, looking as if he was thinking the same thing as Jane.

"Did I leave my purse up here?" said Jane as she entered the office.

None of the police or the technicians looked up. They remained at the door and two men were crawling around under the desk. Ramey was talking on his cell phone just outside the front door. He poked his head in and looked questioningly at Jane.

"I thought I might have left my purse over there," said Jane softly. Ramey watched her for a moment as she scanned the area, then he reminded her that he would want to talk to her again. She nodded, but he was already back outside the door, talking on his phone.

Jane walked over behind the desk in the opposite corner where either Spade or Marlowe sat hatless at the typewriter. Careful not to touch anything, Jane took a pen from her pocket and carefully lifted up a corner of the drooping onionskin paper. The letters were only faintly visible, showing the age and dryness of the old machine's ribbon, but the message was legible.

`Good job, Mr. Bumbles. Well done.`

19

The day had been full of secrets and surprises. Jane had found the bow tie, proof that Mr. Bumbles had been at the scene of Marvin's "accident"; had possibly been flirted with by her old teacher, Mr. Havens; opened up the door to Freddy's theater club; met at least thirty identical Mr. Bumbles; heard a demonstration of Margaret's ventriloquism; stumbled onto Marvin's full life as Geppetto, the carpenter/guru; met Rick Kendell and found him dead; and now, as before, found that all roads always led back to Mr. Bumbles.

"And Nellie," said Jane. "She was the ingenue who everybody loved."

Oh parked Jane's car in front of a convenience store. "We're getting you a sandwich because at some point today, your body will realize you haven't eaten."

"I'm already an hour late for rehearsal. I haven't looked yet, but I bet I have a million missed calls from Tim."

"He knows what's happened. I've spoken with Claire. She needed to prepare Margaret. First it was just to see her brother, and now this. Margaret will have to meet with Detective Ramey this evening. This will all be difficult for her. She is fragile at best and when it comes to her brother, she is like glass. Apt to shatter."

"Why do you despise—" Jane began, then corrected herself. "Why did you despise Rick?"

Jane realized after she said it that this might be the first time she had ever asked Oh a direct and personal question. She was surprised that he answered so easily.

"I dislike people who take advantage of those weaker than themselves, Mrs. Wheel. You already know that. Rick Kendell coaxed his mother into giving him the Florida property, he stole from Margaret, he tricked people into supporting his gambling habits . . . he fooled everyone but Freddy. Freddy tried to protect Margaret. That's why Claire is so upset about the missing art and antiques. She thinks that's how Freddy tried to provide for Margaret, knowing that any money would either be lost by her father or gambled away by Rick. As soon as I saw him, I was sure he was here to steal from the house, but then when I heard about the lease on the building, I thought perhaps he would hold the key to Mr. Marvin's accident. If Marvin died before he could exercise his option to buy the property for Freddy's low price, Rick could sell the property out from under Geppetto Studios and find a way to keep all of it, or most of it, from Margaret. As much as I disliked Rick Kendell, I was pleased that we had so easily found our murderer."

"Until he was murdered," said Jane, "although being murdered doesn't mean you aren't a murderer. He could have gone to talk to Marvin last night and found him unreasonable and thrown the beam down on him, but . . ."

"Unlikely, I know. A big man, not light on his feet, escaping through the woods? Doubling back to get into a rental car and . . ."

"Mr. Bumbles," said Jane, taking a bite of the plastic-looking sandwich she had found in the refrigerator case. Although it was labeled "turkey," she could not taste anything recognizable. She wrapped up the rest of her dinner and threw it back into the plastic bag and took out a dark chocolate bar. Reliable food.

"Mr. Bumbles left his tie there. Whoever was with Marvin, whoever knocked the beam down on top of him, had Mr. Bumbles with him. That wouldn't have been Rick."

"Freddy made sure there were dozens of those dummies. He called them his alter egos. It is certainly possible that Rick could have had one, although I agree it's unlikely. I'm going to drop you at rehearsal, then check out his story about when he got in and checked into the hotel. The police will already have entered his hotel room. I think I will also go make friends with Detective Ramey."

Jane had Oh drop her in front of the theater building and entered through the front lobby. So many people had been in and out of her day, she found herself taken aback when she saw such a warm familiar figure standing and staring out of the window next to the box office.

"Daddy?" Jane said, immediately correcting her grown-up self. "Dad?"

Don turned around and held out his arms and Jane gratefully accepted her father's giant hug. Jane and her dad had never called this massive embrace a bear hug; instead, they had always shared what they named "ow hugs." The idea was to hug the other person so hard you made them say "ow."

"Ow," said Don. "Must have been a hell of a day."

"You look a little beat-up yourself, Dad," said Jane, noting the deep lines around Don's eyes and mouth. Did they look deeper? Or did Jane try not to notice how old her parents were getting?

"I was just thinking about a cigarette," said Don.

"No, Dad," said Jane. Don had quit a three-pack-a-day habit seven years ago.

He shook his head. "Not *having* a cigarette. I was thinking about the first time I saw your mother."

Jane waited. Don, unlike Nellie, was an expansive storyteller. He liked to reminisce and spin a tale or two. But he liked to take his time.

"Your mother was in a play. Not this one, but another one Freddy wrote. I had a date who dragged me to the dress rehearsal because she had friends in it. I had never seen anything onstage except when a movie had a live show—you know, they had those traveling shows at the Majestic downtown. Your mother came onstage and Henry Gand was playing some weasel and he lit a cigarette for her. She was great, so pretty, and I believed everything she said, but she couldn't smoke to save her life. Wrecked the whole thing, I thought.

"After the play, we went to a party and all the actors were there and I went up to your mother and offered to teach her to smoke a cigarette."

"I never knew how you two met, Dad. That's a great story. You helped her become a better actress," said Jane.

"Hell no," said Don. "She said she didn't want to learn to smoke a filthy cigarette. Next thing I know, she goes and talks to Henry, comes back to me, and asks me to drive her home. She quit the play. Said she didn't want to make a fool of herself onstage anymore, doing unnatural things and being something she wasn't. My date ended up going home with Henry and taking Nellie's place in the show."

"And you've always wondered if she regretted it?"

"Nope. But I've always known Henry regretted it."

Jane walked over to the doors to the house and listened for what scene they were on. Henry, as Perkins the gardener, was doing his speech about his unrequited love for Marguerite.

"Isn't this the part of the play where you're supposed to be coughing and causing trouble?" asked Jane.

"Your mom put the pillows into the bed. She went out for some air. I was watching her, but now she's out of sight. I was just going out to get her; it's getting too dark for her to be out there."

"I'll go," said Jane.

"Come out of the woods, you chicken, and pick on somebody your own size."

Jane came up behind her mother, who stood next to Marvin's table saw and spoke directly to the trees behind the building. Jane had often wondered if she had inherited the stealth qualities Nellie employed when she sneaked up on Jane, and she knew the answer as soon as Nellie, without turning to her, said, "Where the hell you been all this time?"

No. Jane would never be able to catch Nellie by surprise.

Jane tried to explain efficiently what had happened at Marvin's memorial, since she had a few questions to ask her mother, and standing in the approaching darkness, away from all of the other cast members, might be the best place to get a few honest answers.

"What did that doofus Rick look like as a grown-up?" asked Nellie.

"He spoke highly of you," said Jane. "Perhaps you should be more respectful—"

"That little juvenile delinquent never spoke a straight sentence in his life," said Nellie. "If he spoke highly of me, which I doubt, he meant just the opposite. He was a con man when he was a teenager. Freddy knew it, too. Freddy loved Margaret, who was a nice little girl, but not that Rick. Slimy bastard."

"He was just a kid when you knew him," said Jane. "How can you say that?"

Nellie inhaled deeply, then exhaled through her mouth. If

Jane didn't know better, she'd think that Nellie was practicing her cigarette-smoking technique out here.

"Look, just because somebody's a kid doesn't mean they don't have their personality yet. Age—young or old—doesn't give anyone a pass to be a liar. Rick was phony. He kept telling me how pretty I was and what a good actress I was, stuff like that. Pretty soon, he was asking if he could borrow my key to the theater club, because he'd lost his. Like Freddy would ever trust that little crook with the keys to the kingdom. Or he'd ask one of us to buy him beer. He was probably thirteen, the little brat. Stuff like that. He'd buddy up to get his way."

"Wait? You had a key back then? What about the ones we found?" asked Jane.

"Freddy kept spares in the chest on the porch, in case we ever needed to get in. He was always worried about us. I think he saw us as a bunch of misfits and thought we might need a place, you know. And he was protective of all of us. Like he was of Margaret."

"So anybody who had worked with Freddy had access to the theater club all these years, even you?"

"Yeah, I got the old key somewhere," said Nellie, flipping the new key, the one Jane had found, and the chain around her neck to the outside of her collar. "Unless Freddy changed the locks, I could have gotten in if I wanted to."

"Great," said Jane. "I'll add you to my list of suspects."

"You know who did it. That dummy was here," said Nellie.

"Right, Mr. Bumbles. The same Mr. Bumbles who was put back into the closet at the theater club. So whoever was here got him out and brought him here and . . ."

A small floodlight attached to the back corner of the theater building clicked, illuminating the table saw as well as Jane and Nellie. Jane wasn't aware that they had moved to activate the motion detector, but she knew it could have been a breeze tossing a leaf, a squirrel, a . . .

"Bat," said Nellie, pointing up to the light.

Jane covered her head and ducked. When Jane was young Nellie had always warned her that the bats flying around the streetlight in front of their house were just waiting to swoop down, nest in her hair, and infect her with rabies. It was an effective means of getting Jane to come in from playing as soon as it got dark enough for the streetlight to turn on. Even though Nick had done his best to convince Jane that bats were really friends and the best means of mosquito control, Jane had never quite shaken the earlier lessons of Nellie.

"You know, you're not necessarily right about the person who killed Marvin bringing Bumbles here," said Nellie.

"Yeah, right, I forgot," said Jane. "Bumbles acted alone."

"No Smarty Pants, I was thinking maybe Marvin was the one who had the dummy with him. Bumbles had a broken leg, right, and Claire said you found out that the guy who was restoring and repairing those dummies was Marvin. Maybe Marvin had old Bumbles out here to fix him and whoever was here and pushed the beam saw Bumbles and decided to take the dummy back."

"Why?" asked Jane. "Why would it matter?"

Jane noted that one corner of the cover on the table saw had come untied, and she reknotted the lace to keep the tarp down over the equipment.

"Well, maybe it was somebody who wanted to play another trick with him," said Nellie. "Freddy was always playing tricks with those dummies. Leaving them around holding notes for us, spying on us. Creepy as hell."

"Or maybe it was someone who didn't want anyone to connect Marvin with Bumbles or the theater club," said Jane.

"What if someone wanted Marvin out of the picture . . . and then saw he had Bumbles with him and knew that the dummy would connect Marvin to Freddy and the family and the club and . . ."

"Nellie," called Don. "Tim wants you onstage for this scene."

Nellie shook her head and muttered something, but went into the theater.

Jane remained looking out into the woods and continued with her train of thought. What if someone knew something about this play or the theater club and wanted to stop anyone else from discovering a connection to that group? If Jane hadn't been working on the sale with Tim, if they hadn't been connected to the Kendell mansion or family, and they had just found these scripts and decided to put on the show . . . all of the theater club stuff would be forgotten. Buried with Freddy. But if someone came out to talk to Marvin or just saw Marvin with Bumbles, they would know that someone might connect Marvin with Freddy. So they came out back and saw Bumbles and tried to take him away and maybe Marvin tried to stop him? No, Marvin was at the saw when the beam fell—no sign of a struggle. He had his back to the tree where the beam had been leaning.

Jane could hear the actors speaking onstage. Rica Evans and Mary Wainwright were doing their big mother-daughter scene, after which Rica would turn to Marguerite in the hospital bed and deliver her monologue, her apology for running off to New York. It really wasn't such a terrible play. Melodramatic, sure, but some of the speeches were really well-written. Maybe if Freddy had kept at it, he really would have written a play that could have provided for Margaret.

"We meet again . . . same place," said Chuck Havens. "Keep this a secret, okay?"

At first, Jane thought he was teasing her about keeping

their meeting secret, but when she looked at him, she saw he was referring to the cigarette he was lighting.

"I don't want it to get out that I relapsed," said Chuck. "Last time I gave in and had a cigarette, Mary threatened to tell my students, which would have made my life a daily hell."

Jane shook her head and placed a finger over her lips.

"I wanted to smoke in the play, you know, to give me an excuse, and besides, I'm a suspect. Everyone thinks I did it so I might as well be a smoker. These days, though, if you smoke cigarettes, it's worse than being a murderer."

Jane only half-listened. What if it was something about the theater club connection that made Marvin a target? Penny Kendell was the first person to be injured—Bryan was a theater club member, and the accident could just as easily have been staged for him. What if they were all at risk because of something connected to Freddy and Freddy's club? What did they know that others might not? Henry and Nellie were also part of the theater club. . . .

A crash and a scream came from inside the theater. Chuck dropped the cigarette, crushed it out, and popped a mint Life Saver in his mouth in one fluid motion. Illicit smoking on or near high school property had clearly given him some practice in quick response and cover-up.

Jane beat him into the theater in time to see Don onstage with his arm around Nellie. Although she was shaking her head and insisting that she was okay, she wasn't wiggling out of his grasp as Jane was more used to seeing.

Peggy, one of the extras playing a party guest, had run down the steps at stage left and come around to the front of the stage. Standing between the front row of seats and the edge of the stage, her head was at eye level with the stage floor.

"I can see it, it's this front leg on the right," she said. She then corrected herself. "Stage left."

Standing directly in front of the raised stage made it easy to look under the hospital bed, now sloping sharply toward the floor. When Jane joined Peggy at the edge of the stage, she could see that one of the legs had telescoped, which would have thrown Nellie to the floor had she been lying on the bed when it happened. Peggy explained to Jane that Nellie had tossed a heavy bag full of books onto the bed, books that were going to be placed around the set and in the bookcase stage left, but which Nellie thought were right in the way of some of the actors. She had hefted the bag onto the bed and the leg had collapsed with such a loud crash that Rica Evans, pacing upstage, had screamed.

Peggy also told Jane that Don had bounded onto the stage like a real hero and grabbed Nellie, who Jane could hear now had reclaimed her wits and begun swearing like a sailor.

"Who in their goddamn infernal wisdom decided to mess around with this bed? I could have fallen off and broken my neck. Was it you, Lowry? I told you I didn't want it up any higher, that it was just fine the way it was."

"Take a ten-minute break everyone," said Tim. "We'll fix this and start the last scene in ten."

Tim looked toward the back and Jane was afraid he was going to call out for Marvin. In fact, Jane started when she thought she saw Marvin himself come out from offstage, but it was Henry, dressed as Perkins the gardener—the pants and shirt so similar to what Marvin had been wearing last night.

Jane took the steps up onto the stage two at a time and knelt next to Henry.

"It's these adjustable legs," said Henry. "Somebody moved the bed and this little knob got pushed so that it was about to come out. See how you push in these buttons together and the legs slide up and down, then you let them out and the leg catches? When weight hit the bed, the leg just slid on down to the lowest position. Could be when somebody made the bed, they just moved it and the thing gave. Feels solid, doesn't it, Jane?"

Jane squeezed the buttons and with one arm supporting the frame, could feel that the adjustable leg adjusted, sliding up and down with ease. Jane also knew that it would take more than moving the bed or making the bed to make one of these legs become precarious enough to collapse when weight hit the bed. Besides, the "someone" who made the bed was either Jane or Nellie, and Jane knew she hadn't moved it off its marks. And Nellie? She could make a bed with perfect hospital corners, tight enough to bounce a dime on the sheets, and never move the bed frame an inch. This bed had been deliberately rigged. If Nellie had flopped down on the mattress as she did every night—a dramatic drop backward that always got a laugh from the crew when places were called—she could have slid right onto the floor. She could have been injured as seriously as, say, someone who arrived home to a darkened house where marbles had been spilled on the floor. Jane Wheel knew it didn't take a Jane Wheel to figure out this was another one of Bumbles's prank accidents.

Jane decided not to mention this to Henry, who was checking all of the legs to make sure they were locked.

"Henry, that plaid shirt looks just like the one Marvin wore," said Jane, gently, conscious that she was reminding him of his lost friend.

"Yes, I borrowed some of his work shirts for my Perkins wardrobe. I didn't have the right thing in my closet, and you know we all pretty much self-costume around here," said Henry. "Makes me feel a little closer to him now," he added, his blue eyes wet and bright.

Henry evened up the legs of the bed and sat on it himself, bouncing a bit to make sure that the frame was solid. Don had come over to Jane's side, watching Henry along with her.

"Seems like old Henry knows how to fix it," said Don.

Jane looked at her father.

"Henry could always take things apart and put them back together."

Don strolled back to where Nellie was putting on a large nightgown over her clothes, arguing with a crew member who had suggested she remove her sweatshirt and slacks so the nightgown would not be so bulky.

Jane looked over at Tim. He was decked out as suave Detective Craven but looked more like a trench coat–wearing six-year-old holding back tears. Rica Evans had gone off into a corner, her lips moving, going over lines. Mary Wainwright was still clinging to a script, or more accurately, *scripts*. She must have snagged scripts from the extras if not the principals since she had several opened and bookmarked to her various scenes. She planted them all over the stage. Jane saw one on the bar, one tucked under the pillow on the hospital bed; another was balanced on the rim of a potted plant. Chuck Havens was stroking his imaginary beard, Henry Gand was stashing his tools in the wings and vocalizing, and the other cast members—Peggy and the rest who played the dinner-party guests—were chatting and milling about.

"Enough," said Jane, loudly enough to silence the cast and two volunteer crew members who were underutilized and bored silly. She looked over at Tim with her brows raised. She didn't have to ask the question out loud. Tim answered by giving an enthusiastic nod and raising his hands in the air in surrender.

"I'm taking over as director," said Jane, "and we're going to have this play ready to open in two days. We're running through this final scene now, double-time, really fast, to make sure everyone has lines and blocking—then we're taking it from the top. Speed run-throughs to set everything. Tomorrow night, we are treating dress rehearsal as a performance—and you are all going to be ready."

Jane walked through the set, snatching up Mary's scripts.

"Mary, you are now officially off book. You know more than you think you do. Trust yourself and when you need a line, call "Line," and Don will give it to you," said Jane, handing her father a script and explaining his new duties as prompter. Jane trusted that Don's sense of duty and the concentration necessary to stay on book would prevent the coughing and sneezing attacks that began whenever Henry had a line.

"Chuck," said Jane. He smiled up at her, his right hand cupping his chin. "You don't have a beard. Stop that gesture now. We can't hear your lines if you cover your mouth.

"Tim, lose the phony accent. You go from Brit to German to some weird Scandinavian and it's a distraction. This play takes place in the Eekaknak Valley. That's *Kankakee,* people. Be articulate without being affected. Got it?"

Tim nodded, beaming. No one had ever looked so pleased when publicly berated.

"Rica, what you're doing is lovely, but you need to vary your seriousness. I know you're trying to balance the scenes you're in, but don't worry about the others. You can be playful with Craven and still be true to your character." Rica looked so pleased to be given a note that Jane noticed she had a lovely smile, which no one in this cast had ever seen.

"Henry, you're a little erudite for a gardener, so unless you know a secret about Perkins's life, you can tone it down a bit.

"Cousin Flip, party guests, and other cast and crew? Quiet when you are offstage. This is no longer a recreational and social activity. People will be paying money for tickets and they expect to see a coherent story effectively told onstage. They don't want to hear offstage giggles and gossip. Crew members, I've asked you to wear all black for the entire week," said Jane, looking over her volunteers, one decked out in a red T-shirt and khaki cargo pants and the other in jeans and a Hawaiian shirt. "Do so tomorrow and wear gym shoes so you are quiet and fast and efficient when you dash out to set props. And stop making eye contact with various people in the front of the house. No interaction with the audience, please.

"And Nellie," said Jane, squaring off and facing her mother. "No more using pillows as your stand-in. You need to be in the bed, remaining still and quiet. No muttering, no huffing and puffing and critical remarks, and no tossing and turning. No sound, no movement during the speeches of the other actors. You agreed to do *this* part, Marguerite, in *this* play, so please do it or allow us to find a substitute right now."

If the cast and crew had been standing at attention as Jane asserted authority, the new stillness, when she ordered Nellie to straighten up and fly right, raised the ante on silence to an otherworldly level. All the clichés of quiet—hearing a pin drop, quiet as a morgue, still as death—were dwarfed by the collective breath-holding, muscle-freezing, airless, zero-gravity atmosphere that enveloped the theater when Jane and Nellie faced off. Time did not exactly stand still, but it did hold its breath until Nellie began nodding her head. Standing there in her five-foot majesty, wearing an oversized white nightgown over her clothes, she looked from side to side at the gaping cast and crew of *Murder in the Eekaknak Valley*.

"What the hell are you looking at? You heard her."

With that, Nellie climbed into the now solid hospital bed, pulled the sheets up to her chin, and folded her hands on top of the covers, the very epitome of the well-behaved comatose matriarch.

As everyone scattered to their places for the final scene,

Jane walked over to the bed and peered down at her mother. Nellie opened her eyes and gave her daughter a Nellific version of a smile, one corner of her mouth grudgingly curving upward while the other remained resolutely in place. She then winked.

"It's about time you took over," said Nellie in a raspy whisper. "Now let's get this show on the road."

Jane liked doing fast run-throughs. When she was in college, a director she knew had always started rehearsals with a speed run-through as a warm-up. It was fun, energizing, and the perfect introduction to a rehearsal session that would eventually be filled with starts and stops. During a speed run-through, however, there were no stops. If an actor got lost or forgot a line, the scene progressed, one actor coming in to just continue, just keep the story moving forward. When it worked, it clarified the story and livened up the action. Actors usually discovered something brand new about their characters when they zoomed through their scenes.

Jane's speed run-through of *Murder in the Eekaknak Valley* did liven up the actors. Once Tim stopped struggling with his accent, he became more relaxed and playful, doing a credible job with Craven, which was essential for the plot twist at the end of the play. Jane wasn't sure that anyone in the audience was going to be surprised by the ending of Freddy's play, since he had clearly cribbed much of his work from every mystery melodrama he had ever seen or read, but at least Tim was now fun to watch.

Rica Evans blossomed. She had always been in control onstage, but now she felt free enough to smile and flirt with Craven and her soon-to-be-ex-son-in-law, Malachi, whose scheming and blackmailing words, now that Chuck Havens had removed his hand from his face, could finally be understood.

Mary Wainwright struggled, but stammered through her scenes better than she had when trying to find her place in the various planted scripts.

Nellie was quiet. She remained still, a hint of a Mona Lisa smile playing around her mouth. Tim had suggested one of the extras come in as a nurse/caretaker, helping her to turn, so her face could be hidden and she wouldn't be under any pressure to keep her eyes closed and her face rigid, but Jane didn't like the interruption. Instead she suggested that Rica come over and adjust the covers so that they were higher under Nellie's chin, and her expression hidden.

It was a tender moment when Rica adjusted the covers and spoke to her mother, explaining why she had left so many years before, abandoning both her mother and daughter for a career, with Perkins the gardener and Hermoine, her daughter, listening in at the French doors at the back of the stage.

When Jane dismissed everyone for the evening, the actors gathered their notes and their bits of costuming that they needed to take home and iron or adjust, and in groups of two or three left by the lobby door. Tim told Jane to wait while he locked up the rear and side entrances to the building. Don wanted to wait, too, but Nellie was antsy about Rita waiting at the house for a bedtime walk and snack.

Jane sat in the empty theater, alone in an aisle seat, sixth row, and stared at the set. It was a miniature of the Kendell house, just as Freddy had instructed in the script. The paintings were hung in the precise spots, the candelabra was centered on the upstage left dining table. The black urn sat on the mantel, allegedly holding the ashes of Myra's stepfather, Marguerite's ne'er-do-well second husband, who, it would be revealed, had actually driven his stepdaughter out of the house and out of the

Eekaknak Valley. Jane made herself a note to actually fill the urn with gray sand so when it was thrown at the end of the play, the audience would see the ashy remains scattered throughout the set. She also made a note to have a crew member double-check the hospital bed between acts, not just before curtain.

"Jane, could I have just a moment?"

Jane thought Mary Wainwright had left with Chuck, so she started at the voice behind her. Damn, she had perfected the throaty, raspy voice she had been practicing since they were teenagers. Jane thought it suited her much better now. She turned to Mary, who stood in the aisle looking apologetic and a little fearful. Jane couldn't help but think that if she could use that look in the play when Hermione confessed to her mother, Myra, that she had read her diary, it would be much more convincing.

Another thought came in for a hard landing when Jane turned to Mary. Mary had been a friend of hers in high school. They had been rivals, yes, but they had also been friends, and it was only after high school, after years had risen up between them, that Jane had let her resentment about the competitions between them grow. Looking at Mary now, Jane realized that she had missed her. Jane didn't have any old friends besides Tim, and no girlfriends at all. She had been so hell-bent on leaving Kankakee behind and having a career, and so caught up with Charley and Nick and all of her stuff, that she had forgotten that she had a younger self. And wasn't her resentment of Mary partially constructed from her own guilt of leaving behind everyone, except Tim, who wouldn't let himself be left behind, and never bothering to look back, never trying to keep in touch?

Damn, it was the magic of sitting in an audience, working on a play, in a now-empty theater. It always got to Jane, making her nostalgic for what might have been. She could hear the squeaking wheels of the stage light, the naked safety bulb, which Tim must be bringing out onto the set before they closed up.

"Jane, did you hear me?" said Mary.

"No, actually, I didn't. I'm so tired and I haven't really eaten all day. I was a million miles away," said Jane.

"I'm sorry," said Mary, and then added, "about the scripts."

"Oh Mary, don't worry about that. You have the scenes down, you don't need the crutches anymore. I remember," said Jane, smiling, "that you were excellent as Lady Macbeth when we did the Shakespeare scenes junior year. And that was a lot harder to memorize."

"You remember that?" said Mary. "I think that might have been the most fun I had in high school."

Mary looked so wistful that Jane knew she wasn't the only one who grew nostalgic in an empty theater.

"Anyway, I'm sorry about all the scripts. I shouldn't have taken them. Here are some more," Mary said, laughing. She handed Jane five more play scripts.

Jane noticed each of the covers was a slightly different shade of yellow. One had the title *Murder in the Eekaknak Valley* printed in red rather than black.

"Where did these come from?" said Jane. "You have more scripts than there are extras in the cast."

"I didn't get them from the cast members," said Mary. "I got them from Freddy's studio. He had this space over the garage that he used for a theater club where—"

"How?" asked Jane, standing. "How did you . . ."

Mary's apologetic look returned.

"I'm the Realtor who listed the house. The key to Freddy's club was on the ring that Rick Kendell gave me. I took it off so that no other agent could have access to the garage or coach house. Rick called me and insisted I do that once he realized he had given me the whole ring of keys. I was not to open that space during an open house. Rick and Margie were supposed to go up there before we could show it. I figured it was just storage, but I had the key and I wanted to see the whole property so I decided one day to just pop in. I saw all these scripts on the shelf behind Freddy's desk and I grabbed them all. I planned on photocopying my lines and planting them around the stage, just in case, but I hadn't had time so I just figured I could plant scripts. But it made things worse. Every time I picked up a script to study lines, I got them all jumbled. I even remembered the cues wrong. Whenever we practiced together, I accused Chuck of gaslighting me—you know, making me think I was crazy because it seemed like his cues were different all the time. I made him show me in his script where he was and where I was. Honestly, I think I really might be losing my mind."

Jane looked at the five scripts Mary had given her. She stuck them into her tote bag with the other three she had confiscated from the set.

"Do you have the key to the coach house with you?" asked Jane.

"No, the key's at home. I heard about Rick Kendell. He was a jerk, but still . . . ," Mary shook her head. "Still a terrible thing that somebody killed him. Made me feel even worse for going against his wishes and sneaking into Freddy's club."

Right. Jane was sitting here all smug about turning around the play and holding a decent rehearsal, completely blocking out the fact that the evening had started with a murder.

Mary patted Jane's shoulder awkwardly and turned to leave.

When she was almost to the door to the lobby, Jane called out, "How did you hear about Rick Kendell?"

Mary thought for a moment, then shrugged.

"Rica, maybe? Everyone in the cast was talking about it.

Most of us had been at the memorial and every time one person mentioned what a creep Kendell had been, rubbing it into Suzanne's face that she was going to lose Geppetto Studios, somebody else would tell them he had been murdered. I heard we all have to talk to the police. Got around pretty fast," said Mary. "I'll have to talk to Margaret about the listing on the house now, but it can wait."

Mary waved and turned to leave. Tim had jumped down from the stage and was now rubbing his knees, muttering about what a stupid thing that was to do, when Jane turned to him.

"Do you remember who told you about Rick Kendell?"

"What about him?" asked Tim.

Don and Nellie were sitting at the kitchen table eating ice cream when Jane and Tim walked in. Rita had been walked and treated and looked grateful to have all of her humans back in the same place again. It wasn't easy guarding your loved ones if your loved ones kept drifting away and leaving you behind.

Nellie jumped up and without asking first got up to scoop out two more bowls of ice cream.

"Any chocolate sauce, Nellie?" asked Tim, following her to the refrigerator and peeking in over her shoulder.

Nellie got out jars of hot fudge and caramel sauce, ignoring Tim's presence, almost closing the refrigerator door on his head.

"So what happens to the sale now?" asked Nellie. "Can Margaret okay everything by herself?"

"Nope," said Tim. "At least I don't think so. They were the heirs and now, I assume, Margaret is the sole heir to the property, but it's possible Rick could have left his half to someone. Maybe he has a significant other down in Florida?" Tim looked around the kitchen, waving the jar of hot fudge. "Still no microwave?"

Nellie grabbed the jar out of his hand and placed it into the pan of hot water she had already coaxed to a simmer.

"Don't need a microwave," said Nellie. "You all are going to grow tails if you keep using those inventions."

Tim looked like he might start up an old argument, just for fun. He even opened his mouth to protest but then closed it just as quickly and shrugged. He was too tired to engage. Don patted the chair next to him and Tim crossed the kitchen to sit down and wait for Nellie to spoon the hot fudge on his ice cream—just as she had done since he was a little boy.

Jane swiped her finger over "end call" on her cell phone and came over to the table. When Nellie pointed to the hot fudge, she nodded. Like Tim, she knew that if she sat down, Nellie would serve her up a giant sundae.

Nellie wasn't always in the kitchen, on duty, when Jane got home from school. She was usually still at the EZ Way Inn, finishing up the dishes from lunch, waiting for the three o'clock rush when the Roper Stove boys poured into the bar, but when Nellie was around—on weekends or after dinner—she waited on Jane, and when he was tagging along after her, Tim, too. Jane acknowledged that she and Nellie never had a particularly warm mother-daughter thing going, but at least Nellie treated her like a favorite customer. Even now, Jane smiled when she saw her mother give her an extra dollop of hot fudge and drizzled caramel over the top.

"Mom, I need to know some stuff about Freddy's theater club," said Jane.

Nellie shrugged and crouched down to rub Rita's ears.

"Freddy was a nut who always wanted a group of people around him, so he wrote plays and got us to practice and—"

"Yeah, I get all that, but what was the group like without Freddy? Were you all friends? Did you hang out together?"

"Jane, you know all this. I didn't go to high school. I worked at the hosiery factory. You think all those country club kids wanted to hang out with me? I lived alongside the tracks, remember?"

Jane nodded, remembering the Sunday visits to her Lithuanian grandmother's house. They sat in her spotless kitchen, Nellie nodding along to her mother's soft broken English, and then the rumbling and vibrating would start. Six times a day, the Illinois Central roared by, shaking the little house, stopping all conversation. The Schaltis family did, indeed, live on the side of the tracks.

"Well, it wasn't just the side, it was the wrong side, and all of them at Freddy's knew it. I was just the best memorizer," said Nellie.

"And the prettiest," said Don.

"Shut the hell up," said Nellie, passing out napkins to everyone.

"They're so cute when they get all romantic," said Tim.

"But you dated Henry, right?" said Jane. "Sorry, Dad, but I've got to figure this out. At first it was just all the valuables missing, but now Marvin's dead and Rick Kendell. There's something about Freddy's club—"

They all heard the knock at the kitchen door.

"Oh," said Jane.

"Who the hell comes by at this time of night?" said Nellie.

Don stood and motioned for Nellie to stay in her chair, but she ignored him and beat him to the door.

"Oh," said Jane. "I forgot to tell you that he was coming by. I wanted to look at the receipts that Claire had for all the art and antiques she had purchased for the Kendells."

Oh came in apologizing for intruding. Claire came in behind him, carrying a woven leather briefcase. It was nearly midnight and she still looked cool and calm and put together in tan slacks and a navy blue fitted jacket, a scarf tied at her throat.

Jane could feel hot fudge dripping down her chin. Without turning to look at her, Nellie handed Jane another napkin.

"Ice cream?" Nellie asked.

The Ohs shook their heads, and Nellie nodded, crossing to the stove and putting the kettle on. She busied herself getting out tea bags and sugar and lemon, but Jane could tell her mother remained at alert. All ears, all systems go.

"Claire wanted to bring the receipts herself," said Oh.

Was there a note of apology in his voice?

"I have a notebook and some photos, but I just thought I could explain some of the pieces better than little scraps of paper could," said Claire.

Don had pulled up two more chairs to the round kitchen table.

"How's Margaret?" asked Jane.

"It's been grueling," said Claire, "but I think she's pulling through okay." Claire looked at Bruce Oh, who nodded.

"We waited to come here until she was asleep. Identifying a relative for the police is never an easy chore, and for Margaret, even though Rick was not a good brother, he was the last relative," said Oh.

"Bryan and Penny Kendell?" asked Jane.

"Oh, they're just spongers," said Claire. "Distant cousins waiting for some crumbs to be tossed their way. Margaret said Penny had wanted to visit her at the motel this afternoon, but she was able to put her off."

"This afternoon?" said Jane. "Wasn't Margaret at the house with you washing dishes . . . and I saw Penny at the memorial for Marvin."

"We left the house around three, didn't we, Nellie?" asked

Claire. "Margaret wanted a nap and I wanted to go over this book again. I keep thinking I've missed something in that house," Claire paused, cocking her head as if she surprised herself by what she had just said. "And I never miss anything."

Jane did a little time check in her head. The memorial probably ended around three thirty. At least Rick had stopped his petty little speech by then. People had remained chatting and consoling Suzanne, but Jane had been talking to the carpenters and looking around the shop. Could Bryan and Penny have said their good-byes, met Rick out in front, and, between the two of them, switched the mannequin, encouraged him to sit and talk family business, then killed him? Then Penny might have called Margaret, hoping to get rid of her, too, so she and Bryan would be the last Kendells standing? Jane really hadn't paid attention to who left when. She envied those fictional detectives who always had just glanced at the clock before they heard a scream or the witnesses who had checked their watches the minute they heard a shot. All Jane knew at this point was that she and Oh had arrived at Geppetto Studios shortly after lunch, had momentarily gotten hung up in the stage set office where Marvin had set up the Lew Archer/Sam Spade dead detective tableau, or whatever the hell it was supposed to be, then walked through the doors that hid the enormous workspace from the front, walked the length of half a block through the scene shop area to the partitioned-off back where the memorial site was set up. Jane had found Rick Kendell's body around five? Five thirty? That did it. Jane promised herself she would start wearing a watch. She knew it was after seven by the time they left, after reporting the murder, after talking to Ramey.

And after finding the typed note from Mr. Bumbles.

"Look at this," said Claire. "That silver vase, eighteenth-century American? I found that for Margaret's mother, when she still had money or thought she did. Artistry, function, and history. A piece by this silversmith sold a few months ago at auction for over a million. And that's in this economy. Museum quality," said Claire. Jane watched her stroke the pencil sketch of the piece with her index figure. Jane wondered why a sketch.

"Oh I have digital photos on file, but I don't print everything. I just sketched this one out because I bought a few pieces at the same auction and I wanted to be clear about which client took which piece."

Nellie snorted as she handed Claire her tea. It was subtle, but Jane heard it. It was the sort of sound her mother made whenever anyone pronounced the word *vase, vaaaz.*

"That *vaaaz,*" said Nellie, "looks just like one of my sister Veronica's bowling trophies."

Jane paged through the receipts Claire had brought while Tim filled Oh in on Jane's takeover of *Murder in the Eekaknak Valley.*

"She was a theater major in college, you know, and she hasn't lost a step," said Tim. "She was masterful."

"Perhaps one never loses the mastery of one's first true vocation," said Oh.

"Avocation," said Jane. "I only *thought* I was called to the stage."

Jane selected three receipts for paintings. "Are these the ones that were supposed to be sent to auction?"

Claire nodded.

"Did you go with Margaret to identify her brother's body?" Jane asked Oh.

"We both did," said Claire. "Bruce had texted that Rick was in town, which I told Margaret. She was pleased enough that she wouldn't have to go through the house sale business alone. I'm not sure she believed Rick had stolen those pieces anyway. She didn't think he'd come to town if he had taken them. Anyway, I told her to rest up so she'd have her wits about her when we confronted Rick. I went back to my room to make some business calls.

"We had vowed to find someplace in this town for dinner where the main course wasn't breaded or deep-fried. So after Bruce called the second time to tell me Rick was dead, I went to Margaret's room and she was getting ready for us to go out. Bruce arrived and we told her together and she was pretty strong, I'd say."

"Yes," said Oh. "Identifying a body is more than difficult, but she managed the task."

"Keep in mind, Bruce, she's always had a fragile nature, but she has a fine mind, a tough mind. She wanted to be a doctor, so maybe that helped today," said Claire. "Her work as a scientist."

Jane looked up from the receipts.

"Margaret has a job?" asked Jane. "I didn't know she actually worked."

"Well, no, not a job, but she went to college and I think she majored in math and science."

"Like you majoring in theater," said Nellie to Jane.

"But Freddy wanted her to go into show business," said Claire.

"Freddy wanted everyone to go into show business," said Nellie.

Don waved from the doorway, yawning.

"Maybe you theater folks can stay up all night, but saloon keepers need their beauty sleep."

As hard as she tried to resist, Jane caught the yawning from her father. It had been one of the longest days she could remember—after a fairly short night. Oh handed her a copy of the police report that Detective Ramey had shared with him.

"Nice guy," said Jane. "Nicer than any of the other police I've met here."

"He's new, Mrs. Wheel. He isn't familiar with your penchant for finding bodies in Kankakee."

"It was a nail gun," said Jane, reading. "That's what I thought I heard them say." She wondered why there wasn't more blood at the scene. Everything had been so clean. Oh would be able to explain the reason, but she really didn't want to ask the question and have that conversation before going to sleep.

"Jeez," said Nellie. "That's a new one. Who the hell would think of using a nail gun?"

"A carpenter?" said Oh. Claire had already stepped outside and Oh turned back from the door. "All of those scene builders who were there?"

"The Geppettos," said Jane. She waved, covering another yawn with the other hand.

"And Suzanne," she added. "I'll bet Suzanne knows her way around a nail gun."

21

Amazing what six solid hours of sleep could do. Jane opened her eyes and stretched, reaching for her phone and the notebook she had parked on the table next to the bed.

First she sent Nick an e-mail, telling him it was practically opening night and his grandma's stage debut. It was easier to type *debut* than try to explain *comeback* using this tiny little cell phone keyboard. She gently reminded him that it might be nice to try to call Nellie over the weekend if they went into town. He had been so good about keeping in touch with her and, as he had requested, Jane had kept her part of the bargain, joining Facebook and Twitter, even if she was a reader and lurker. She followed all of the news and tidbits about the dig, then sent Nick private messages. She hadn't wanted Nick to know that he was her only Facebook friend, but how could she hide all that information on the side of the screen? It wasn't that she wanted other imaginary online friends—she couldn't help it—she thought of all the Facebook friends and tweetees as imaginary. Even so, having only one friend made her sound lonely—in a not-so-imaginary way.

Jane watched today's slideshow of the artifacts they were finding. Seeing Nick looking so tanned and tall and grown-up, holding his own among the college students who were all there for credit or the graduate students who were there for internships, warmed her absentee mother's heart. This was a good summer for Nick. And Charley? He looked good, too. It would catch her by surprise, seeing Charley in a photograph. He wasn't in many. Jane assumed that was because he was usually the photographer, but every once in a while, his crinkled half smile would take her by surprise.

Jane had spent the winter mourning the loss of her marriage, but not because she thought it should continue. She knew better. She and Charley had chosen occupations that kept them from each other, their passions were separate—equal maybe, and sometimes even equally respected by the other, but certainly separate—and that should have been the biggest clue that things were ending. But Jane didn't like to fail at anything. And she didn't love Charley any *less* exactly. But she had to be honest with herself. She didn't love him any *more,* either. And to stay married to someone, to really make it for the long haul, Jane knew you had to keep loving the other person more.

Jane let the screen on her phone go dark.

She jotted down things she needed for tonight's dress rehearsal. Tim had informed her just before leaving last night that there might be a few extra people in the audience tonight.

"How many?" Jane had asked. "Who?"

Tim had shrugged and just said that the president of the theater board had left a message for Tim on his cell phone that he would see him at the invited dress.

"It's an invited dress?" asked Jane. "Why didn't you tell me?"

"I didn't invite anybody," said Tim. "Probably just a few board members are coming. No big deal," he added, obviously unaware of what an invited dress could turn out to be.

When Jane appeared in a play in college that held an invited dress rehearsal, it was treated like an opening night. The actors invited their friends and other students in the department came. For some of their shows, the audience on the night of the free invited dress was larger than any their entire run. Tim might be right that just a few board members would be attending, but Jane didn't want to take any chances. She planned on inspecting all the props and checking everything onstage herself long before they raised the curtain at eight. The cast was called for six, so that gave Jane the entire day to run errands, hem her mother's stage nightgown, pick up sand at the hardware store or think of something else that could represent the stepfather's ashes, and maybe even figure out who killed Rick Kendell. And Marvin. Poor Marvin. Jane thought about how unfair it was that a first murder was so often forgotten in the face of a second.

Nellie was in the kitchen making breakfast when Jane came in, searching for coffee. When Jane asked her why she hadn't gone in to work with her dad, Nellie shrugged.

"It's practically opening night, ain't it? I took the day off."

Jane looked at Nellie, who turned away quickly, flipping pancakes expertly, catching one after the other in the frying pan. Something was different. Was Nellie wearing makeup? Eyeliner? Mascara? Jane thought of a dozen different jibes, payback for all of the times Nellie teased her about a different haircut or laughed at her outfit or said her earrings were too dangly or told her if she consented to wear lipstick, she ought to at least pick out a nice shade. Jane smiled and touched her mother's shoulder.

"You look so pretty," said Jane.

Nellie slid the pancakes onto a plate.

"Thank you," she said.

Jane poured coffee for both of them.

"Is this okay for tonight?" asked Nellie, waving her hands over her face.

Jane nodded. "Maybe a little stronger on the eyeliner, but that's all. You don't really need blush, being that you're in a coma and all."

"Yeah, but I come out of it at the end," said Nellie, pouring syrup on a pancake for herself and cutting up a plain one for Rita, who sat at her feet.

Jane did not want to argue with her mother, not with her wearing makeup and serving up blueberry pancakes when it was only a Thursday, but Jane didn't think Nellie's interpretation of the smile on Marguerite's face at the end of the play was accurate. Nellie had said all along that when Marguerite smiled, it meant she woke up and had known who committed the murder all along, but Jane saw it differently. From her first reading, she had interpreted the beatific smile that was on Marguerite's face to mean that she had died a peaceful death when her daughter and granddaughter were reconciled and the killer unmasked.

Since there were no final lines given to Marguerite and the stage direction was simply *Marguerite, breathing softly in her hospital bed, smiles as the lights fade,* Jane figured there was no reason to argue the interpretation with Nellie. She had told Tim's friend Bill, who was running lights, to fade the spot on Marguerite quickly, just in case Nellie decided to turn the enigmatic smile into a wide-eyed grin. That should ensure a peaceful final curtain.

Jane dragged her large leather tote bag over to the kitchen table. She had scored the bag at a garage sale for next to nothing and it had become her favorite accessory. Tim always fought her on the use of that word: *An accessory accessorizes, dear; it adds glamour and glitz and style and pulls your look together.* Jane preferred to think of accessory as essential, something that added to her effectiveness, and this tote held almost everything she needed in her day-to-day.

Reaching into the bag and fishing through the mini-notebooks, hand sanitizer, packages of plastic gloves, energy bars, digital tape recorder, tissues, antiseptic wipes, Gummi Grapefruits, scissors, stapler, double-sided tape, she finally found the object of her desire.

The sewing kit was the only item she had purchased at her first estate sale. She had wandered among the piles of linens and stacks of dishes and precariously balanced china cups, musing on the life of this elderly woman who had died alone in an upstairs bedroom, according to one of the neighbors gossiping to whoever would listen. Jane was so overwhelmed with the stories told by each of the items, the contents of her drawers and jewelry boxes now turned out and exposed to the world—gold portrait stickpins wrapped in tissue, a celluloid box with two pale, dry, four-leaf clovers tucked inside—she could barely focus enough to select one thing to buy. She found the sewing kit on a dressing table, reached for it as another person pushed past her and, with a satisfied smirk, grabbed a rhinestone encrusted hand mirror. Jane had no desire for the mirror, no desire to see herself—she wanted to see the old woman, to hold something in her hand that had been held by her, something that had been of use, that had been cherished and needed. The sewing case. For one dollar, Jane bought a share in another's history. Soft baby-blue leather with a sturdy zipper and button flaps opened to reveal threads, needles, a finely balanced pair of scissors, and a silver-engraved thimble—EDS. Jane made up a name for the original owner of the thimble and, today, hoped Edna Dolores Savarin would smile down on her and aid her in hemming Nellie's nightgown. Jane thought this might be the closest she came to true prayer.

Jane set the sewing kit on the table and pulled out the scripts she had confiscated from Mary last night and the five additional she had voluntarily surrendered. Jane lined them up on the table in front of her and got up to replenish her coffee.

"Mom, bring me your costume and I'll get started hemming it so you can manage your curtain call," Jane called. "And a spool of white thread, too." Jane knew that the threads in the case were no longer strong, and she couldn't bear to unravel them from their tiny Bakelite spools.

She could have left this chore up to the costume helper or Tim for that matter. He could sew a better hem than Jane could. But there was something soothing about this work. It made it okay for her to dawdle over coffee and sit in her mother's kitchen. Besides, the hardware store didn't open until nine and hand sewing would help her think.

Each of Mary's pilfered scripts looked slightly different. They varied in usage—from new-looking to worn and bent—but their differences were greater than their individual condition issues. The shades of yellow on the covers varied from a pale butter to an orange-gold. On one of the covers, the lettering was in red rather than black and two of them had a variation of the author's name. The others were all by Frederick Kendell Junior except for two that were more casually attributed to Freddy Kendell.

Jane opened up one of the scripts.

> I dedicate this play to my grandchildren, Ricky and Margie. Follow your muse, children, and you will never take the wrong path.

That was slightly different from the dedication in the script Jane had been using, wasn't it? She opened the next script, which she noticed had a faded number four penciled into the inner corner.

> To Rick and Margaret. The future is yours.

Odd. Jane opened up each of the scripts and found five different dedications. The one that interested Jane the most was the one in the script with the title printed in red.

To Margaret . . . your future is here. I have done my best.

Jane opened up the script and began to read the play. When Nellie came in with a spool of white thread and a giant sewing basket, she looked at the scripts spread out on the table and saw Jane engrossed in a copy. She set down the basket, refilled her daughter's coffee cup, and left the room. If Jane hadn't been totally absorbed in what she was reading—yes, *Murder in the Eekaknak Valley,* but a considerably different version than the one that was to have its invited dress rehearsal that very night—she would have heard her mother heaving open the door to the attic, pulling down the creaky ladder, and climbing up to a small storage space under the rafters. Jane, however, was oblivious.

Since she was familiar enough with the play to skim through many scenes that were the same or almost the same as the version they were doing, Jane was midway through by the time Nellie returned to the kitchen.

"I apologize," said Jane, looking up at her mother.

"It's about time," said Nellie.

"Do you know what I'm talking about?" said Jane. "Why I'm apologizing?"

"Maybe," said Nellie, pouring herself a cup of coffee and topping off Jane's mug.

Jane leafed through another script until she got to the second act. In the first one she read, Marguerite was not in a coma. She was ill, and in and out of consciousness. She revealed the family secrets that had driven Myra away from home: the abusive second husband, the affair with Perkins the gardener. In the next script Jane chose, she compared the same scene, and Marguerite revealed that Perkins the gardener was the father of Myra.

"Holy Toledo," said Jane. "Freddy was a real writer, wasn't he? He never stopped rewriting."

"Yeah, he drove everybody crazy. He would have a new idea every day," said Nellie. "And when he was afraid we'd all get mad at him, he'd have that dummy, Bumbles, announce there was a new version. It was creepy, but then Henry would yell at the dummy about memorizing lines and we'd all start laughing because it was so goofy to be arguing with the doll and Freddy would just jolly us all up again and we'd start over."

"So the play was never produced, but . . ."

"You ask me, Freddy never wanted the play put on. We'd be almost ready and Freddy would give us a new script. He liked writing and he liked rehearsing, having everybody around for the club, but he didn't give a damn about the play being put on."

"Maybe that's why all those little Mr. Bumbles notes were stuck in the scripts. They were Freddy's way of warning people away from the play itself," said Jane, picking up another script and paging through. "After he had his heart attack and couldn't keep the club going, maybe he couldn't bear to destroy the copies of the play, but he worried about somebody coming in and finding all those scripts."

"Like Lowry," said Nellie.

"Yup, just like that. What do you know about the club and the group who was rehearsing the play after you dropped out?"

"Well, I met your dad and I walked. If I thought we were really going to do the damn play, I might have stuck with it. But Don came along just when I was getting fed up anyway," said Nellie. "Tell you the truth, I never really saw the people from the club after that. Henry kept calling for a while, but he got fed up, too. He wanted to be an actor so he moved to California. And Marvin wanted to make sets for plays that really got put on, so he moved to Chicago. I'd see him around every once in a while, though. Came back here a lot. Let's see," said Nellie. "Rica Evans's mom passed away, and that Bryan Kendell married one of the girls in the group, not that Penny but—"

"Rica Evans's mother?" said Jane.

"Yeah, I didn't know her very well, she was a lot older than me. But Rica looks like her, so I asked her and she said her mom was Barbara, who I remember from rehearsals and stuff."

"Was there anybody in this town who wasn't in Freddy's theater club?" asked Jane.

Nellie shook her head. "Don't know about that, but Freddy wouldn't have turned anybody away who wanted to be. He saw himself as a combination playwright and director and camp counselor and child psychiatrist or something. He said there wasn't enough places for creative types and artists and sometimes kids didn't feel at home in their own homes and he wanted them to always have a safe place to come to."

Jane looked at her mother and remembered she had been forced to quit school and work in the Bear Brand hosiery factory to bring in a paycheck to help her family.

"Was Freddy's club a safe haven for you, Mom?"

"Hell, no. I had a home and my own mom and dad. I just wanted to put on the goddamn play."

Jane took the script Nellie offered her.

"Was this the final one, the one you were rehearsing when you met Dad?"

Nellie nodded. "Probably not final, but Freddy had that heart attack pretty soon after I left, so I don't know if he kept writing after this one."

Jane read the dedication.

For my dear grandchildren—Margaret and Frederick III

Jane knew a treasure when she held one in her hand. It wasn't because this script revealed anything new about Freddy and the club. This was an earlier version than some of the scripts spread out before her. She could tell by the dedications that grew increasingly more pointed about the play being the inheritance Freddy was earmarking for his grandchildren. This particular script's value was in Nellie's margin notes, her underlined part. This was part of the Nellie archive that Jane hadn't even known existed, Nellie's life before Jane and her brother, Michael; before the EZ Way Inn; before Don. This little volume had some power.

"May I hang on to this?" asked Jane.

Nellie nodded. "What about the rest of these?"

"I think this is the order they were written. Or rewritten, actually," said Jane, who had lined up the scripts on the table. "Mostly, it looks like he played with Marguerite and Myra's scenes. They go back and forth between Marguerite in a coma or explaining things at the end. And the stepfather who is long gone—his character changes, too. He's revered, then he's a villain. In the last script, his ashes up on the mantel are a shrine—at least until the end. In the earlier ones, they talk about throwing the ashes in the trash bin."

Nellie picked up one of the scripts and read a few pages. "Freddy's still bossy. He tells everybody exactly how to do everything and what kind of couch should be on the stage and what kind of painting is on the wall. He even makes it part of the speech. Like here, he's got Perkins saying something about the cow in the picture. You can tell Freddy put that in so you'd know that's the picture he wanted up on the wall."

"A lot of playwrights are pretty specific about stage direction and props, but Freddy's right up there with the most particular," said Jane. "He even specified the lamps and the wallpaper and the urn for the stepfather's ashes, all of the vases and even what kind of flowers should go in the vases," said Jane. "It was really important to him that the Kendell mansion be re-created as the stage set. I think that's why he was so specific. But if the script is some kind of a treasure map, I'm just not following yet."

"Don't we have things to do before the play tonight?" asked Nellie.

"We?" said Jane. "Tonight's your debut. You should just relax . . ." Jane stopped and looked at her mother. Nellie looked back at her, head cocked to one side, defying her daughter not to give her a job.

"First, walk Rita, then I can go to the hardware store and pick up some sand or potting soil or something. We have to put something in the urn that will seem like ashes spilling when it gets tipped in the fight. I'll call Oh and find out what he knows from the police and see how Margaret's doing. We can take it from there," said Jane.

Nellie nodded and grabbed Rita's leash. Rita sat waiting for Nellie to snap it onto her collar, but Nellie held up and gestured with the leather braid. "Now that you've seen all of them scripts when Marguerite knows all the answers, don't you think at the end, she wakes up?"

"Yeah, Mom. Marguerite probably knows what's going on the whole time."

Jane waited until Rita led Nellie down the street, then she picked up her phone to call Oh. As she told Nellie, she wanted to ask after Margaret and find out if Oh knew anything more about Rick Kendell, alive or dead. If, for example, they knew more about why he had shown up, they might know more about who had killed him.

"Mrs. Wheel," said Oh. "I was just about to call you."

Jane smiled. As Nellie and Rita had rounded the corner at the end of the block, she had sat down on the top step of the porch, planting herself in the only triangle of sunlight allowed by the not-quite-fully-leafed-out trees in Don and Nellie's front yard. In another few weeks, there would be no sun-warmed step; the shade would keep everything dark and cool all day long. Jane wrapped her arms around her knees and leaned her head against the porch rail to listen to Oh's report.

"Then I decided to wait until I arrived."

Jane sat up straight, aware of her silly grin and schoolgirl pose on the steps as Oh pulled his car into the driveway.

Both continued holding their phones until Oh sat down beside her on the steps. Shaded and cool. *Appropriate,* thought Jane. *She, exposed and sunlit, Oh, shaded and cool.*

"Rick's autopsy is scheduled for tomorrow morning," said Oh. "Margaret decided she would let Bryan help her with the arrangements. He's really the only relative, and although they were never close, Margaret needs to depend on someone. Claire, of course, has already done most of the advising. Margaret just needs a relative to help her to agree and move on."

"Everybody in Kankakee had a key to Freddy's theater club," said Jane. "How do we figure out who our particular Mr. Bumbles is?"

"Everyone, Mrs. Wheel?"

Oh had remarked before on Jane's tendency to exaggerate, which prompted one of Jane's attempts to get Oh to laugh. "Yes, you've told me a million times not to exaggerate," Jane had said to him. Oh had not laughed, but he had almost smiled. "At least four times, Mrs. Wheel," he agreed.

"Nellie. Henry. Marvin. Bryan. Suzanne. Mary Wainwright, the Realtor. Apparently Rica Evans's mother was in the club."

"Margaret and Rick," added Oh.

If Freddy was playing child psychiatrist and social worker to young people and giving the artists in town a safe haven, almost anyone could have had a key. Anyone could have known that there were valuable items in the house, in the theater club space. The missing valuables could have easily been removed by any number of Kankakee residents. Jane herself had opened up the back gate and could have unloaded anything from the studio into her car without a neighbor around to see.

"So why kill Rick Kendell?" asked Jane. "It wasn't about stealing from the Kendell estate. That could be accomplished without much interference."

"According to Rick, presenting himself as the new landlord at Geppetto Studios, Suzanne would lose her workspace and her home," said Oh, looking at his vibrating phone.

He nodded to Jane and answered the phone as if it were part of the conversation they were having. When he clicked off, he told her that Ramey wanted to meet with them at the police station.

Nellie and Rita returned and Jane gave her mother a list of chores to be accomplished before the six o'clock call. Jane promised to keep in touch and apologized for not finishing hemming the nightgown.

"Anybody can sew a hem," said Nellie. "You got more important things to do today."

Jane felt herself blushing and before Nellie could squirm out of her grasp, she managed to give her mother a decent hug.

At the police station, Jane repeated what she had told Ramey the evening before—that she and Oh had shown up to ask questions about Mr. Bumbles, and stumbled into the memorial service for Marvin.

"But you knew Marvin?" asked Ramey.

"Yes, of course. We were working together and I was there when he . . . when the accident . . ." Jane stopped. How could she pretend to believe it was an accident? Marvin was dead and Jane thought whoever killed him could be connected to the Rick Kendell murder. It was time to act seriously about a serious subject.

"I'm not sure Marvin's death was an accident," said Jane. She was already picturing the swarm of police around the back of the cultural center, the taping off of the area, the closing down of the play after everyone had worked so hard. Ramey was distracted by something that flashed onto his computer screen.

He held up one finger and picked up his desk telephone, listening. After a one-syllable reply, he hung up and stood.

"That was the coroner calling on Kendell. Full autopsy scheduled, but we already know how— What did you say about Marvin?" asked Ramey.

"Nothing. Just said we showed up at his memorial accidentally," said Jane.

Oh, standing in the corner of the room, cleared his throat and turned away to look out the window.

"I've had a question about Rick Kendell since I found him," said Jane. She wasn't sure whether or not she wanted to claim the discovery so firmly, but maybe it would make her question seem more appropriate.

"Why wasn't there blood? I heard the officer tell you a nail gun was used and it seems like that would be messy, but the site was not— There wasn't really any blood."

"A sharp object inserted into the brain stem, right at the top of the spinal cord," said Ramey. "It's a fairly clean death."

"Clean?" asked Jane.

"Very little blood. It's how my teacher used to kill frogs for biology class," said Ramey.

"Oh my God, sophomore-year biology. Sister DiBlasi asked for volunteers. I remember that," said Jane.

"Pithing," said Oh.

Jane and Ramey both looked at him.

"It's called 'pithing.'"

That's just the kind of thing that Oh would know, thought Jane. She reminded herself that she should never agree to play Scrabble with him. As soon as she pictured the two of them sitting at her kitchen table leaning over a game board, she felt flushed, embarrassed that such a domestic thought had crossed her mind. Why would she and Oh ever spend an evening spelling out words together? And who besides Jane would ever think that an intimate enough pastime to be embarrassed by it?

"Are you all right, Mrs. Wheel?" asked Oh.

Jane nodded and finished giving her statement, managing to avoid the subject of Marvin's accident. Jane did tell Ramey about the note from Bumbles in the other typewriter, to which he nodded. They had the note and Jane told them that Mr. Bumbles's notes had appeared in the scripts, at the Kendell house, but that everyone at Geppetto Studios knew about the reference to Freddy's dummies.

"And do you have any idea who this Mr. Bumbles is?" asked Ramey.

"I honestly think some of the notes in the scripts might have been left there years ago by Freddy Kendell," said Jane. "There's something about the handwriting, the language . . . but as far as our contemporary Bumbles?" Jane shook her head.

What did she know? What facts? There was valuable property missing from the Kendell estate. Marvin had probably been killed by someone who wanted to keep his connection to Freddy's theater club quiet, and that Rick Kendell might have been killed by almost anyone who wanted to keep Geppetto Studios alive. In other words, she knew nothing that would be of value to Ramey. On the other hand, if she babbled on about her suspicions concerning Marvin's death and all of the interconnected members of Freddy's club, it was highly likely that the show would not go on this weekend, and Jane believed positively that if the show did go on, the murders of both Marvin and Kendell would be solved.

All of the answers were there—like all of those Scrabble tiles mixed up together in a bag. If she could just draw out the correct ones, the answer to the puzzle would be spelled out.

Ramey was thoughtful when he told her she was free to leave. "We'll talk again soon, Mrs. Wheel. It might help to continue to puzzle this out together."

Jane nodded. She had no idea whether Ramey was being kind or if he felt she was keeping something from him.

"Both," said Oh when they were back in the car and she asked what he thought. "Detective Ramey knows that you, too, are trying to figure out who is responsible, but I think he knows you have not yet reached any conclusions. I wouldn't be at all surprised if Detective Ramey and his team decided to attend the theater this weekend."

Jane asked Oh to make a stop at the hardware store, where she bought a small bag of sand, a bit of potting soil, and some granulated charcoal bagged for use in terrariums. She needed to mix up some concoction to be heavy enough that it could be seen from the audience when it spilled, but not so sandy and fine that it would be inhaled by the actors or fly into their eyes and blind them mid-scene.

Oh asked Jane to come with him to pick up Margaret and Claire at Bryan and Penny Kendell's home. Jane was sorely tempted because she wanted to see for herself how Bryan and Penny were handling the news about Rick. If they had anything to do with his death, they would be anxious to work their way into Margaret's affections, although that might be the case anyway. They were the only other Kendell relatives that Jane knew of, and perhaps Margaret would be sharing some of the household with them. Or they might just be trying to be helpful because they were her only relatives—maybe they just wanted to be helpful. When exactly had Jane begun to believe that everyone in the world had an ulterior motive for everything they did?

"No, thanks. I want to talk to everyone about Rick and I especially want to know when Bryan and Penny left the memorial, but you can find out all of that as well as I can," said Jane. "I have too much to do at the theater. Director tonight, detective tomorrow."

Jane walked into the cultural center and waited for that warm feeling of opening-night excitement to wash over her, but this time, being alone in the audience and looking up at Marvin's impeccable set did not give her the inexplicable giddies. Her footsteps echoed, and despite the warm sunshine outside, the theater felt dark and chilly.

She plopped her giant bag down on a front-row seat and dug out her notebook, folded it open to her list, and stuck it into the pocket of her jeans. She opened up her hardware store bag and looked at the mix she had asked them to stir up while still at the store. Did it look like cremains? She wasn't sure. She had never really seen the ashes of a cremated body, so she did not know if they were as ephemeral and delicate as fireplace ashes or if there was substance, bits of bone and such, that would give them more weight. She counted on the actors making such a fuss that the audience wouldn't have much time to reflect on the authenticity.

Jane filled the urn and replaced it on the mantel. It had two handles, like the loving cup Nellie had mentioned—her sister Veronica's bowling trophy. It was painted a thick, flat black and felt like chalkboard to the touch. Jane adjusted the urn so it was centered in front of the painting, a pastoral scene specified by Freddy in his notes.

Jane measured out the placement of the hospital bed, twelve steps from the stage right entrance in the first act where it was discussed that Marguerite would soon be coming home from the hospital and spending her final days there at the house with her daughter, Myra, and granddaughter, Hermione. Thinking about Mary's portrayal of Hermione, Jane paced the stage and checked out the hiding places where Mary had previously hidden the scripts to make sure no extra copies lingered.

Next, Jane made the bed, bouncing up and down on the mattress to make sure the legs were firmly slotted into place. She would ask her stage crew to double-check the bed between acts, too. Jane walked out the upstage French doors that were supposed to lead into the garden. Henry's garden rake was leaned carefully against the rear wall so he could grab it before entering. The small tin box he was to uncover that held the diary revealing the family secrets leading to the climactic final scene was also placed on a small table that held other personal props that actors would check and double-check for themselves.

Jane walked over to the bar, downstage left, and held up the bottles to see that there was enough "alcohol"—in actuality, weak tea left from rehearsal, for Myra to pour for her guests in the first act. Jane held up the cut-glass decanter she had found labeled as the appropriate prop in Freddy's trunk. The liquor looked real enough.

In fact, it looked so real, that Jane unstopped the heavy crystal and sniffed the liquid. Scotch. Who put real alcohol in the bottle? Rica was the only one who poured drinks . . . no, Malachi poured himself a drink and sipped while he reminisced aloud to Marguerite. Jane had suggested Tim add that bit of business since it gave Chuck Havens something to do with his hands, preventing him from stroking his imaginary beard. Had he planted real alcohol so he could have a belt midway through the play? Jane knew he secretly smoked; maybe he was a man of more than one vice.

Jane replaced the scotch with tea. She didn't want to take the chance that someone would grab that decanter and cough their way through a stage drink. Chuck would have to wait for the cast party for cocktails.

A large bulletin board hung backstage. There the actors could leave notes for one another, Jane and Tim left notes for the actors and each other, and the stage manager posted the calls. Next to the board hung a large clipboard. Jane used it to communicate directly with the stage manager, a young woman named Mandy who had been efficient throughout the rehearsal process. Jane checked off all she had done and wrote in a few chores she would expect Mandy to attend to. She signed it, *See you all at the cast party—break a leg! JW,* just in case she didn't get a chance to speak to everyone individually before they went on. After all, she had promised Tim he could still do the quality-of-life directorial stuff—all the preshow pep talks and rituals. Jane would just tend to the concrete directorial chores. Next to the hook for the clipboard, an envelope was stuck to the wall with a piece of wide masking tape. J AN E W H E E L was printed on the envelope.

Jane hoped it wasn't from the electrician who had stopped in yesterday to check the fuse box and lighting board. Her hope was for no surprises, not on opening night. But why would it say Jane Wheel? Until last night, Tim Lowry had been the director to whom any message would be addressed. The envelope wasn't sealed.

> Why isn't Mr. Bumbles appearing in your play? Bumbles doesn't like to be left out.

The letter provoked the chill Jane was sure it was meant to do. She had passed by this message board space only a few minutes before, pouring out the alcohol and replacing it with "alcohol," and hadn't noticed the envelope. She decided to take a chance that whoever was in the theater with her couldn't see her in this dark backstage corner. She carefully folded the message, reinserted it in the envelope, and retaped it to the wall. She hoped the Bumbles who was in the theater with her would not know that she had received the ominous note. Better to be the one setting the trap than the one for whom it was set.

Jane walked purposefully across the stage, skipped down the steps to the front row of the audience, and fished out her phone from her tote bag. She scrolled favorites, swiped her finger across a number, and hoped that there would be a real person on the other end. When instead she got a message, she pretended to converse through it, loudly, with as much enthusiasm and sincerity as she could muster, hoping that whoever might be in the theater to hear her would be convinced she was having a real conversation.

"I know where all the stuff is—the paintings, the silver. Yes, of course. It was so obvious. You knew it, too? That's great. Yes, as soon as you get here."

Jane clicked off the phone and hoped she had accomplished her mission. Speaking to Oh's voice mail, she hoped to lure out the Bumbles who was lurking in the theater, imply that she wasn't the only one who had the information, and stress how important it was for the cavalry to arrive.

"Jane Wheel! Hey, Jane Wheel!"

It was only a matter of time. Jane knew that. But as much as she tried to steel herself for this moment, it was still creepy beyond creepdom to look up at the stage and see Mr. Bumbles calling to her from the loveseat. He was seated on the back of the piece of furniture, and whoever was working his mouth and head must have been hiding behind the couch.

"Margaret?" called Jane. Margaret was the only one of this crowd who Jane was sure could throw her voice and knew how to work Mr. Bumbles.

"Oh come now," an equally creaky voice, this time from behind her, called out to Jane. "You don't think Margaret is the only one Freddy taught the fine art of ventriloquism?"

When Jane turned, another Mr. Bumbles, this one dressed in a khaki suit and intact bow tie was sitting about six rows back.

Jane couldn't have designed a better nightmare if she had tried. Not one, but two ventriloquists? Or was it one, throwing his or her voice to both dummies, and did she just imagine the jaw moving, the eyes rolling? She looked down at her phone, still in hand, and checked the time. Nearly five thirty. Someone would arrive any minute. The call was for six. Mandy, the stage manager was always on time, and Tim was usually early. He might walk in at any minute.

Jane stood in front of the stage facing the audience. She knew that one Bumbles was onstage behind her and one was directly in her sightline as she measured the distance to the front of the house. This was her make-or-break-famous-detective-heroine moment. How many times had she watched the stupid girl in the movie or, on occasion, the mindless boy, run deeper into the maze, climb higher into the attic, crawl farther into the tunnel instead of breaking into a zigzag run (harder to aim at) out of the enclosure—whatever it was—and head straight for the door. *Go toward the light* was what Jane was thinking, but before she started her run down the aisle, she heard a voice from the last row of the audience—right at the place she was focusing as her finish line.

"Don't think about running off toward the lobby, Jane Wheel. I can see Nellie walking down the street from where I am, and if you don't do as we say, your mother and your dog might have to do our bidding. Is that what you would prefer?"

The thing about ventriloquism is that the voice is thrown. Was there really someone in the lobby who could look out and see Nellie barreling down the street, leash in hand, right into the line of fire? Or was this a bluff from someone on the stage, hiding behind the couch with one hand up a puppet's behind?

Jane knew that the timing was right for Nellie to arrive. Forget Tim or the stage manager; it would be Nellie walking first through the lobby door. But she wouldn't have Rita with her, would she? Whenever had they brought the dog to rehearsal? It was someone who had watched them, who knew about Rita and knew that Nellie walked her, but Nellie wasn't heading toward the theater on foot right now. Bumbles was bluffing.

Jane wrapped her arms around her tote bag and took a deep breath, ready to head for the lobby, but forgot how to exhale when she felt what was, unmistakably, the cool cylindrical barrel of a gun in her back. The voice had been thrown, the Nellie threat wasn't real, but the gun and the ventriloquist behind her were metal, flesh, and blood. She might not have fallen for the actual bluff, but it had worked just the same, costing her the time she could have used for breaking out of the theater. And the squeaky voice that seemed to come from the rafters, telling her to turn slowly, keep her eyes forward, and walk backstage, might be misdirected sound, but the gun made it a pointed command that had to be obeyed.

The person prodding Jane from behind was either throwing his or her voice to confuse Jane or there was someone else in another location. When Jane tried to turn, the gun was pushed harder between her shoulder blades and she was told to keep her eyes straight ahead. A man? A woman? Who was this? Once they were backstage left, the voice of Bumbles instructed her to unhook the flimsy chain that blocked off a staircase that only went down. Jane had assumed the steps led to a storage area, and as she was pushed and prodded down the stairs, she was already thinking about what kinds of items might be stored under the cultural center theater stage. Furniture, props, costumes? And now, Jane Wheel? Damn, why had she left such a comprehensive note for Mandy? She even included a "break a leg," like she might not be around to say it herself. Would they even begin looking for her before six thirty or seven? After all, she didn't have a makeup or costume call, and even though Tim and Nellie would expect her to be there early, they wouldn't really panic if she wasn't there when they arrived.

Any girl detective manual would advise her not to go into a dark and enclosed space, but any manual worth its salt would also argue against denying the request of the person holding the gun. And so Jane walked through the door into what she thought was going to be a closet but turned out to be a much larger space, lit by an industrial work light hanging from a hook in the ceiling. Neatly stacked tables and chairs ringed the room. It was a pit-trap room, just like the one under the Playhouse stage at her college theater. The space extended beyond where Jane guessed the proscenium would be. They could even do musicals here with a small pit orchestra. Jane looked up at the low ceiling. She could barely make out some hinged squares. She hadn't even realized that this theater was so well equipped, so versatile. If they had wanted Marguerite's house to have a wine cellar, so Myra could send Perkins "downstairs" to fetch a few more bottles of the good stuff, they could have opened a square on the stage floor, built a little railing for effect, and placed a small staircase directly below—Jane saw one wheeled into the corner of the trap room—and Henry could have realistically descended into the "cellar" and climbed back up with his two prop bottles, previously placed on a table in the pit-trap room.

Jane stepped forward and Bumbles gave his creaky laugh. "Far enough, Jane Wheel, we're here."

Whether it was because Jane had just been thinking about Perkins the gardener and picturing him descending into the pit-trap room or whether she had caught Don's distrust of the man, Jane found herself curiously unsurprised to see Henry Gand standing in front of her, pointing a gun when she tentatively turned around. "Henry, why in the world are you doing this?"

"My dear girl, I heard you not more than five minutes ago say you knew where all the expensive Kendell treasures Freddy hid away were, so that means you know what they are and what they would fetch. What is it that you young people say? It's all about the Benjamins."

Jane knew how serious this situation was, but she couldn't help but be amused at Henry's characterization of her as one of the youngsters, and the fact that he thought Puff Daddy was the au courant slangmaster. He wasn't even Puff Daddy anymore, was he? You had to love someone a little for trying to keep up, even if they were holding a gun on you.

"Could you just tell us where they are, then we'll give someone a note and they can let you out after the play?" said a squeaky voice from behind her. She turned, expecting to see Bumbles sitting on the couch. Henry was good. She hadn't seen his lips move at all.

Looking at the figure on the love seat, she realized she hadn't seen Henry's lips move because Henry hadn't said anything. Instead, Suzanne was now doing the talking, still in a Bumbles voice, but as herself, sitting on the couch with a black hooded scarf folded neatly in her lap.

"You look surprised to see me," said Suzanne.

"I thought you didn't leave the studio. I thought you were agora—"

"No! No! Who told you that? Rick Kendell? He always called me the vampire, that little brat. I just have an illness. I can't be in sunlight. My eyes, my skin . . . I only go out at night, that's all."

"It's still light out now," said Jane.

"It's a special occasion," said Suzanne, refolding her scarf and face covering.

"We have to hurry, Jane," said Henry. "Just tell us and no one in the cast, not you or anyone, will be hurt. Right after the play, Suzanne will go her way, I will go mine—and you'll be discovered and released."

Jane had been facing Suzanne while Henry was talking. She saw her flinch when he said she would go her way.

"Where will Suzanne go?" asked Jane. "She won't be able to return to the studio. You'll have to help her find a safe place, won't you?"

"Of course, of course. I have some places in mind for her already," said Henry.

"If Marvin were here," said Suzanne, "none of this would have happened."

If Jane could keep them down here, if she could stall them long enough, cast and crew would arrive. Henry wouldn't be able to slip up the stairs unnoticed.

"What would Marvin do?" asked Jane.

"Marvin wouldn't have killed anyone!" said Suzanne.

"Don't start this again," said Henry. "You did what you had to do."

He handed his gun to Suzanne and told her to train it on Jane while he emptied her bag. He pried the tote from her hands and dumped its contents onto the floor. All of the scripts scattered, Jane's sewing kit, a flashlight, all of her notebooks, and three lipsticks rolled under the loveseat. Jane kept her eyes on Suzanne, who held the gun, but shook her head, pressing her lips together until they were pale lines on a paler face.

"No gun?" said Henry. "Don and Nellie said you were a detective. No gun?"

"I'm a beginner," said Jane.

Henry pocketed Jane's cell phone.

"I'll give everyone your message—that you decided to go and pick up some special treats for the after-party in the lobby. It's a tradition you know, after invited dress. And if you're held up, you told me to tell everyone to break a leg. I'll even drive Don crazy by blowing Nellie a kiss and saying it's from you."

Jane could fight these two people, they were her mother's age for heaven's sake, but the gun gave them an advantage.

"Suzanne, I'm padlocking the door from the outside. I've got to get up there. I hand your mother a sip of water in the second act, Jane. Remember? I'm not supposed to give her anything, but I think she looks thirsty and hold the glass up to her lips?"

Jane nodded. She was afraid of what was coming.

"If I don't get a signal from Suzanne that you've told her where everything is, that glass will have poison so fast-acting and so subtle that no one will know until the curtain call that anything is wrong. She won't recover, *capiche*?"

Puff Daddy, *Goodfellas*, who was this guy really? Jane could hear Don muttering that Henry Gand was a hell of an actor.

"You loved my mother, you wouldn't . . ."

"No, dear. She was a good actress and years ago, I wanted her to be in a play. Freddy kept recruiting idiots and runaways for his little club. Nellie could memorize lines and she had a kind of . . . empathy. But I didn't love her then and I don't now. I just like making Don squirm."

"He'll know it was you. My dad knows you're just faking it all. He's been watching you," said Jane.

"Oooh, I'm scared." A voice came from behind Jane. It was a Bumbles voice, and it was Henry and his lips did not move. He was a good actor and a good ventriloquist.

Henry slipped out the door and locked it. Jane heard the key turn and the thud of the padlock against the door.

"May I put my purse back together?" asked Jane.

"If you tell me about the paintings and stuff while you do it," said Suzanne.

"What if I really don't know?" asked Jane.

"We heard you on your cell phone and we know you've worked at the house," said Suzanne. She smiled. "We also know you were talking to voice mail. You should turn down the volume, because we could hear the recording click on and off as loud as we could hear you. So we know you were pretending that the guy you were talking to knew, too. Henry said it made sense that you knew by now—he said that's why you took over directing the play."

"Look, Suzanne," said Jane, fanning out the scripts, compulsively arranging them in the chronology she had figured out. She leafed through the most recent, the one that was probably printed a few years before Freddy died. "I thought the answer was here, in the script, but I haven't figured it out yet. I don't know, I honestly don't. And you're in so much trouble now, I mean two people have died and maybe, because of your illness, maybe they would take that into consideration?"

"I have porphyria," said Suzanne. "I'm not crazy, I just can't be in the light. And," she added, "I didn't kill anybody, so there's nothing to take into consideration."

Jane looked down at the script. There were black smudges all over the yellow cover. Jane opened her hand. Her fingers were covered with a powdery black substance. The fake cremains?

This stuff wouldn't brush off like the ash and soil and charcoal mix would. She wiped her hands on the back of her jeans.

"That's the damn spray paint," said Suzanne. "Freddy wanted the chandelier to be black and a bunch of the chrome and silver stuff, so we spray-painted all of that old plate for Marvin. And the boys found that the only stuff that gave coverage at all just flakes off and gets all powdery. If the play was running more than a weekend, we'd have to repaint it all."

Why did everything have to be sprayed black? The silver would reflect light better onstage, silver would make everything look richer, wouldn't it? Jane started flipping through the script. She found the spot where the cremation urn was described. Double-handled, a metal bead around the edge, a triple-edge pedestal? Three graduated blocks? Even for Freddy Kendell, this was mighty specific.

"Suzanne, Marvin is dead and Rick Kendell is dead. Rick was killed with a nail gun in your studio. Do you expect me or anyone else to believe you didn't kill Kendell?"

"Henry says he didn't do it, but if he didn't, who did? He told me where to put the nail gun so we could scare Rick and I probably could have killed him if Henry couldn't have gotten him alone. I was mad enough to do it. I would have put a nail right through him, like the bolt on Frankenstein's neck. I was so mad. But when I went in there, he was already dead. Henry keeps saying it was me, but it wasn't. I think it had to be Henry."

"He's going to pin it on you, Suzanne. He's setting you up for Rick Kendell's murder."

Jane heard footsteps on the stage. They were testing the hospital bed. She couldn't make out the words—everything was muffled—but it wasn't the actors, it was the stage crew putting on the finishing touches. Suzanne looked up, too. She waved the gun.

"Tell me where the paintings are, where Freddy hid his stuff."

"Suzanne, Henry made you place the nail gun, so your fingerprints are on it. Henry probably wore gloves and he'll say he saw you take the gun. That's the place he has in mind for you, Suzanne. Jail."

"Henry says he didn't do it because he doesn't even know how to use a nail gun, and he probably doesn't. He says he was helping Marvin with the set, but Marvin said Henry didn't know one tool from the other." Suzanne paused. She was agitated and unused to talking this much, but she was beginning to think things through. "Just because Henry couldn't do it, that doesn't mean that I did it. They won't think I did it," said Suzanne.

Jane could hear Nellie's voice but couldn't make out any words. She could hear the staccato rhythm of Rica Evans's heels pacing the floor. Who was that singing and vocalizing? Henry and Tim.

"That's exactly what they'll think, Suzanne. You were the one who was going to lose her business and her home. And maybe at the time, you thought Rick was responsible for Marvin's death?" said Jane.

Where was Oh? He would get her message and know that she hadn't gone out for party food. And Nellie—wouldn't she know that Jane would be there for their unofficial opening? Then again, she had left a pretty comprehensive checklist for the stage manager. Nellie would have no reason not to believe Henry that Jane had dashed out to get a cake and champagne.

Suzanne held the gun steady but looked uncertain. Jane's best chance was to chip away at any confidence Suzanne may have placed in Henry. Suzanne made it clear that her faith was in Marvin. He was the one who had taken care of her.

"Suzanne, you weren't responsible for killing Marvin. He was your best friend. It was still light out when that board fell on him. You weren't there. And he was so careful . . . do you really think it was an accident?"

"Marvin didn't think Freddy had any treasures. He thought he was just a nutty guy who wanted us to find each other. Marvin loved Freddy. He would have had to go work at the factory with his dad if Freddy hadn't taught him about theater and set design and taught him that all kinds of people could work in theater. Theater wasn't fussy—that's what Freddy always said. Rich or poor, if you had the talent and could work hard, it would take you in. That's why . . ."

Jane edged closer, setting down her bag, ready to sit next to Suzanne as soon as she looked like she'd accept her.

"Why what?" Jane asked.

"Marvin told Henry if he didn't stop talking about Freddy's treasures, he was going to stop the play and tell the director what was going on, that all the old theater club members agreed to be in it because they thought Freddy left clues in the play about where the valuables were. Until your friend Tim found the scripts, everybody had forgotten about what Freddy used to tell us. He was going to make this play the inheritance for his granddaughter. We all thought he was just trying to write a good play, but then Henry lost his money, that Wainwright girl's father lost everybody's money, and Henry told Marvin there had to be money or stuff worth money in the house or—"

"Suzanne, did Henry search the house? Did he use his key and—"

Suzanne wasn't listening to Jane. She had her head cocked and was listening to the sounds on the stage above their heads. Henry was leading the rest of the cast now in vocal exercises.

"Henry didn't know how to use a nail gun. But . . ."

Jane watched Suzanne's face crumple and rebuild itself.

Her pain at losing her friend and protector Marvin was now as fresh as it had been two days ago. In her mind it had just happened and she saw it unfold. This time, seeing it as Jane had described it.

"Henry tried to make the play seemed cursed, didn't he, Suzanne? He left notes and arranged accidents to slow everything down, maybe to stop the whole thing, now that he had the script in his hand again and realized his old theater club key would get him into the studio where he thought he might find the treasures. He tried to scare Tim and me away from having a house sale. And he decided to cause another accident to scare everyone, but this time, it wasn't just a scare," Jane said, edging closer to Suzanne. "Henry had brought the Bumbles to Marvin so he could fix it and maybe Marvin got mad at him for going into Freddy's studio. Maybe they argued about Freddy's play and what Freddy meant when he talked about treasures. Maybe Marvin said he was going to tell Tim and me about what Henry was up to, and Henry saw the four-by-four. Maybe he was really trying to just make it seem like a scary accident, but the beam hit Marvin and—"

"Henry killed Marvin. He said it was a Bumbles accident. Henry had a Bumbles with him. It was the curse of Bumbles. Then Rick Kendell came and said he was going to take away Geppetto from us . . ."

"And Henry's going to say you killed Rick Kendell."

"I didn't kill him," said Suzanne.

Jane believed her. Jane had faced other people who waved guns in her face. Most of them were crazy or mean or desperate. Suzanne was a little crazy and a little desperate and a whole lot of lost. But she hadn't killed anyone. Yet.

"Henry must have—" Jane began, but Suzanne stopped her, shaking her head.

"Henry didn't kill Rick Kendell," said Suzanne.

Detective Oh was in Jane's head. *Wait for it, Mrs. Wheel. Listen to the answer to the unasked question.*

"Henry can't stand the sight of blood. He faints dead away. Even if somebody gets a splinter and I get out my tweezers, Henry's gone. There's no way in the world," said Suzanne.

"But there wasn't any blood. The nail went in at the top of the spinal cord, the base of the brain stem, and Rick died instantly. No bleeding," said Jane, thinking back to what Ramey had told her when she and Oh had been at the station earlier.

"How in the world would Henry know how to do that?" asked Suzanne. "All he knows how to do is to pretend to know how to do stuff. He's been an extra out in California for years, pretending to all of us that he was some big shot. He wanted me to help him take care of Rick, he said, and he told me I should put the nail gun out there. We could scare Rick into signing over the place to me is what Henry said. And then after you found Rick dead, Henry started saying it was okay that I killed him, that it would work out even better now. But I told him I didn't kill Rick Kendell."

Suzanne's voice had gotten softer and softer. Jane held out her hand. "If you'll give me the gun, I'll make sure everyone hears what you have to say," said Jane. *Don't overpromise,* she told herself. "Please Suzanne, we have to make sure Henry doesn't hurt Nellie."

Suzanne nodded and, just like that, it was over. Except for the fact that she and Suzanne were locked in the pit-trap room and Henry was going to poison Nellie if Jane didn't give them the information she had only bluffed about having. Until a few minutes ago, she really didn't know if those treasures of Freddy's were real or not. Now she knew exactly what they were and where they were, but if she didn't get out and stop the onstage action, one of them was going to be ruined. Oh, yes . . . and Nellie was going to be poisoned.

"How were you supposed to tell Henry I had given you the information?" asked Jane.

"At the end of the first act, when the hospital bed is wheeled center stage and they bring in Marguerite?"

Jane nodded.

"Perkins the gardener pounds the floor with his rake to see if the electrician is finished in the basement, when they talk about plugging in the electric bed. I was supposed to knock back twice if you told me and three times if you hadn't."

"But we never even rehearsed the knocking back part," said Jane.

Suzanne shrugged. "Henry said the play's such a mess and that Tim Lowry is such a bad director, nobody will notice anything that's different."

Henry was probably right about that.

They could hear many voices now, the rolling waves of sound that an audience makes with its muttering and murmuring, reading aloud program notes to their seatmates and the helloing across aisles when they see someone they know. Even with the sounds muffled, Jane could tell it was a large audience.

"Invited dress, my eye," said Jane. "Sounds like a full house."

"Oh, yes," said Suzanne. "That's the tradition of the invited dress here. The theater board sends out so many invitations, to try to get new people in. It's kind of like giving free tickets, but they know the people who always come will buy seats, so they make a big deal out of invited dress to get new people. They serve food and wine afterward in the lobby. Henry said the house would be full and that was good because he and I could disappear in the chaos."

"I have a feeling," said Jane, looking through the prop

furniture and rolling out the small portable stairway, "that Mr. Bumbles has left a note somewhere about poison in the liquor and that note will be traceable to you. It's probably pinned to the dummy you were using with your fingerprints all over the thing." Jane looked at Suzanne to see if what she was saying was sinking in.

"Henry could have even found his poison in your scene shop at Geppetto Studios."

"I hate actors," said Suzanne, confirming Jane's longtime suspicions about the way designers and techies feel about the so-called talent.

"The play's started," said Jane, whispering. "There might be some kind of intercom down here. How else would someone know her cue?" Jane took the compact flashlight out of her tote and began scanning the walls. She found a panel speaker with a switch below and flicked it to the on position. The speaker had to be clogged with years of dust and debris, but Suzanne and Jane could hear muffled onstage voices.

"I was surprised to be invited to your welcome-home party, Myra. Things being the way they are between Hermione and myself," said Chuck Havens as Malachi.

He was mumbling. Jane was sure he had reinserted the imaginary beard-stroking in his nervousness over the size of the audience. Some of the regular community theater folks might be expecting the invited dress to be an opening night, but neither she nor Tim had known, so they gave no warning about the preopening opening.

"Malachi! Who invited you? Mother, you didn't, you couldn't, you wouldn't . . ." Mary Wainwright made it out on time and hit her mark, but she didn't, couldn't, and wouldn't say the right line because she had no idea what it was.

Chuck came to her rescue. "Don't worry, Hermione. I won't bother you tonight. I came because I heard Marguerite would be here and you know I always adored your grandmother."

Unfortunately Mary's stage fright prevented her noticing that Chuck had bailed her out. Apparently, she was going to be one of those actresses determined to say her lines, all of her lines, whenever she remembered them, even if someone had already said them for her.

"It must have been Marguerite who invited you. She always adored you."

Pause.

"Yes, yes she did," said Malachi.

"Put aside your differences for a moment, you two. Can't we just pretend for one night that a homecoming is a glorious event? A night to be celebrated? Can't we be them?" said Rica. Jane knew she was now gesturing to the painting over the mantel. It was a sentimental pastoral scene in which a shepherd drove his flock toward the barn and a woman waited with a lantern.

Jane knew now, however, that underneath that amateurish scene was another canvas. It was a painting called *A Homecoming*, described by Claire and the auction house that received another painting in its place as having an auction estimate of $250,000. If Rick Kendell had wrapped up the wrong painting, it wasn't on purpose. He just couldn't find the right one since it was disguised and stored in Freddy's props closet.

That was why Freddy kept changing the lines and rewriting the play. As soon as he was able to spirit something out of the house, away from the foolish selling off of property and blind investing and gambling of his son, he had to camouflage it somehow and add it as a prop to his play. Freddy's legacy was in his play, all right, but the treasures were literally, not figuratively, present. Freddy's promises were not about royalties; they were literally promises of valuable properties—props. Jane crouched down next to the rolling staircase and tried to lock it in place.

"Can you help me steady this thing?" asked Jane.

Suzanne shook her head but came over and with one hand pushed the lock down on each of the wheels. "You were an actress, weren't you?" she asked.

"A long time ago," said Jane. "Now I prefer to be behind the scenes."

Jane carefully climbed the stairs and unlatched the lock on the hinged square on the ceiling/stage floor. She could tell by where the actors were standing that this was the farthest trap from the downstage action. If opened, the placement should be right next to the French doors leading to the garden.

"Why, Detective Craven, I wasn't sure you'd come," said Myra.

Silence.

"And now, here you are," said Myra.

Silence.

"How could you miss my homecoming party, after all? I'll bet you wouldn't miss a chance to visit this old place in a million years, would you, Detective Craven?"

Rica, as Myra, was good, but Jane could hear a note of desperation creeping into her voice.

Silence.

Jane tiptoed up the now-locked stairs. She hoped her spatial sense had not failed her and prayed that the hinges would not squeak as she opened the trap. She knew the action was taking place downstage and there was no danger of dropping an actor through the floor, but she also hoped that no potted plant or set of fireplace tools would come crashing down.

Slowly she opened the hinged panel. The trapdoor would swing open downward and once it was open an inch, she held the door steady and peeked out. Just in front of the panel was a huge brass pot filled with geraniums marking the entrance to the garden. The perfect screen. No actor would be coming near the now unlocked trap. Peeking out, she could see she was directly behind Tim. The hem of his trench coat was just above her eye level.

"Detective, may I offer you a drink?"

Jane could hear Myra walk toward the bar. The silence onstage was palpable. Jane could hear the clink of the crystal stopper being removed from the decanter.

"I'll have a scotch. Neat," whispered Jane. "Get it together, Timmy, it's just a dress rehearsal. Say your lines."

"Scotch," said Detective Craven. It came out as a parrot squawk. "Neat," he added with a little more force.

Myra laughed and bless her, she ad-libbed a cover and gave him his cue.

"I was afraid my celebrity might make you nervous, might make you forget that I am just a hometown girl at heart."

"You were many things, Miss Davis, but you were never just a hometown girl."

Jane noticed that Tim had brought back his Norwegian/Manchester/Australian accent, but the fact that he could speak at all was good. Perhaps those in the audience would not figure out that the Eckaknak Valley was their very own Kankakee on Backward Day. Perhaps they would buy Detective Craven's accent as the Eekaknakian vernacular.

Three more lines and Perkins would enter through the French doors, so Jane closed and latched the panel.

Suzanne had left her spot on the couch and was going through Henry Gand's messenger bag. She took out cough drops and a water bottle, two energy bars, a Swiss Army knife, folders filled with papers, and as she opened one of the folders, his passport fell out on the floor. She opened it and nodded.

"Good picture, Henry," she whispered. "You son of a bitch."

She twisted and pulled at the passport with a wringing motion and managed to tear out the photo page. She handed Jane a printout with flight information. An e-ticket.

"We don't have much time, Suzanne. You say Henry couldn't kill Rick, but I do believe he's capable of poisoning my mother. We have to get out there and—"

"The padlock is on the outside. He locked us both in, remember?"

Jane pointed up with her finger. "This is the way out."

"I cannot go onstage," said Suzanne. You can go out and come around for me, but I can't go onstage."

Jane looked at the woman and saw the pure panic in her eyes. There was stage fright and there was *stage fright,* and this was the latter. Paralysis would set in before she could climb the stairs.

Okay. By this time Detective Oh would know she was in trouble. He would have called Ramey, he would be prepared to lead the cavalry, but there was no way for him to know exactly where to charge. Claire and Margaret would probably be with him, probably sitting in the audience. Margaret might not feel like seeing Freddy's play tonight, but they wouldn't leave her alone in the motel room.

"Cook tells me they're bringing your grandmother home tonight." Henry Gand was in fine form as Perkins. When had he gone Scottish?

Silence.

Mary Wainwright again, probably scrambling for a script in a potted plant.

"Just say *yes,* Hermione, for God's sake," whispered Jane.

Suzanne shrugged and walked over to the intercom speaker. "Yes," she whispered directly into it.

"Yes," said Hermione.

Jane mimed applause. Suzanne nodded and whispered, "Actors are morons."

"Morons," said Hermione, matter-of-factly.

Jane motioned Suzanne away from the speaker.

"What's that you say, lass?" asked Perkins.

"When did this play become *Brigadoon*?" whispered Jane.

"I said . . . I said, the morons from the hospital should be arriving any minute," said Hermione.

"That's good, Mary, just go with it," muttered Jane.

Jane weighed her options. If she popped out onstage and yelled "cut," she would certainly stop the action and there was a chance they would be able to grab Henry Gand before he could gather his wits and run from the theater. Jane was sure Oh would have the place surrounded, or at least the entrances and exits guarded. The problem as she saw it—and she was thinking quickly—was that Henry believed Suzanne had killed Kendell and so would everyone else. He could pin everything on her. The police had identified her prints on the nail gun by now and Henry would have made sure that the notes and the dummies would be traceable to Suzanne. He would present himself as an old man who was persuaded to help his old friend, before he realized what she had done. He would say he had no intention of poisoning Nellie, he was afraid for Jane's life since Suzanne was holding a gun on her below. It would be Jane against Henry. And, as Don had said himself, Henry was a hell of an actor. But if Henry really didn't kill Rick, as Suzanne insisted, someone was out there who did. Bumbles was still at large. And somehow, Jane popping up and stopping the action might put more people at risk. She had to find a way to make sure Henry couldn't follow through on his plan, but make sure no one was tipped off too early about Jane's plan. Oh yes, and she had to figure out a plan.

The actors had limped through the first act and Jane

realized she could sneak up right now, during the intermission, and no one would be the wiser. She knelt down in front of Suzanne, who had reclaimed her spot on the couch. Suzanne might still be capable of running a scene shop, but right now she looked scared and sick and every bit her age. She was still holding what was left of Henry's passport.

"I'm going up there and we'll work this out, okay? You won't be left alone in this," said Jane.

Suzanne nodded.

Jane climbed up the stairs and opened the trap, but instead of seeing the lights of the theater stage, the square that should have allowed her to exit was blocked.

"Damn it, they've already moved the couch back to make room for the hospital bed downstage," said Jane.

She pushed on the bottom of the sofa, but it was impossible to move or slide the heavy piece from her angle below at the top of the stairs. The couch was dead center over the trap. She climbed back down the portable stairs and moved them under another trap, upstage left. If she were right again about the placement, this door would open next to another large pot of flowers, on the other side of the garden entrance/exit.

There was a music cue that signaled the beginning of the second act and Jane heard the first chords. So much for the window of time during the intermission. Now the second act would begin, the second act where Perkins the gardener would offer Marguerite/Nellie the forbidden sip of water.

Jane looked around the perimeter of the pit-trap room. Besides the furniture piled up to the low ceiling, there were a few freestanding wardrobes. Jane slowly opened one, listening for squeaks. She slipped a denim work shirt off its hangar and over her yellow T-shirt. Heavy red stitching accented the seams and pocket flap. She tied a white canvas carpenter's apron around her waist and slipped in a screwdriver and a wrench. They were the heftiest tools she could find that would fit in the pockets. She unfolded a large print pocket square and tied it in her hair. She looked at Suzanne for approval.

"Rosie the Riveter?" Suzanne whispered, and gave her a thumbs-up.

They could hear several pairs of footsteps over their heads. It was the opening scene when the dinner-party guests were all mingling in the parlor after the body had been found in the garden. Craven had announced at the end of the first act that no one must leave and the second act opened with the "mumble, mumble, rhubarb, rhubarb" of fake chatter among the guests. Jane stood on top of the stairs, her hands on the trap, waiting for the guests to disassemble and the action to begin farther downstage.

"The rest of you can wait in the garden or in the library," said Craven. "My men will call each of you individually."

The extras muttered and "rhubarbed" their way out the side and rear exits.

Jane could hear Myra speaking softly to Marguerite, now tucked in the hospital bed downstage. Hermione, Malachi, and Craven should have been, if they all remembered their blocking, standing in a triangle in front of the bar.

"Detective Craven, I'll be happy to answer any questions, but I'm sure Hermione will tell you she never let me out of her sight all evening," said Malachi.

Silence.

Poor Mary.

"Although I'm sure Hermione might agree she saw you for part of the evening, there was surely a window of time during cocktails, when she was talking to me, where she couldn't account for your whereabouts," said Craven.

Convoluted, but Tim was trying to throw her a bone and let the scene continue.

Silence.

"Indeed, there was that time when I fixed myself a dry Manhattan and needed to get more garnishes from the kitchen," said Malachi.

Garnishes? A Manhattan? They were drowning out there and Chuck Havens had no idea where to throw out the life preserver.

"You'd like to think we were together all evening," said Hermione, her voice switched onto autopilot, "but you left to fix yourself a cocktail. It was a martini, wasn't it?"

"Manhattan. I said Manhattan," said Malachi, sounding much more like an angry Chuck Havens.

"I'm sure it was supposed to be a martini," said Mary.

Rica Evans swept in as Myra to save the day.

"Stop bickering, you two. Detective Craven has a murder to solve. We must remember that Mama . . . Marguerite . . . might be in a coma, but she can hear us, I know she can. For her sake, we must stop our petty squabbles."

At this point, Jane imagined Malachi nodding, chastened, and Hermione hugging her mother, Myra, that is, if Mary remembered her blocking better than she remembered her lines. Although the script was being shredded by the actors, the action seemed to be limping along as it should. At this point in the play, Perkins should be lurking upstage right, gazing at Marguerite tucked into the hospital bed, waiting for his opportunity to get close to his old love.

Of course, imagining the play from below the stage floor wasn't exactly the best method of capturing the action. Jane knew that none of her people in the audience—Oh, Don, or Claire and Margaret—would be able to give her an accurate report of how the play went. Oh would be looking for Jane, Don would be watching Nellie like a hawk, Claire would be dissing the furniture and artwork, and Margaret? What would Margaret be thinking?

Her family all dead and her legacy somehow tied up in this ridiculous murder mystery/melodrama. Freddy, apparently the only family member who loved Margaret enough to put her ahead of himself, leaving her the crazy messages and ramblings about her fortune and *Murder in the Eekaknak Valley,* often delivered by a wooden dummy named Mr. Bumbles? It was enough to . . . wait . . . the cue Jane had been listening for . . . two lines ahead of where it was supposed to be since Mary once again was lost in space.

"Is mother's bed fully functional?" asked Myra. "May I raise the head of it so we can feel like we are including her in the family discussion?"

This was where Mary was supposed to fuss around with the cord on the electric bed and ask Perkins if he had made all the arrangements with the electrician. The answer, according to the script, was going to be no since that would give them an excuse for leaving the bed flat. Tim had been too afraid of Nellie's mugging for the crowd if they had actually raised the head of the bed.

Silence. Jane pictured Mary gaping, holding the electric cord in one hand and looking heavenward for some dialogue.

Jane knew what would come next. Henry, as Perkins, would bang his rake on the floor and wait for Suzanne to signal back. Jane took a deep breath as the stood on the middle stair. She shook out her arms and hands, quietly cleared her throat, and readied herself. Jane Wheel was about to make her comeback.

22

Enter upstage left, the electrician, a woman oddly dressed for the period, muttering about the antique wiring in the old house.

"Following the wiring in these old houses is like walking a maze, you know? Not to mention the places where the mice have just chewed through walls and wires," said Jane as she stepped fully onto the stage.

Everyone—Rica Evans as Myra, Chuck as Malachi, and Henry, standing with his rake poised to strike the floor—stared openmouthed as Jane muttered something about closing the cellar door so no one would fall in. She slammed the trap shut and wiped her still paint-smudged hands on the back of her jeans.

Jane could hear Tim in the wings, waiting to come on as Craven, hissing at her to get off the stage.

The only actor who seemed to take Jane's unannounced cameo appearance in stride was Mary Wainwright. Since she had planted all of those different versions of the script around the stage, picking up a different one each night to use for memorizing her lines, Mary thought she was losing her mind when her cues changed all the time. Seeing Jane onstage actually seemed to give Mary some confidence. At least everyone else now looked as confused as she had always felt.

"Would you like a drink of water, Rollo?" asked Mary, looking directly at Jane, when no one else said anything.

"Rollo?" said Jane.

"That's what it says on your shirt," said Mary, fully in character as Hermione.

"Oh right," said Jane, outlining the embroidery on the pocket of her work shirt with her finger. "I must have grabbed Rollo's shirt today. I'm . . . Nellie. Nellie the electrician," said Jane. She thought she could hear group yawns coming from the audience.

As Jane announced her name, the only one she could think of on short notice, Marguerite, snug under her covers in the hospital bed, snorted.

"Perkins," said Rica, snapping out of her shock and deciding to ride whatever crazy wave had just rolled onto the stage, "Give Nellie the electrician a glass of that water so she can explain what's going on. With the electricity, I mean, of course."

"Of course," said Henry, who was carrying a pitcher and a glass.

He crossed to where Jane stood and held up the glass.

"No, no water, thanks," said Jane.

"Then I'll just let Miss Marguerite have some to wet her lips, she looks—"

"No, I said," said Jane, knocking the glass from his hand. It fell but thankfully didn't break and rolled toward the back of the stage.

"Sorry, but no one should drink anything. When I was in the basement I noticed the pipes were contaminated. Until I can get a crew down there, nobody drinks anything here, understand?" Jane tried for a plumber/gangster attitude.

"I thought you were the electrician," said a puzzled Malachi. Chuck Havens had stopped stroking his imaginary beard and was talking in a regular voice. His normally amused tone had given way to total confusion.

"I'm the plumber, too. You know," said Jane, "electrical and plumbing . . . like heating and air-conditioning. You've really got to offer both these days."

Was the audience aware of her babbling? No matter. Jane knew the second act had only just started, but she had to find a way to wrap this up and get the curtain down fast, before Henry could—

"I got this from the bottled water I keep in my shed," said Henry.

How had he slipped offstage and on in this short time?

"No, I said. No water." Jane reached over to knock the glass out of his hand, but this time Henry was ready and backed up a step, holding the glass over his head.

"Why no bottled water?" asked Craven. Tim had strode onto the stage—mystified, but wanting in on the action. The play had, after all, at one time, been his directorial debut.

"Bad for the environment. All that packaging waste and so few recycle, really, especially if there's no curbside pickup . . ."

Everyone stared at Jane. *Murder in the Eekaknak Valley* might be written as a half-witted murder mystery, but it was a fully realized period piece. In its earliest incarnation, it took place in the 1930s, and in Freddy's later rewrites, he had brought one version up to 1951 in order to insert some "current" references. Tonight's version, as conceived and directed by Tim Lowry, was staged and set as the thirties showpiece, complete with art deco barware and gorgeous vintage dresses for the ladies. Even the music cues were thirties-era Ted Weems and Fred Waring. Jane Wheel, in jeans and a gray work shirt might pass for a weird offbeat individual of that time working in the plumbing trade—at least with this undemanding audience—

however, the reference to curbside recycling made everyone onstage freeze.

A full beat that felt like a lifetime passed. Anyone who has ever been onstage when something goes terribly wrong knows the quality of the silence. Every actor could hear his or her own heartbeat. Who would have ever imagined that Mary Wainwright would throw out the life preserver?

"Are you from the future?"

Jane tried to look inconspicuous as she paced the stage checking both right and left wings. Ramey now had officers stationed at each entrance and exit. The cavalry had indeed arrived. Jane's message to Oh had been interpreted as a call for backup, but Jane hadn't known at the time and had no way of communicating exactly who the cavalry was here to thwart. And since the theater was filled with an audience and the stage was crowded with every cast member—no one wanted to miss this master class in improvisation—neither the cavalry, nor Officer Ramey, nor Detective Oh was going to set off a panic.

Instead, they were going to send in another actor.

Jane was prepared to answer that she was indeed from the future and they all had to evacuate, single file, stage left, because something terrible was about to happen when one more tradesmen entered through the upstage garden doors.

Wearing one of Marvin's plaid flannel shirts over his own dress shirt and vintage tie, Detective Oh came in holding a piece of pipe he must have picked up backstage. From third-row center, Jane and the rest of the cast and audience heard a loud "Bruce, what in heaven's name are you doing up there?" No question about where Claire and Margaret were seated.

"I have come to assist you in all your plumbing needs," said Oh formally.

"Didn't we need an electrician?" said Rica, sounding ready to give up.

"No, Mother, we needed both and, lucky for us, Nellie and her assistant are here, maybe from the future, to help us," said Mary. She had never spoken Freddy's lines with the confidence she now displayed.

The audience had been mumbling for a while and at least a few of them began to be aware that this play was not the one described in their program.

Onstage, Jane managed to nod her head in the direction of Henry Gand, and Oh circled around behind him.

While all of the unannounced comings and goings of new characters kept the actors' attention on Jane and the improvised dialogue, no one had been paying attention to the character who was supposed to be the focal point of the second act. Marguerite, in and out of consciousness, was supposed to be at the heart of the action, hence the placement of her hospital bed downstage, just left of center. Perkins was getting very close to the bed, which was plugged into a live outlet. Jane noticed he had set down the glass but still carried the pitcher of water. Did he think he could cause an electrical short with that water pitcher, with Nellie still under the covers? Or was that pitcher full of some other caustic substance that could harm her mother? Jane had tried to preserve the appearance of the play long enough and she had plenty of backup, so it was time to call for the arrest of Henry Gand.

"Stay right where you are everyone," said a squeaky voice from upstage, behind the actors.

Jane turned slightly and saw Suzanne, who had opened another trap and climbed onstage, holding Mr. Bumbles in one hand and the gun Jane had taken from her but left behind in the pit-trap room, in the other. Suzanne hadn't lost her stage fright. Her face was a solid expressionless mask more wooden than that of her dummy companion. But she must have realized if she talked through Bumbles, she would be able to speak.

"Thank God," said Henry Gand. "This group of tradesmen are fakes and phonies. They've come to rob you, Myra, and to harm my Marguerite."

At that point, Nellie threw off her covers and stood up, looking from actor to astonished actor. Jane noticed that her nightgown had been hemmed, albeit unevenly, and the sweatpants Nellie insisted on wearing underneath were unrolled and completely visible hanging out from under her prim old-lady nightie.

Francis the breadman, somewhere out in the middle of the house said loudly, "Finally. There's Nellie. I told you she was in this show."

Henry was making a grab for Marguerite, but Nellie was too quick at standing and he was left grasping the air.

The actors all waited, looking at Nellie for a clue. Rica managed to find her voice and reached toward her stage mother. "You're in a coma," she said.

"I'm better," said Nellie.

Myra and Hermione tried to get close to Nellie and embrace her, ad-libbing their joy at her unexpected recovery. Henry, by this time, had come around the bed, dumping the pitcher and tossing it, to use both hands to pull Nellie in front of him, pinning both her arms to her side.

Mr. Bumbles opened and closed his mouth, not quite in synch with his words—the same ones as before—shouting for everyone to stay right where they were.

"Let's get Marguerite out of this madhouse and back to the hospital," said Henry, looking at Suzanne and gesturing toward the back of the stage. He had spotted the police at both side exits but knew if they could get out offstage through the French doors, there was an exit that led directly outside to where Marvin had set up all of his power tools. There would be police there, too, but Suzanne had the gun and he had Nellie.

"No, Perkins, you let go of her and stand still, too," said Bumbles.

Jane could tell Suzanne was trying not to look at the audience and was growing more and more uncertain of her next move.

Mary Wainwright remained the calmest actor on the stage, and for some reason decided to return to the script. Picking up the urn on the mantel, the one that was supposed to contain the ashes of her stepfather, Mary took a deep breath, ready to curse his name and fling the container that would bring them to the final five minutes of wrap-up in the play.

"This is all your fault, Father," shouted Mary/Hermione.

Jane judged the trajectory of the urn, which they had never really practiced throwing onstage before. Tim had suggested it for dramatic effect and instructed Mary to hurl it hard toward the garden doors, so if the "ashes" flew up and out, the actors wouldn't choke on them. If Mary threw it now, it would hit the floor hard, and the vessel would undoubtedly get dented beyond recognition. This would not, of course, matter if the urn were the worthless piece of spray-painted silverplate that everyone assumed it was when they found it in Freddy's prop storage closet, marked as the only urn to be used in *Murder in the Eekaknak Valley*. Jane looked at the traces of black paint still on her hands and held them both up.

"Stop! It's not the ashes of your father," said Jane. "It's the ashes of Cornelius . . . Cornelius something. He was a famous American silversmith."

"Oh my God," shouted Claire Oh from the audience. "That's it!"

Mary, surprised that Jane wasn't properly appreciative of her dramatic efforts to save the play, and annoyed that she would interrupt her most highly charged moment onstage, screamed out that she didn't care whose ashes they were and let the urn fly.

Jane made a flying leap toward the airborne object, now raining potting soil and sand all over the stage. She caught it before it hit the ground, slipped, and landed at Suzanne's feet, cradling the urn in her arms. Was this how holding a million dollars was supposed to feel?

When Henry got dirt in his eyes, he had to use one hand to reach up to his face, which was all the break Nellie needed.

"What the hell do you think you're doing, Henry, grabbing me like that?" Nellie said, pulling loose. She cocked her fist, letting go with a punch to Henry's jaw. "I'm a married woman."

Don entered, stage right, just in time to see his wife knock out Henry Gand cold.

"I would have liked to do that myself, Nellie," he said, putting an arm around her.

"Next time," Nellie promised, allowing his arm to remain for a second or two before shrugging free.

Several in the audience applauded the punch and knockout.

"It's all over now, Suzanne," said Jane, standing and brushing herself off. "I'm going to help you explain what happened. Detective Oh will help, too."

"Who?" said Suzanne, in her own voice, dropping Bumbles onto the couch.

"Oh," said Bruce Oh. "I am the plumber's assistant."

Suzanne handed the gun to Jane, who handed it to Oh, who passed it on to Ramey, who joined them onstage.

Claire and Margaret reached the stage and Claire snatched the urn from Jane's arms. "This, my dear, is your fortune," said Claire, holding the urn up to Margaret's face.

"The paintings, too," said Jane. "Underneath those paintings are the ones that should have been sent to auction. I don't think your brother sent the wrong ones on purpose. Freddy had been spiriting valuables out of the house for years and disguising them for use in *Murder in the Eekaknak Valley*. That's why he kept rewriting the play—it was to accommodate the props. You might want to check that jewelry chest. I thought it was all costume, but there might be some real treasure in there."

"No, I didn't kill Rick Kendell," said Suzanne. "You can't arrest me for that, I didn't do that."

Jane turned and saw Ramey nodding for another officer to come and take Suzanne away.

"She didn't do it," said Jane.

Now Ramey was giving her the look she usually saw on the faces of Kankakee policemen. The uh-oh-now-is-she-going-to-tell-me-how-to-do-my-job look.

"Did she, Margaret?" asked Jane.

Claire Oh looked from Jane to Margaret and back.

"How dare you . . ." Claire began.

"There was no blood. Whoever killed Rick didn't put a nail in his neck like Frankenstein's bolt, which was how you said you'd do it, right, Suzanne?" said Jane. "Whoever slipped in that front door and killed Rick Kendell knew something about science, knew exactly where to place that nail," said Jane.

"Knew about pithing," said Oh with a small sigh.

"It's how we killed the frogs," said Margaret, looking up at Claire. "Remember in biology class? You didn't want to do it, but I volunteered to come in early and take care of it for everyone? It didn't hurt them. I'm sure it didn't hurt them."

Ramey now signaled for his female officer to transfer her attention from Suzanne to Margaret.

"Rick was going to turn out all of those people that Freddy took care of. And when he asked me to meet him at Geppetto Studios, he accused me of stealing the treasures from the house. He was a horrible man. He had lost all his money and now he was going to take all of mine and lose it. He was just like our father."

Margaret took a deep breath and looked over at Mr. Bumbles, sitting askew on the couch where Suzanne had dropped him.

"But you were always more like your mother," said Bumbles.

"Yes, I was," said Margaret, nodding at the dummy. Jane had to admit that Margaret Kendell was a fine ventriloquist. Her lips never moved.

23

Only after Margaret stood up straight and allowed Ramey and a female officer to escort her from the stage did Jane look out into the audience.

A full house stared back at her, many of them leaning forward in their seats, straining to catch all the action, some of which had begun to be played out in much quieter voices.

Suzanne and Henry Gand had also exited, stage right, accompanied by police officers, and Jane was sure that although Henry was, as Don had pointed out, a hell of an actor, thanks to Nellie's punch, he was too groggy to be able to lie outright to the police about his argument with Marvin and his impulsive shove, which had brought the board crashing down on Marvin's head.

Remaining onstage, in addition to the cast of *Murder in the Eekaknak Valley*, were Oh, Claire, Don, and Jane. Tim had signaled to Mandy, the stage manager, to close the curtain, but she seemed to be in shock and had been talking rapidly on her cell phone, apparently giving a play-by-play of what was going on, ever since Jane had crashed the party in the middle of the second act.

Nellie walked down to the apron of the stage and Jane thought for a moment she was going to make a speech to the audience. Still facing front with a smile, arms straight, she reached her hands behind her. Rica Evans and Mary Wainwright understood immediately and stepped forward, each taking one of Nellie's hands and reaching their own back for the rest of the cast. Don took Claire's elbow and they walked forward and joined the line of actors. Jane and Oh looked at each other and approached the line from the other side. The entire line, holding hands, with Tim breaking into the center between Nellie and Rica Evans, took a deep bow. Only then, when the audience broke into thunderous applause, did Mandy realize she was supposed to bring down the curtain.

The cast remained in place for a second curtain call, but Jane and Oh took advantage of the briefly closed curtain, stepping offstage and into the wings.

"I got your message, Mrs. Wheel," said Oh.

"I'm sorry I wasn't clearer," said Jane.

Oh shook his head. "You were quite clear. I knew someone was listening and you were bluffing that someone else knew what you had figured out. I only wish I had actually figured it out in time to save you the discomfort of being held by Henry and Suzanne underground."

"The pit-trap room," said Jane. "This is quite a theater. If they ever give Tim another shot, he can put on something fairly complicated here."

There was a third curtain call, and Jane had a feeling Tim might try to milk it for a fourth, so she told Mandy, rather loudly, to leave the curtain closed and bring up the houselights.

"Poor Margaret," said Jane. She knew she should be saying poor Rick, since he was the murder victim, but there was something about that fragile woman. It was so clear that she never had a chance at normal, let alone happy, and that prompted sympathy.

"I should have seen it," said Oh. "Her brother had tortured

her as a child. Claire told me stories Margaret shared with her when they were in boarding school. He was a bad man and to have him for a brother with those parents . . ."

Jane saw Don and Nellie and Claire heading toward them from the other side of the stage. Only then did Jane become aware that she and Oh were still holding hands. She quickly untangled her fingers from his and walked toward her parents.

"Are you okay?" she asked Nellie, knowing the answer.

"I might have to ice my hand," said Nellie, sounding surprised at her own admission of weakness. "I haven't punched anyone in a while. I forgot what it feels like."

"He feels worse," said Don, pleased.

"Glass jaw," said Nellie.

Claire looked at Oh sadly, then turned to Jane. "When did you know?"

"Not until tonight. When Suzanne said she and Henry planted the nail gun but that neither of them did it, I thought about what Bruce had said about pithing and what you had said about Margaret being strong because she was a scientist. And to tell you the truth, I still hoped I was wrong."

Claire nodded and walked over to the paintings that Jane had asked Mandy to take down and put in the wings. Jane was sure that three of them were the masterpieces Claire had been searching for, but it was possible there were even more treasures hidden on the set. One of the stagehands had gone down into the pit-trap room and gotten Jane's bag for her and she had pulled out all the scripts. She handed them to Oh.

"Claire should read these. She might recognize allusions to more stuff that Freddy hid in plain sight."

Tim was encouraging everyone to go out front and mingle with the audience. When he came to Jane, he hugged her, and through smiling, clenched teeth, talked into her ear. "If you ever do anything like this again . . ."

"You'll what?" asked Jane. "Hang a ventriloquist's dummy from a chandelier to scare me?"

Tim pushed her back and held her at arm's length.

"What are you talking about?" he asked.

"Let's go out to the lobby and get some food," said Jane. "I'm starving, and something tells me this crowd is going to want to applaud your success."

"It was a disaster and how did . . . ?"

"Three curtain calls, Timmy, and you couldn't have done it without me," said Jane.

"You turned my classic whodunit into Dr. Who meets the Marx Brothers," said Tim.

"Trust me, you're going to miss me tomorrow when the play really opens," said Jane. "The audience loved this new and improved version."

"Yeah, they did, didn't they?" said Tim, acknowledging congratulatory nods and shouts from across the lobby.

"Next time you want to interest me in a job, you don't have to go to such creepy and elaborate extremes," said Jane. "Shame on you."

"How . . . ?"

"The foyer at the Kendell house was dark when we went in. Even with the light on, there was no way to tell that was an Hermès silk scarf tied to Mr. Bumbles. Only you would have picked out something so classy and only you would have freaked out when you saw the scissors in my hand to cut it down."

The president of the theater board waved Tim over with a big smile. Jane could tell he was going to tell Tim how happy he was about the job he had done spicing up this old chestnut. Jane hoped for Tim's sake that the prez wouldn't be coming back tomorrow to see the real play.

Jane could see from the lobby that Claire was directing the

volunteer stagehands to pack up several items and load them into her car. At least Freddy's legacy would help Margaret find a good lawyer.

Oh came up behind her and placed a glass of champagne in Jane's hand.

"I think you deserve a drink, Mrs. Wheel," said Oh.

Someone tapped a utensil against a glass and the theater board president cleared his throat.

"Congratulations to Tim Lowry as a first-time director—we hope he'll agree to participate in many more productions, and we'd also like to thank the cast and crew. We'll be dedicating the weekend performances to Marvin, who was such a friend to . . ."

Jane saw Nellie roll her eyes at what promised to be a long-winded speech. Nellie clinked her own glass with a fork, interrupting.

"Yes, let's drink to Marvin and Freddy and the old theater club and to *Murder in the Eekaknak Valley.* If anyone can put on an ass backward show in Kankakee, it's Tim Lowry," said Nellie.

Everyone laughed and continued to talk and eat and drink, and then Jane heard it again. That noise. That buzzing vibration that sounded like a loose fan belt inside of her brain. This time, though, she knew what it was. Ramey had returned her cell phone to her after she had asked him to check Henry's pockets.

The vibration announced a message from Nick. They must be in a town or somewhere they could get a signal.

was tonite grams opening? howd it go?

This tweeting was going to kill the English language. What was the expression Nick had been using for everything? Jane tweeted back.

Killer. It was killer.

Jane slipped her phone back into her jeans, slipped off Rollo's work shirt, and grabbed a mini quiche off the tray. Jane looked around at the happy crowd of EZ Way Inn regulars who surrounded Nellie, the theater board who surrounded Tim, and began to walk across the lobby to where her partner, Detective Bruce Oh, stood, alone and patient.

As she threaded her way through the crowd that separated her from Oh, Jane allowed herself only a moment to reflect on this long year of sleepless nights and recriminations, loneliness and guilt, and she silently toasted the end of her marriage and a new beginning of . . . something . . . although she wasn't sure what that something would be. Like all the collectibles that crowded her shelves, the objects of her affections and desire, she really didn't know what they were until she saw them. That's how she felt about the next chapter of her life: She'd know it when she saw it. She accepted a second glass of champagne from one of the theater board members who congratulated her on her performance. Laughing, Jane Wheel decided to join the party.